The Glass Magician

The Glass Magician

CAROLINE STEVERMER

TOR

A Tom Doherty Associates Book
New York

This is a work of fiction. All of the characters, organizations, and events portrayed in this novel are either products of the author's imagination or are used fictitiously.

THE GLASS MAGICIAN

Designed by Greg Collins

A Tor Book
Published by Tom Doherty Associates
120 Broadway
New York, NY 10271

www.tor-forge.com

Tor® is a registered trademark of Macmillan Publishing Group, LLC.

The Library of Congress Cataloging-in-Publication Data is available upon request.

ISBN 978-0-7653-3504-3 (hardcover)
ISBN 978-1-4668-2083-8 (ebook)

Our books may be purchased in bulk for promotional, educational, or business use. Please contact your local bookseller or the Macmillan Corporate and Premium Sales Department at 1-800-221-7945, extension 5442, or by email at MacmillanSpecialMarkets@macmillan.com.

First Edition: April 2020

Printed in the United States of America

0 9 8 7 6 5 4 3 2 1

This book is respectfully dedicated to Nell Odella Newton, better known as Dell O'Dell, whose stage magic appeared not only in vaudeville, but on television. Her long career inspired this novel.

Without Moshe Feder and Ellen Kushner, this story would never have been started. Without Frances Collin and Claire Eddy, it would never have been finished. Please accept this dedication as proof of my gratitude.

The Glass Magician

Chapter One

Thalia Cutler, the stage magician known as the Lady of the Lake, stepped nimbly aside to avoid the singer coming offstage at Keith's Vaudeville Theater in Philadelphia. A plate spinner had already taken the singer's place, and onstage the show went smoothly on. Backstage was the usual bustle for an evening performance, invisible to the audience out front, essential to the performers.

"Look alive, sister." Eulalie the Trader Nightingale, known offstage as Ermentrude Ulrich and as ordinary a Solitaire as Thalia, gave her a cold stare as she bumped her. "Coming through."

Thalia spoke through clenched teeth. "I'm not your sister, Trudy." Beneath her costume, she wore a pigeon squeezer, a homemade contraption that held the doves she used in her act. The singer's clumsiness had driven one of its hidden wires between the bones of Thalia's corset. It hurt.

"Shut up, Blondie." The red-haired singer swept past. "Make way for the talent."

Thalia reminded herself she was a consummate professional. Therefore, she resisted the urge to step on the train of the singer's gown as she passed. The gown, because it was supposed to belong to a Trader, was the last word in luxury, coral silk with jet beads and egret feathers that matched Trudy's picture hat. Damaging it wouldn't accomplish anything, and Thalia knew she was above all that nonsense. Anyway, she had work to do. The Lady of the Lake was next on the bill.

Just offstage, inches out of the audience's line of sight, David Nutall stood talking to one of the stagehands. Nutall—like Thalia, a white Solitaire—was looking paler than he usually did, his straight black hair and pencil mustache a greater contrast even than usual.

Thalia tried to pick out their conversation. Both spoke in murmurs. Thalia had to come close to hear them.

"No, Horace." Nutall smiled but his voice was firm. "This time, you're wrong."

"Think about it, that's all I'm saying." Horace, a black Solitaire whose nose testified that he'd been in many fights, was holding a rope but had his entire attention focused on Nutall. "'Deeper than did ever plummet sound I'll drown my book.' If Shakespeare wasn't a Trader, how could he write dialogue that fancy? He knew how Traders like that talk because he was one."

"Birnam Wood came to Dunsinane, does that make Shakespeare a Sylvestri?" asked Nutall.

Horace was offended. "I never said he was Sylvestri. I said he was a Trader. No Solitaire would ever be so fancy, you have to admit."

"On the contrary. I've known some tremendously fancy Solitaires in my day." Nutall turned to greet Thalia as she took her spot beside him. "There you are."

"Shakespeare was a Trader?" Thalia murmured.

"No." Nutall was firm. "He certainly was not. William Shakespeare was a Solitaire."

"Just like you and me?" Thalia asked.

"Exactly," said Nutall.

"If you say so. Good evening, Miss Cutler." Horace, stoic in the face of Nutall's skepticism, turned his attention firmly back to the plate spinner at work onstage.

The theater was nearly full, the audience happy but not boisterous. The pit orchestra struck up Thalia's music. Nutall gave her a brilliant smile. "That's us."

Together they took the stage. Blinking to focus in the glare of the lights, basking in the attention of the audience, Thalia felt the whole world sharpen around her. Shoulders back, head held high, she took her mark onstage. She did not walk, but glide.

Nutall's deep voice provided the narrative to the act. "Ladies and gentlemen, Solitaires, Traders, and Sylvestri, I present to you Thalia Cutler, the Lady of the Lake, here to amaze and entertain you."

Clad in a shining white gown with medieval sleeves, with her fair hair loose over her shoulders, Thalia stood center stage and made doves appear from thin air. Thalia turned cards into coins and changed them back again. She turned a wooden staff into a snake that slithered off into the wings.

The audience was rapt throughout, applauding each trick enthusiastically. The music and the sleight of hand went smoothly.

At the climax of the act, Nutall declaimed, "For her final trick this evening, the Lady of the Lake will defy the incredible danger of the Siege Perilous." On cue, the curtain behind Thalia swept aside to reveal a simple throne of rough-hewn wood. This was no flimsy stage prop, but a solid chair with arms and a high back, approximately medieval in appearance.

Above the chair was a rope-and-pulley rig that held a sword suspended, point down, over the wooden throne. The pit orchestra played a little waltz while Nutall paid out the rope to bring the sword down to demonstrate how sharp it was. He sliced an apple with it, then hauled it back to its menacing position. He produced a candle, which he set in a wrought-iron stand. It was placed so that, once lit, the flame would touch the rope.

Thalia, with due ceremony, took her place upon the throne. Nutall took up the manacles that dangled from chains welded to the arms of the throne. He called for a volunteer from the audience to witness that the cuffs were made of genuine steel and that the chains were just as solidly made. When the volunteer went back to the audience, Nutall closed the manacles on Thalia's wrists, trapping her in the chair. He placed the key—the only key—in his waistcoat pocket and walked away.

Thalia sat tall and did her best to look queenly and brave—but not too stupid to realize her danger—while she let the audience take in her plight.

Nutall stepped to the candle stand and produced a box of lucifer matches. "Ladies and gentlemen, please give the Lady of the Lake your undivided attention."

The orchestra fell silent, save for a snare drumroll. Overhead, the sword gleamed in the stage lights. Thalia could sense the audience's anticipation. She could smell the apple Nutall had sliced in half. When Nutall struck a match to light the candle, Thalia could smell the sulfur of its flame and then the scent of burning hemp as the candle flame licked the rope.

Nutall raised his hands and the inner curtain closed, concealing Thalia from the audience. The drumroll continued.

The moment the curtain hid Thalia from the audience, she set to work. The handcuff key hidden in her left sleeve dropped into her hand, and with a twist and a tug, she freed herself from the manacle on her right wrist.

Thalia could have picked the locks, but it was far more efficient simply to lie about the number of keys. She used her free right hand to release the catch that held the seat of the throne in place. With the faintest of clicks, the seat dropped from beneath her like a trapdoor, clearing the way to the open trapdoor in the stage below. All that remained was to unlock the manacle on her left wrist, bundle up her skirts, and drop through both openings at once to hide beneath the stage.

With the key in her right hand, Thalia worked to unlock the remaining manacle, keenly aware of the dwindling seconds she had before the rope, treated to burn slowly, would part at last.

Something inside the lock jammed. Thalia worked in vain. She was stuck.

Thalia took a wild look around. The sword was directly overhead, but not for much longer. On the other side of the curtain, the audience waited, attention rapt on the candle burning through the rope. The drumroll still sounded.

Thalia could smell greasepaint and her own sweat. Her entire focus was on the last chance she had: to slip her hand through the locked cuff.

It never occurred to Thalia to call for help. This was her profession, her birthright. The show simply must go on.

Thalia dropped through the trapdoor in the throne as far as the length of chain allowed. The links of the chain kept the seat from snapping back into place as it was meant to. That alone would certainly ruin the trick. When the sword dropped, it would strike her, but perhaps not fatally.

The numbness in Thalia's left wrist had turned to fire. Stubborn to the end, angry with herself for failure, Thalia was still twisting the key in the jammed lock, while straining to pull her hand through the cuff despite the impossibly tight fit.

Thalia's arms, her whole body, went from numbness to pins and needles everywhere. She looked up, ready for the sword, angrily resigned to pay the price for her clumsiness with the jammed cuff. But Thalia could not see her left hand. She saw something white, something she didn't understand. It could not be what it seemed, white feathers forming a shape like the tip of a bird's wing. Before she could make sense of what she saw, Thalia fell at last, free of the cuff.

The chain, free of Thalia's weight, was rigged to slide to the outside of the throne. It slithered upward out of sight. The trapdoor in the throne clicked shut as Thalia fell into blind darkness beneath the stage. The numbness held her. She couldn't see, but she could hear.

The sound the crowd made, the collective gasp of horror and delight, told Thalia the candle had done its work at last.

The rope parted.

The thud of the sword overhead made Thalia flinch. From far away, applause told her the curtain had drawn back to reveal the empty throne with the sword lodged harmlessly in the wooden seat, the empty manacles dangling.

Thalia lay there, swiftly becoming aware of her situation. She had arms again, not feathers. She was lying on a mildewed mattress directly beneath the trapdoor in the stage overhead. She was herself again, not pins and needles, not fire, not numbness.

Thalia crawled off the mattress, vomited on the dirty floor, and spat. She drew a shaky breath. What she had seen in that elongated second before she fell had been her own hand transformed into something she could not put words to. Something with feathers. Thalia knew that Traders changed that way, Traded one shape for another, as easy for them as breathing. Thalia knew she was only a Solitaire. Yet somehow, she had changed. What did that mean?

Far above, as the applause died away, the pit orchestra took up Thalia's music again. Thalia found herself on her feet, staggering toward the door that would take her to the back of the theater. Nutall would be watching for her so he could point her out to the audience.

As Thalia made haste, her head cleared. She found herself counting the bars of music. If she hurried, if she ran full tilt, she could still make her cue. She must not miss her cue.

Chapter Two

Thalia finished the performance only by refusing herself permission to think. She moved as if mesmerized, taking her bows with Nutall, clearing up her props, removing her stage makeup in the dressing room shared by all the chorus girls, and changing out of her costume and into a tan walking dress and her favorite hat.

At last, in the dark street outside the theater, Nutall offered her his arm and an unconvincing smile. "What happened?"

They set off toward the Solitaire boardinghouse where they had rented rooms for the duration of their stay in Philadelphia. It was a chilly night in early April. The air was not precisely fresh but it was cool on Thalia's face as she matched her steps to Nutall's. It cleared her head and made her feel more like she was awake and less like she was still lost in a dream.

"What's wrong?" Nutall prompted.

Thalia cleared her throat. "I Traded."

Nutall stopped in his tracks. Thalia released his arm and stood facing him, wishing the nearest streetlight were bright enough to show her more of his expression.

"Not here." Nutall led Thalia back to the boardinghouse parlor. Most of the other residents had long since retired for the night. Nutall turned up the gaslight and gestured Thalia to the horsehair settee while he pulled a spindly chair close. "Keep your voice down and tell me everything."

Thalia drew back her glove enough to show Nutall her left wrist, swollen, scraped, and already bruised. "I couldn't unlock the cuff."

"I saw one manacle was open and the other shut. I assumed you'd pulled your hand through."

"The lock jammed. I tried to." Thalia described her experience. "I Traded, didn't I?"

Throughout her account, Nutall had grown more and more rigid and still. His dark eyes blazed into hers. "Why didn't you call for help? Why didn't you stop the act?"

"I didn't think of it." Thalia rubbed her wrist. "Are you upset because I Traded or because I didn't stop the act?"

"I am surprised and concerned," said Nutall. "Milk bottles are upset."

Whenever anyone said they were upset, it was a sure thing that Nutall would say that. Sometimes Thalia said it herself without meaning to.

"You may well have demonstrated the ability to Trade. Whether you did or not, I am angry with myself that I didn't train you better. You should have stopped the act. On that point,

I admit I find myself torn between fear for your safety and pride in your courage."

"Oh." Thalia took a moment to let that sink in. Fear had ruled her. She'd known Nutall would be frightened too once he saw the locked manacle. It was strange to think he'd felt proud of her for her single-minded stupidity.

"Did you Trade spontaneously after twenty years of Solitaire behavior?" Nutall went back to glaring at Thalia, but she could see the raw concern behind his stern expression.

Into the resulting silence, Thalia ventured a reply. "Yes?"

"Well, good." Nutall did not seem to think it the least bit good, but he was as calm as ever. "In the morning, I will make some inquiries. We will find someone who knows about these things. For now, rest. You need sleep."

Thalia regarded him with disbelief. "How on earth can I sleep? I may have been wrong about myself all my life. What if I'm not a Solitaire at all? What if I am a Trader?"

"Don't sleep, then. Go to your room and practice your card passes instead. No, I take that back. Let your wrist recover before you resume your practice." Nutall gave her a genuine smile, not one of the artificial versions he'd tried before. "In the morning, we'll look into this properly."

Thalia surprised herself by sleeping most of the night. The rest must have done her good, because by the time she and Nutall finished breakfast with their fellow boardinghouse residents, Thalia felt perfectly well. Last night's trick gone wrong had dimmed in her memory. It was only a nightmare now, not something she jumped back into every time she closed her eyes.

Nutall led Thalia away from the rather sticky breakfast table, and they readied themselves to go out. Nutall was his usual spruce self, boot-polish-black hair combed flat and gleaming beneath his elegant hat. Thalia was wearing her best walking suit, dark brown wool with amber-brown velvet lapels the same shade as her eyes.

"Where are we going?" Thalia adjusted her hat and pulled on her gloves. April in Philadelphia could be lovely, but this morning it was not. There was a damp cold wind that promised rain to come.

"I've made some inquiries," Nutall replied. "We are going to pay a call upon Professor Philander Evans, an authority on Trader literature at the University of Pennsylvania."

Thalia fell into step beside Nutall as they walked along the broad cobblestone street in the direction of the university. "Why Trader literature? Don't we need a Trader scientist or doctor?"

"But we have an appointment with the only Trader authority who had time to speak with us before we catch the New York train." Nutall looked chagrined. "It's not ideal."

Thalia agreed. Their booking in Philadelphia was over. By evening, they would be in New York City, working at the next theater on their vaudeville circuit.

As they marched, the row houses on either side of the street grew in dignity as the greenery, trees, and ivy on many of the dark brick walls grew more dense. Nutall drew up in front of a particularly appealing house, with elegant leaded-glass windows and holly bushes on either side of the front door. There were yellow tulips growing all along either side of the front walk. "Here we are. Professor Evans is expecting us at half past nine."

Thalia consulted the plain little watch pinned to her bodice. "It's already five minutes past that. Why are we waiting out here?"

"One mustn't abuse courtesy with promptness." Nutall checked his own watch, a handsome repeater that he'd once won at cards. "Give it another minute, and then we'll dawdle up the walk."

Thalia drew a calming breath as she waited for Nutall's cue. It felt ridiculous, consulting a strange academic about her experience of the night before. What would a professor of literature know about turning into a Trader?

Nutall gave Thalia a meaningful look and tugged at his right earlobe. On that signal, Thalia started for the front door, Nutall just behind her.

When they rang, the door opened immediately. "Mr. David Nutall, I presume?" said the bright-eyed old white man standing there. He was dressed in tweeds and sported a magnificent snow-white beard that curled into ringlets on his chest. His nose was redder than the rest of his face. "This will be Miss Cutler, I trust. Please come in. I am Philander Evans, professor emeritus of the Strawbridge Chair of Trader Literature. Do follow me."

Thalia followed the old man from the foyer into a study abounding in books and papers. The room smelled of pipe tobacco and hair pomade. Professor Evans cleared two chairs of approximately twelve pounds of accumulated paper and motioned for them to be seated. When Thalia had seated herself, Professor Evans sank into his own chair behind the oaken desk and set about filling his pipe. "How may I help you?"

Thalia cleared her throat. "Last night I Traded. I think."

Professor Evans dropped his pipe. "I beg your pardon?"

"I changed shape. My hand turned white." Thalia faltered and fell silent at the expression of astonishment on the professor's face.

"Perhaps it will be helpful to put this in context." Nutall told Professor Evans the story as Thalia had told it to him. "I can feel nothing but gratitude for whatever this phenomenon may be, as it spared Miss Cutler severe injury if not something much worse."

Professor Evans had regained his composure during Nutall's explanation. Now he lit his pipe and puffed on it in silence as he stared at Thalia. When he spoke at last, it was with far less friendliness. "May I see the afflicted member? Show me your hands, Miss Cutler."

Thalia removed her gloves and held out both hands. The left wrist was bruised and scraped, swollen visibly in comparison with the right.

Professor Evans peered at her for another three puffs of the pipe. "Your parents."

It took Thalia a moment to realize that Professor Evans was asking her a question. "Dead, sir."

Professor Evans gave her a thin little smile. "You have my sympathy for your loss. Tell me all about them."

"My father was Jack Cutler, a stage magician like me. He died three years ago. That's when I took over his act."

"Was he a Trader?" It was clear that Professor Evans expected the answer to be no. When Thalia had identified her father's profession, his face had fallen in disappointment.

"He was a Solitaire," Thalia replied.

"What of his parents?"

"I don't know." Thalia looked to Nutall for help. "He was an orphan."

"That's right," said Nutall. "Jack Cutler knew nothing of any family. He was my dearest friend for many years. He was a widower when we met and never spoke of any relations, alive or dead."

"Did he ever display signs of Trader behavior?" Professor Evans asked.

"He wasn't as rich as Croesus, if that's what you mean," answered Nutall.

"I mean nothing of the sort. Was he adept at some particular field of business or study? Was he musical? Did he have a singularly mercurial temper?"

Thalia looked blankly at Nutall, who looked back with eyebrows raised. Thalia met Professor Evans' inquiring stare. "My father was a very fine stage magician."

"He was not musical, nor was his temper at all out of the ordinary. He earned his money. It didn't come to him from any trust fund." Nutall added, "He was as fine a Solitaire as I have ever met."

"Your mother, Miss Cutler, who was she? Was she a Trader?"

"She died when I was just a child," Thalia replied. "Her name was Margaret Cutler."

"Margarete, actually," said Nutall. "Before she married, her surname was Gruenewald. She came from Vienna."

"And you?" Professor Evans turned his full attention to Nutall. "You are an uncle, perhaps?"

"I am no relation to Miss Cutler at all. As I said, her father was my closest friend. Anything I know of Miss Cutler's mother's antecedents comes from stories her father told me. Before he died, he asked me to watch out for Thalia. So I have." Nutall gave Thalia a smile, but it did not warm his grave expression.

Professor Evans turned back to Thalia. "So as far as you know, both your parents were Solitaires."

"That's right," said Thalia.

Nutall cleared his throat. "Not exactly."

"Not exactly? What does that mean?" said Professor Evans.

To Thalia, Nutall said, "Your father told me about your mother. He said they met in Vienna in 1873."

Thalia had heard that story from her father many times. "He was performing at the Vienna World's Fair, yes."

"They married and your father brought her with him when he returned to the States. Your father told me that your mother's family had been most unhappy about her decision to marry and leave them behind."

Thalia frowned. "I never knew that."

"He also told me that both your mother's parents were Traders."

Thalia gazed at Nutall, thunderstruck. "Traders?"

Professor Evans said, "That means your mother was a Trader as well. That's most interesting."

"Mother was a Trader." Said aloud, the words sounded quite normal. Which was absurd.

"That's right." Nutall smiled encouragingly. "I'm glad you're taking this so calmly."

"I am not *calm*." Thalia stood up and paced across the cluttered room to the door and back. "My mother was a Trader."

"Precisely so," Professor Evans stated. "She was a Trader. It is not surprising that you believe you Traded."

"Don't be silly," Nutall said. "She didn't know about her mother until just now."

"Really? I wonder." Professor Evans rubbed his chin. "Children can be very perceptive. But let that go. Miss Cutler, your injury is very interesting, but I believe it to be consistent with pulling your hand through the locked cuff. In emergencies, we are sometimes spurred to do what cold reason tells us we cannot hope to accomplish."

Thalia crossed to the professor's desk and leaned over it to stare at him. "My father knew nothing of the family he came from. Isn't it possible he could have come from Traders too? Then I would have Trader blood on both sides."

"It is not impossible," Professor Evans admitted. "Merely highly unlikely. As it is highly unlikely you actually Traded."

"You honestly find it easier to believe that I pulled my hand through a locked cuff than that I Traded?" Thalia kept her voice low and steady. It required effort.

"Honestly? Yes. Looking up at you like this is hurting my neck. Please resume your seat. It's a question of age, you see. You're what, eighteen years old, Miss Cutler?"

Thalia sat. "I'm twenty-one." This was not strictly true, but she had been twenty for three months, which was nearly twenty-one.

"Forgive my error. You are twenty-one years old. Have you ever in your life before experienced anything remotely similar to your difficulty last night?"

This, Thalia had to be honest about. "No."

"Yet if you were truly a Trader, your experiences with Trading from one form to the other would have begun soon after your menarche. When Trader children begin to mature, that is when their poorly controlled Trades begin. You can imagine how closely their parents watch their progress."

Thalia nodded, but Professor Evans went on without giving her a chance to speak. "Once a Trader child learns to control the urge to Trade, once they can resist it or change at will, they are given an ordeal to prove their proficiency. There are poems and novels, even plays about these ordeals. Perhaps you've seen the *Metamorphoses* of Lucius Apuleius Madaurensis? It's better known as *The Golden Ass,* but delicacy demanded it be renamed when one of the Latin professors here adapted it for the stage. Selections from it are sometimes performed by the graduating classics students."

Nutall scoffed. "You have a quaint notion of entertainment. Although she has grown up in theaters, you may safely assume that Thalia has never seen a classical play of any kind, Trader, Sylvestri, or Solitaire."

"Really? What a pity." Professor Evans turned his attention back to Thalia. "Only if the Trader child succeeds in performing that ordeal, only then are they deemed complete Traders, fully adult, and safe to travel the world freely. By the time a Trader reaches the age of twenty-one, they are long past the kind of experience you described." Professor Evans paused for breath. "You are much too old to have Traded for the first time."

Nutall folded his arms and frowned. "What if you're wrong?"

Professor Evans sat back in his big chair. "Then Miss Cutler is a Trader with no training, no family support of any kind, let alone the usual Trader family financial trusts, and a future I can only call grim. Until they are able to control their Trades, young Traders can be prey to attacks by manticores. Manticores, although rare, still live by feeding off the magic of Traders who cannot control their powers. Should a young Trader survive unscathed by a manticore, know that most Traders have lost their mental acuity by the time they are seventy. Many Traders choose to spend their declining years in their animal form. If I am wrong about you, Miss Cutler, not only do you have my sincerest apology, you have my profound sympathy."

There was silence while Thalia and Nutall absorbed this information. When Professor Evans spoke again, it was with a bright, false smile. "You have one Trader parent, it seems. You are not a Trader. I have one Trader parent myself, and believe me, you will never meet anyone more Solitaire than I am. Congratulations, Miss Cutler. You are safe. You are in no danger of attracting the attentions of a manticore."

Thalia frowned. "Then what happened to me last night?"

"I don't know." Professor Evans gave his beard a thoughtful tug. "I am a professor of literature. I don't have a scientific explanation. If you force me to opine, then I think the danger you were in overwhelmed your ordinary perceptions. You experienced something very like a visual hallucination."

"I wasn't hallucinating." Nor was it merely visual, Thalia did not say aloud. There was a limit to how much of her time and energy Professor Evans was worth, and she had reached it.

"Something *like* a hallucination," Professor Evans repeated. "The mind is a powerful thing and extreme conditions produce extreme responses, particularly in the weaker sex."

"Right." Thalia put her gloves back on, careful with the bruising on her wrist despite her irritation with Professor Evans and his opinions on women. "But if things were different, if I had Traded last night, what would happen now?"

Professor Evans took his time thinking that over. "Probably one of two things, with one being much more likely than the other. You would experience similar episodes. Even if you are able to master your condition, you will find yourself in a difficult situation, given that you have neither family nor fortune. Or, and this is much more likely, you would be attacked by a manticore, which would consume whatever magic dwells within you, and you would die."

Thalia flinched.

Professor Evans grew gentle. "Solitaire children often dream of being Traders. I did myself, can you believe it? But it is better this way, isn't it?"

"Where do manticores come from?" Thalia had heard of manticores. She knew they preyed on young Traders. She knew they were cunning and relentless. "How will I know one when I see it?"

"*If* you see it," Professor Evans said. "I told you they are rare. A manticore is the fruit of Trader intermarriage. Given the emphasis Trader families put on the dangers of inbreeding, it is considered more desirable to have a child with a Solitaire, or even a Sylvestri, than to risk giving birth to a manticore by binding family lines too tightly."

"Inbreeding," Thalia echoed faintly. That sounded disgusting.

Professor Evans continued. "A Trader takes two shapes, their human form and the form of the animal to which they Trade. A manticore has two shapes, their own dreadful form and the imitation of a human to which they shift."

"So a manticore is really a Trader," said Thalia.

"Never say that to a Trader unless you wish to offend them," said Professor Evans, "but in a sense, you're right. Solitaires and Sylvestri dislike the manticore, but they have almost nothing to fear from them. Traders, on the other hand, loathe the manticore. The manticore returns the sentiment. Traders wish to destroy all manticores forever. A manticore preys on the magic found in Traders too young to control their transformation. Once the Trader can control the Trades, the manticore cannot feed upon them any longer."

"So manticores eat young Traders," Thalia repeated.

Professor Evans shook his head. "They consume their magic. The body remains, almost untouched. They eat the intangible. Where a manticore has fully fed, what remains cannot sustain life any longer."

Thalia cleared her throat. "That's horrible."

"To us, it is. To Traders, it is unspeakable. They go to great lengths to protect their young from the risk of a manticore attack. All the larger cities employ a Skinner specifically to deal with any manticore that dares to venture into civilization. Freelance Skinners work more remote places. All are promised reward."

"What are Skinners?" Thalia had seen the term in newspapers, but the dismissive way the professor pronounced the term made it clear he thought there were better jobs to have.

"Just people. They can come from any background, but most often a Skinner will be a Solitaire who has the senses of a hunter and no other honest way to earn money." Professor Evans added, "Any further questions?"

"Just one," said Nutall. "Are there any members of the faculty we could speak to who are actually Traders themselves?"

Professor Evans chuckled. "Very wise to seek a second opinion. Unfortunately, Traders in academia are rare. There are none on the faculty here. It is an unusual Trader who loves learning so much they will spend their limited time finding it. They know it will be the first thing they lose when their days of clarity come to an end."

"Thank you for your honesty, Professor Evans." Thalia had endured about as much honesty as she could stomach for now. She rose and held out her hand.

Professor Evans rose as Nutall did and leaned across his desk to shake hands with them in turn. "Thank you for consulting me. I hope you will keep me advised of further developments. I may decide to write a paper on the theme of Solitaire children with one Trader parent."

Thalia was glad to leave the professor's house behind. On the street outside, she drew a few deep breaths to banish her anger and the smell of pipe tobacco. "What now?"

Nutall gave her a crooked smile. "Now we catch a train. No more Siege Perilous for you. Tonight, we'll make do with the snake transformation."

"No!" Thalia caught his sleeve and shook Nutall's arm in her excitement. "Tonight we'll try the Bullet Catch!"

"Too dangerous," Nutall replied instantly.

"Nonsense! The snake transformation isn't going to be enough for an audience of New Yorkers. We need the big gun." Thalia held Nutall's gaze until her enthusiasm melted his restraint.

Nutall conceded defeat in their staring contest. "Oh, very well. The Bullet Catch it is. You will be careful."

Delighted, Thalia pulled him onward. "I always am."

Nutall gave her an old-fashioned look. "You never are."

"I will be from now on, I promise." Thalia set aside her fear of the night before. Stage magic was what she knew. Stage magic was her livelihood. She was a professional. She would give her performance every ounce of skill and determination she possessed. The audience would witness the kind of magic only a Solitaire could make.

Chapter Three

Although the Majestic Theater had just as many seats as the theater Thalia had played in Philadelphia, the performance that evening was much better attended. It had been six months since Thalia had last played New York City, but some of the stagehands remembered her.

"Hey, Lady of the Lake," one called when he saw her. "Welcome back to the big time."

"Oh, Ed, I've seen bigger," Thalia replied sweetly.

Ed the stagehand rolled his eyes. "You're too young for that kind of talk, Miss Cutler."

Thalia left Ed behind as she made her way toward the dressing rooms. Although the Majestic Theater was in the Cadwallader Syndicate, not the Keith Syndicate, backstage was no different. It was full of shadows and smells—sweet greasepaint, stale sweat, cheap perfume, and even wet dog hair from one of the animal acts.

The dressing rooms at the Majestic, unlike those at some theaters, were worth the argument it took to get one. Thalia wasn't the headliner, so there was no designated room with a star on the door for her. The rest of the cast shared the two bigger rooms, one for men and one for women. The women's dressing room had mirrors on one wall and a screen to dress behind. It wasn't perfect privacy, but Thalia had experienced much worse. There were theaters out on the circuit with so little thought given to the performers that Thalia had to change in her room at the boardinghouse before the show.

Behind the screen, Thalia buckled herself into the pigeon squeezer, which fitted over her corset and chemise. Once she had the doves safely stowed, she donned the white Lady of the Lake gown with its hanging sleeves. The extra fabric made it easy to produce the doves on cue without giving away their point of origin. Thalia unpinned her fair hair and combed it to fall smoothly over her shoulders and down her back. The gilt circlet of the Lady of the Lake's crown was the finishing touch. Thalia made sure she had it on straight and pinned firmly in place before she shook out her voluminous skirts and stepped forth. A black Solitaire clog dancer in a blue dress immediately took her place behind the screen.

To put on her greasepaint, Thalia had to jostle for room in front of a well-lit mirror. Singers, dancers, and acrobats were doing the same, but Thalia held her own against them all. She finished up her face with a dot of red beside the inner corners of her eyes and put enough kohl on her light brown eyelashes to darken them to visibility.

By the time Thalia joined Nutall in the wings, she was fully in character, head high, back straight, the genuine regal Lady of the Lake with every swoop of her sleeves. She reminded herself to keep her chin up, the better to show off the line of her throat. Thalia knew she was no Lillian Russell, but she strove for that kind of elegant self-possession.

Nutall shifted his attention from the ventriloquist act onstage to Thalia. "There you are. Ready to impress them?"

Thalia gave him her widest smile. "Ready to catch a bullet."

"Don't even joke about it." Nutall squared his shoulders. The ventriloquist finished up and took his bows. The pit orchestra struck up Thalia's music. Nutall smiled back at Thalia. "Break a leg."

Although their act was announced as the Lady of the Lake and the Siege Perilous, Nutall ignored the mistake until it was time to replace the old trick with the new. They moved through the routine dove by dove, until it was time for the big finish.

Nutall's voice was smooth as aged brandy and as deep as London fog, pitched to reach the last row of the seats in the highest tier of the cheapest balcony. "Tonight, for the first time on the New York stage, you will be privileged to witness the Lady of the Lake performing the most dangerous of all feats of stage magic: the Bullet Catch. First things first. Ladies and gentlemen, Solitaires, Traders, and Sylvestri, may I have a volunteer from the audience?"

The man they'd planted in the audience volunteered enthusiastically. Fortunately, the crowd was lively, so there were other members of the audience clamoring to be chosen. Nutall brought him up to the stage, where Thalia opened the case with her father's muzzle-loading rifle. Thalia showed the weapon to the audience with great panache. *Shopping the prop,* as her father had called displaying an item of equipment to best advantage onstage, had been Thalia's specialty since she'd grown old enough to go onstage as her father's assistant.

Nutall issued his next command to the volunteer. "Please take a moment to inspect this deadly missile. Do you agree that it is a musket ball of solid lead?"

The volunteer agreed it was. At Nutall's bidding, he scratched his initials on the surface of the ball with Nutall's own penknife.

Thalia then made the most of the gestures it took to load the rifle—fine black powder, carefully measured out before the performance ever began; then wadding; and finally the rifle ball—then a pantomime of tamping it all down gently with the rod from beneath the rifle barrel. Thalia pretended to present the loaded rifle to their volunteer, but Nutall intervened.

"You have inspected this rifle, sir. You stand witness that the ammunition is properly loaded down to the last grain of gunpowder?"

The volunteer agreed all was as it should be.

Thalia glided across the stage to take her place on a wooden pedestal. She stepped up and struck a queenly pose, holding the enamel cup out in her most regal manner.

"It is my honor to be the man to pull the trigger," Nutall announced. "Solitaires, Traders, and Sylvestri, prepare to witness a living wonder of the modern world. The Lady of the Lake will use her great powers to capture the rifle ball before it can pierce her breast. Her powers are great, but even the greatest stage magician can suffer a mishap." In an aside, Nutall added, "If you have children with you, I suggest you cover their eyes."

Thalia held her cup high.

Nutall called, "My lady, are you ready?"

Thalia, mindful of the circlet she wore, inclined her head only slightly as she nodded her consent.

Nutall commanded the pit orchestra. "Drumroll, please!"

The pit orchestra gave him his cue, a snare drumroll worthy of a firing squad.

Nutall leveled the rifle at Thalia's breast and paused, as if to savor the moment. He took careful aim at the cup in her hands. In his top hat and evening clothes, his shoe-button-black eyes somehow appeared closer set than usual. He was the very picture of a noble English gentleman, entitled to shoot beauty in any form, whether it wore fur, feathers, or a frock.

The sleight of hand was over. Thalia already held the volunteer's leaden rifle ball, the one marked with his initials. She had switched it for a duplicate when loading the rifle, palming the scratched original out of sight until it was time for it to reappear when she caught it in her cup.

Now, with nothing more than the force of her personality, Thalia would convince a theaterful of people that they could not trust their own eyes. She took a deep breath of sheer, delighted anticipation. *This* was the real magic. Traders might Trade. Sylvestri might work wonders with a forest. But no one but a stage magician could show people what it looks like to violate the laws of physics.

Thalia could smell the excitement of the audience. She knew what that meant. The stirring sight of Thalia held at gunpoint, valiant and vulnerable, spoke to something dark inside the watchers. This might be the night the trick failed. This might be the night they saw a woman shot down before them.

Thalia kept her eyes on the muzzle of the rifle Nutall held. She didn't have to look at Nutall. Her entire attention was focused on directing her audience.

The drumroll broke off as Nutall lowered the rifle. Intent on some imaginary flaw in the sight, he inspected the gun while the crowd stirred, speculation fanned hotter by the delay.

Of all the tricks in stage magic, the Bullet Catch was the most dangerous. There was always the chance someone in the audience might join in with a firearm of their own. The spell Thalia wove with her manner and gestures, the spell Nutall wove with his voice, these were all the protection she had from such mischance.

When the drumroll resumed, Thalia kept her shoulders square and her head high. *Here it comes. Make it look good.* With the greatest possible delicacy, Thalia widened her eyes and flared her nostrils, permitting a flash of fear to show in her expression.

Nutall aimed the rifle again, this time with confidence, and squeezed the trigger.

The gunshot rang out; the audience gasped. Thalia mimed something striking her cup with terrific force, jerking as if her knees had tried to buckle, maintaining her balance on the pedestal with great difficulty. As Thalia's balance changed, she made the pass that slid the volunteer's rifle ball into the cup. She let her expression soften, fear vanquished by triumph, but did not permit herself to smile. The pit orchestra's triumphant fanfare was short but perfectly timed.

Thalia held the cup high as she let the rifle ball roll around the interior. Smiling only slightly, she stepped down from the pedestal to permit their volunteer to peer into the so-called Holy Grail. Even though he'd been in on the act from the first moment, still he registered wonderment.

Yes, that was the mark he'd made. Yes, that was the rifle ball

he'd handled. Yes, the Lady of the Lake had caught the bullet in
midair. It should have struck her in the breast. The man gazed at
Thalia in awe.

Thalia stepped away before the man's admiration of her bo-
som crossed the line of good taste. This was vaudeville, after all,
decent entertainment suitable for the whole family. Burlesque had
no business at a respectable joint like the Majestic.

Thalia moved smoothly from one side of the stage to the other,
offering the cup to the audience's view. She made the bullet slide
and rattle as she turned the cup.

Thalia knew to the split second when the applause peaked.
Milking the audience was for performers who earned far less applause. She took her curtain call, sharing the ovation with Nutall, who bowed as she curtsied. She made her stately way into
the wings just before the closing curtain would have swept her
off anyway.

No one over the age of six honestly believed Thalia had caught
the bullet in the cup. But no one in the audience could tell exactly
how the trick had been done. The pageantry that Thalia and Nutall had given them was easier to believe than the laws of physics.
In that place between what the audience knew and what it tried to
guess, that was where Thalia made her living. That was her magic.
That was her power.

The Bullet Catch was just a trick. The danger, however, was
completely real.

Chapter Four

Backstage, as usual, was chaos. Before Thalia's applause had faded, a family act, with six acrobatic Cantonese Solitaire children and a well-trained terrier, had taken the stage. Thalia headed back to the dressing room, intent on getting out of her now-empty pigeon squeezer, with a muttered prayer of gratitude for having her performance before the kids and the dog. Whoever followed them on the bill was going to have a hard time getting the audience's attention back.

When Thalia deemed herself fit for public consumption, she emerged from the shared dressing room in her tan wool walking dress, the one that buttoned right up under her chin. Her outer garment, handed down from her mother, was an opera cloak of fine black wool lined with ivory silk. The ensemble made her feel uncomfortably warm backstage, but she knew she wouldn't be backstage much longer. With her white Lady of the Lake gown safely in its garment bag and her greasepaint already wiped away, Thalia was ready to finish for the night. She took stock.

Thanks to Nutall, the doves were back in their travel cages and the snake was back in its basket. Thalia fed and watered them all. Then she helped Nutall, who had changed out of his elegant stage costume into equally elegant street clothes, to pack away everything involved with the act. It was a finicky process, but Thalia had learned the proper routine from her father. Time taken now would be time saved tomorrow when she was getting ready for her next performance.

"You two. Lady and Gent of the Lake." Andy, the bossy young white Solitaire man who worked the stage door as a combination doorman and bouncer, stepped in front of them, snapped his fingers, and pointed at Nutall. "Manfred wants you."

Nutall spread his arms wide. "My dear boy, the whole world wants us. Mr. Manfred will simply have to wait his turn."

Andy was unimpressed. "Manfred wants to see you in his office."

Nutall waved him away. "I'll look in on Mr. Manfred tomorrow morning."

"Now," said Andy. "In his office. Just you, Laddie of the Lake."

Thalia caught Nutall's eye. "I'm coming with you."

"It's probably nothing." Nutall led the way.

"It's probably something. Do you want me to fascinate him? Shall I turn him to putty in my hands?"

Nutall laughed. "Perhaps some other time."

"I don't know why you're laughing. I could do it."

"I'm sure you could. Let Mr. Manfred be. There's quite enough putty in the world as it is."

Thalia followed Nutall up a narrow flight of stairs to the manager's office. Nutall rapped on the door and they were called in immediately.

"About time. Have a seat." Manfred, a white Solitaire man in his forties, was at his rolltop desk with a ledger open on the blotter before him. The office smelled of wet pipe tobacco and fennel seeds. Manfred waved at a pair of spindly chairs beside the desk. "You don't have to be here, Lake Lady. I just need to talk to your boss."

"I am Miss Thalia Cutler. If anything, I am Mr. Nutall's boss." Thalia considered herself excused from fascinating Manfred. He already looked a lot like putty.

"If you say so. Take a pew."

Nutall and Thalia seated themselves.

"Okay. Here it comes." Manfred lowered his voice and leaned toward them as he blotted his sweaty forehead with a stained handkerchief. "You're canned."

Thalia gasped indignantly, but Nutall was unperturbed. "I beg your pardon?"

"What, are you deaf?" Manfred put the handkerchief away. "I said you're fired."

Nutall folded his arms and settled back in his wobbly chair as if he intended to spend the night there. "My dear chap, obviously there's been a misunderstanding. We have a contract. We're to play here at the Majestic, evenings and matinees, for the next fortnight, with an option to renew."

"A contract is just what you don't have." Manfred popped a fennel seed into his mouth. "You two were signed as Lady of the Lake and the Siege of Peril, whatever that is. Instead, you show up as Lady of the Lake Catches Bullets."

"Surely replacing a dangerous exploit with one yet more dangerous must prove an acceptable substitute," countered Nutall.

"The Bullet Catch," Thalia told Manfred in her kindest tone, "is the most dangerous trick in all of stage magic."

"Right you are, Miss Lake." Manfred took on a kindly tone himself, as if speaking to a half-wit. "Only this theater is part of the Cadwallader Syndicate, so what the syndicate lawyers say goes. What they say is that the Imperial Theater, which even you and Mr. Lake here may have heard of, features a headliner with a special noncompete clause in his contract. Nobody, and I do mean nobody, is allowed to play any other theater in the syndicate with an act similar to his. Which, since the headliner catches bullets himself, yours is. Similar."

"How brave he must be." Nutall did not sound impressed. "Nevertheless, whatever the syndicate's solicitors may have told you, we do indeed have a valid contract."

"Watch who you accuse of soliciting." In his indignation, Manfred's fennel seed went down the wrong way.

"Dear me, I meant no offense." When Manfred's coughing had subsided, Nutall resumed. "Let me try to explain this simply. If we play this theater for the next two weeks, then the syndicate makes a lot of money. Therefore you make a lot of money."

"The syndicate already makes a lot of money, thanks. Without you two."

"Who is the headliner?" Thalia asked. "I've never heard of a noncompete clause for stage magic. Who else does my Bullet Catch?"

"Von Faber the Magnificent, that's who."

As Manfred said *Von Faber*, Nutall made a noise between a cough and a curse.

"He got a noncompete clause out of Cadwallader somehow,"

Manfred continued. "Von Faber always gets his way. No one messes with him anymore. Not unless they want trouble."

Von Faber the Magnificent wasn't famous the way the Herrmanns were, but Thalia had heard of him. The name meant more to Nutall than it did to her. On principle, she looked as bored as possible and shrugged indifferently. "Never heard of him."

Manfred's eyes widened. "Where've you been? The guy is a count or something, says he's from a noble old Bavarian family, but he doesn't use his title. You catch the bullet just the way he does, only his bullet is silver. Your gun is just like his, even the ramrod bit. Your whole trick is like his, only he's a headliner and you aren't. He has an agreement with the Cadwallader Syndicate and you don't."

"Faber?" Nutall bristled. "That nonentity is no more noble than I am. Less so."

"Your parents are your business. The only big difference is, he catches the bullet with a priceless Limoges dessert plate and never even chips it."

"Priceless Limoges poppycock." Nutall sniffed. "The man's a complete bounder."

"Could be, but he packs the Imperial solid every night." To Thalia, Manfred added, "I knew there would be trouble when Mr. Lake here called out bullets instead of perils. Only with you in that white gown, I didn't have the heart to give you the hook. If I may be so bold, Miss Cutler, you made a beautiful Lady of the Lake."

Thalia forced herself to smile at him. She'd had a lucky escape. Fascinating Manfred would have been all too easy. "What if we dropped the Bullet Catch from the act, Mr. Manfred? What would the syndicate lawyers say then?"

"The lawyers were very specific." Manfred looked almost sad. "The wire came fifteen minutes ago, so someone in the audience or crew has tipped them off. Neither you nor your partner here are to work the Majestic, nor any other Cadwallader Syndicate theater. Which I wish you both very good luck finding a decent theater that isn't. I risked my job just letting you stay onstage tonight."

"Sensible of you to let us proceed," Nutall observed. "I hate to think what the audience might have done to your theater if you'd deprived them of this evening's star attraction." His tone suggested uprisings and riots.

"They're not so bad," said Manfred. "The Majestic might not be in the same league as the Imperial, but we get a decent crowd here. They almost never rip the seat cushions or set anything on fire. They don't even throw much rotten produce. Well, not very often. Not very rotten."

Nutall held his line. "Yet you willingly conspire to deprive them of the very act that filled your seats to overflowing tonight."

Manfred helped himself to another fennel seed. "My seats are filled every night."

"Are they indeed?" Nutall lifted one eyebrow. "That's not what the chap in the box office told me."

Manfred's eyes narrowed. "You calling me a liar?"

"If the shoe fits," Nutall agreed.

"That's it." Manfred threw a handful of coins and crumpled bills down on the open ledger. "There's your kill fee. Take it and get out of here. As of now, you belong elsewhere. Get gone."

"What about our props?" Thalia gave him a long reproachful look and added the Lillian Russell lift to her chin for good measure.

After a moment, Manfred relented. "You can pick them up in the morning."

Nutall finished counting the money and put it neatly back on the ledger. "Five dollars? Don't be ridiculous. Our kill fee was negotiated for cancellation without performance. We've performed. That doubles the fee."

Thalia took care to show no surprise. For a kill fee, five dollars was generous. Ten dollars was absurd.

"Limeys! Think you own the world." Manfred opened a desk drawer and produced a tin cashbox. "Seven dollars."

"Ten." Nutall was firm.

Manfred glared at him. "Eight."

Nutall glared back. "Ten."

"Nine and that's it." Manfred added money to the heap of coins, then locked the cashbox away. "Take it or leave it."

Nothing in Nutall's outward appearance changed, but Thalia felt certain he would have settled for eight. She assumed holding out for nine had been what Nutall sometimes referred to as an experiment in Solitaire behavior.

Nutall's martyred sigh was a masterpiece. "Oh, very well. We accept your terms. But we shall take all our props with us tonight, so we'll need a drayman."

"So get a drayman."

Nutall wasn't the only one who could experiment with Solitaire behavior, Thalia decided. She gazed sadly at Manfred while Nutall pocketed their kill fee.

After an uncomfortable pause, Manfred extricated himself from his chair and crossed to the door. "Oh, all right. I'll tell Andy to find you somebody."

Nutall asked nicely, so the drayman let him and Thalia ride alongside him for the journey west from the Majestic Theater's stage door to their boardinghouse. Although the April night was chilly, the ride was short and easy, for the street sloped gently downhill. Professionally speaking, however, Thalia could not help but reflect that their journey might as well have been a hundred miles straight down.

That morning, Thalia had been at the top of the tree, a professional stage magician with a two-week contract at one of the most popular theaters in New York City, and therefore in the entire country. Now, in the wan hours after midnight, she was out of work, with no immediate prospect of another job. No work meant no money. No money meant she and Nutall should watch every penny until they had their next engagement booked.

Thalia caught herself. She might be down, but she wasn't down and out. Far from it. She was simply between engagements. She was simply on the road again, even if their road at the moment was a few blocks down Forty-Ninth Street, just as far as Ninth Avenue.

Nutall tipped the drayman generously, so they had his help unloading the trunks that held the props. Mrs. Morris, their landlady, came down, cheeks pink and eyes shining with curiosity, to see what all the fuss was about. Nutall used his charm to good effect. Mrs. Morris, a buxom white Solitaire well into her sixties, hovered about shushing the drayman as the trunks were hauled upstairs.

While Thalia and Nutall waited for the drayman to finish, Thalia whispered, "A noncompete clause? Is that crazy or can they really do that?"

"I'm sure they think they can really do that." Nutall looked tired. "We will find out for certain tomorrow. Stage magicians may not steal tricks from each other outright, but one-upping each other is a fine old tradition."

"Even if we drop the Bullet Catch, the syndicate bars us, Manfred said. How are we going to find work outside the syndicate?"

"Just because Manfred said it doesn't mean it's true," Nutall reminded her. "First we shall confirm the facts of the matter and then we will investigate all of our options—tomorrow."

The drayman finished up. He touched the brim of his hat and sketched a bow to Thalia and Mrs. Morris as he left.

"It is late," Mrs. Morris said pointedly.

"To be continued, then." Nutall gave Mrs. Morris more than just a sketch of a bow. It was the full exhibit. "I will see you ladies in the morning."

Thalia's boardinghouse room was small, but she didn't have to share it with anyone. The cages for twelve doves and a corn snake made it smaller. Thalia settled them all for the night. Once Thalia had cleaned up at the washstand, she put out the light and lay in bed wondering what they were going to do next.

Could they even find a gig at a theater that wasn't part of the Cadwallader Syndicate? Should they hire lawyers to fight the non-compete clause instead? Lawyers were expensive.

No contract. No gig. It felt strange not to know when her next performance would be. Unpleasant. She would talk it over with Nutall in the morning.

Nutall would have ideas about all this. Nutall knew all sorts of people and all sorts of things. He knew things about her mother and father that even Thalia didn't know. How many more secrets had her father told him?

Thalia thought about her father. If he had been a Trader instead of a Solitaire, Thalia would have been a Trader too. The very idea now seemed ridiculous.

Even if Jack Cutler had been a Trader instead of a Solitaire, her mother's family would have objected to him. Marrying a stage magician probably wasn't something a well-brought-up Trader girl was supposed to do. Even a well-brought-up Solitaire girl would think twice about it.

But Thalia could not imagine her father in any other life. Nor could she imagine herself as anything but a stage magician. But she didn't have a gig. So was she still a stage magician?

Vaudeville performers who were between gigs said they were resting. Thalia decided she was resting. All this could wait until morning. In the morning, she would talk to Nutall. Nutall was sure to have a good idea.

Thalia's next clear thought, though it came to her slowly, was that her crowded little room was full of cold gray daylight. She took a look out the window and saw a slice of cloudy sky that promised rain later. The sounds she heard were the other boarders stirring as Mrs. Morris's lodgers woke up for the day. The smells she smelled were not yet the pleasant odors of breakfast, but a reminder that the doves and the snake needed to be taken care of evening and morning both. Gig or no gig, Thalia had responsibilities.

The chill unpleasant fact that Thalia didn't have a job drove her from her warm bed. Something had to be done about that, and sooner rather than later. Meanwhile, once she had taken care of the doves and the snake, she had to do her finger exercises and practice her daily routine of card and coin passes.

Nutall was waiting for her when Thalia came downstairs, and they went into the dining room together.

Mrs. Morris had eight boarders at the moment, counting Thalia and Nutall. Her dining room table was long and narrow, with plenty of room for four places set at either side. Mrs. Morris and Esther, her white Solitaire kitchen girl, managed the steady supply of eggs, oatmeal, toast, and coffee.

Everyone in the room, including Mrs. Morris, either had something to do or had somewhere to be or both, so table talk was minimal. Thalia confined herself to smiles and nods as she complied with requests to pass butter, salt, and pepper. The moment it was decent to do so, Thalia excused herself from the table and went to get her hat and gloves. As an afterthought, she added her umbrella.

When she came down, Nutall, likewise equipped with his best going-out gear, met her at the foot of the stairs. "There you are. Going somewhere, are we?"

Thalia met his cheerful expression with narrowed eyes. "Aren't we? We need a lawyer, don't we? Let's go find one."

"Ah." Nutall looked pleased with himself. "We can do that if you wish, but first, I would like to pay a visit to the Ostrovas."

"Ostrovas!" Thalia was delighted. "Will we order a new trick? Can we afford that?"

"Possibly. We must certainly look through the inventory of props your father left in storage there. Something might be suitable. It has occurred to me to wonder how Faber's Bullet Catch came to be. I know Faber of old, and he's much more likely to steal than to invent."

Ten minutes after Thalia and Nutall set out from the boardinghouse, it began to rain. Thalia did not let the damp impair her spirits. She felt the rain carried smells better. Today the wind was right, so she could smell the Hudson River close at hand. Thalia liked rivers.

Thalia and Nutall put up their umbrellas and walked through the crowds along Broadway as far as Greeley Square, then another six blocks down Sixth Avenue, doing their best to ignore the sporadic din of trains passing overhead on the elevated railway.

Thalia reveled in the crowds and traffic. Other cities were crowded. Other cities had streets filled with traffic. But nowhere Thalia had ever been could match New York City for that particular sense of purposeful importance. Maybe the people jostling her on the pavement were going nowhere in particular, but everyone had an air of great urgency and immense determination. Thalia loved it.

Despite the rain, it was a pleasant day, no chill in the air anymore. The damp April breeze carried a vivid mix of scent. Over the ordinary traffic smells of horse manure and engine exhaust, Thalia picked out the more enticing aromas of roasting coffee beans and grilling sausages.

Thalia could have found the way blindfolded. The Ostrova Magic Company was the finest purveyor of magical illusions in North America, possibly in the world. To stage magicians everywhere, the name Ostrova meant excellence and discretion. Thalia had grown up playing with the Ostrova children while her father commissioned the Ostrovas to build complex props for the Great Cutler's magic tricks.

Nutall held the door as Thalia preceded him through the professional entrance. This door, completely unmarked, was one down from the entrance of the magic shop, a cluttered emporium of simple magic tricks the Ostrovas made to satisfy the general audience. In contrast to the glass display cases and tall wooden shelves of the magic shop, the reception room at the professional entrance was austere.

To Thalia, the familiarity of the place was delightful. The bell that jangled to alert those within that a visitor had arrived sounded just as she remembered it. Across the room, running the width of the space, there was a wooden counter, like a highly polished bar, upon which gimmicks could be displayed or diagrams could be unrolled for inspection. Thalia recalled being too short to see over the counter even if she stood on the brass footrail and stretched upward. A brass spittoon was still kept nearby, almost as shiny as she remembered.

A pair of wing chairs, upholstered in dark leather edged with brass nailhead trim, still loomed to the left, backs turned to the outer door. In the corner farthest from the outside door was a doorway hung with a bead curtain. Thalia knew the passage beyond led to Madame Ostrova's private office. There was no one to keep the door, no sign warning the caller to stay in the front room. No need for signs. Anyone who ventured this far knew that Madame Ostrova and her family were not to be trifled with.

Thalia drew in an appreciative breath. The place smelled wonderful, just as she remembered, a blend of fresh-cut lumber and pipe tobacco. That was the scent of possibility. That was the scent of wonderful new magic tricks under construction. "Oh, it's good to be back."

Thalia and Nutall moved toward the wing chairs. "I should have wired ahead," Nutall said.

Thalia beamed. "I don't mind waiting."

A step or two toward the wing chairs and Thalia discovered one was taken. The well-dressed white gentleman who sat there sprang gallantly to his feet. "Miss Thalia Cutler, isn't it? The Lady of the Lake? I'm Nathaniel Ryker. Please, take my chair."

The well-dressed gentleman, Thalia realized slowly, had to be a Trader. His clothing was tailored perfectly for his frame, but also for the place and time of day. He was only an inch or two taller

than Thalia herself, but his frame suggested strength and endur-
ance. He was in his mid-twenties. He wore wire-rimmed spectacles
and had a brilliant smile that flickered on and off. It hit Thalia full
force but faded out as he waited for her reply.

Thalia felt herself blushing. "I beg your pardon, sir. I didn't
see you there."

"I was at the Majestic Theater last night, Miss Cutler. Your
performance was strangely compelling."

"Indeed?" Thalia frowned. "What does that mean?"

The bead curtain rattled, and a vaguely familiar young man
with ears like a sugar bowl emerged. "Mr. Ryker, Madame Ostrova
will see you now."

"Thank you, Anton." Mr. Ryker gave Thalia another flicker of
that brilliant smile, and threw Nutall a friendly nod of farewell as
he followed the young man through the bead curtain.

The last time Thalia had seen Anton Ostrova, they'd played
jacks together. He had been a stately ten years of age. She'd have
been about eight. It was difficult to reconcile the memory of the
boy with the man she'd just seen. Only the ears were the same.

"Mr. Ryker, eh?" Nutall looked thoughtful. "One of the Riverside Rykers, perhaps? Traders. Made their fortune in fishing, then
shipping. Now they have a modest assortment of passenger liners.
Well, they'd hardly have dealt in furs. They Trade into seals and
otters."

The bead curtain was still swinging after Ryker's passage when
a bull-necked white Solitaire man in expensively flashy clothes
emerged wreathed in smiles. "I'll fetch your things, sir," said the
younger man—a different Ostrova, although the ears were the
same—escorting him.

Thalia felt Nutall tense beside her. "Faber," he said, as if the name tasted bad.

"Granny Nutall." The flashy man accepted his hat and walking stick from the younger Ostrova. "Haven't you seen my posters? The name is Von Faber."

"It never used to be." Nutall spoke mildly. "Plain Johan Faber, that's who you were when you left the Great Cutler's act in Burlington. Skipped in the middle of the night."

"You must be thinking of someone else," said Von Faber. "I've never been to Burlington."

"You ducked out on your share of the boardinghouse rent there. You also helped yourself to some props and my pocket watch."

"You're getting old. Memory's going bad." Von Faber buttoned his cashmere overcoat as he gave Thalia an assessing look, up and down fast, then up and down much more slowly. "Well, well. Who's this? A fraulein your age here with Granny Nutall? That makes you Jack Cutler's little girl. Last time I spoke with you, you sat on my knee. Shall we try that again?"

Nutall caught Thalia's eye and tapped his nose. That little gesture sent a message Thalia had no trouble interpreting. *Don't let him provoke you.* Thalia's distaste kept her silent.

"Oh, ho. Stuck up, are we?" To Nutall, Von Faber said, "She's grown up to be just like her mother, then. Little Margaret thought she was better than all the rest of us put together, didn't she?"

"I never met her, but from what Jack told me, she *was* better," Nutall said flatly. "What brings you here, Johan? You're the headliner at the Imperial. Surely you've stolen all the tricks you need by this time? What's left for you here?"

"I pack them in at the Imperial," Von Faber agreed, "but it's going to be a long run. I'll need to freshen the act sometime. I've ordered a new trick, a real beauty."

Thalia could not help the tiny pang of envy she felt at the thought of being successful enough to commission a completely new trick from the Ostrova Magic Company. Firmly she told herself she was not the least bit curious about what sort of trick it was.

Von Faber gave Thalia another admiring look. "An artist like me, I see possibility everywhere. Don't you feel left out either, Thallie. I can always use another pretty assistant."

Thalia stiffened and drew herself up to her full height. Von Faber's disrespectful admiration made her skin crawl. The man was old enough to be her father. If he talked like that to her, how did he treat his actual assistant? The man was a bully. Thalia despised bullies. "Don't call me Thallie."

Nutall said, "Stop this impertinence."

Von Faber ignored them both. "I saw a matinee of yours in Trenton. I don't think much of the Lady of the Lake bit. It's old-fashioned. But the chains are good, Thallie. I liked you in chains."

Deep inside, Thalia's disgust stirred her anger. Before she could respond, Nutall's hands closed around Von Faber's throat. Before he could protest, Von Faber was off balance, pressed back against the wooden counter, eye to glaring eye with the Englishman.

Nutall's voice was ice and velvet. "Can I possibly have heard you correctly?" He tightened his grip. "Do you dare to offer Miss Cutler an insult?"

Von Faber's heavy jaw worked for a moment before he got words out. "Unhand me, sir."

Nutall's grip didn't change. Neither did his cold, soft tone. "Thalia, please go find Madame Ostrova. You don't need to see this."

Von Faber had gone beefy red. "Let me go, you sod. Don't touch me." He shoved Nutall back. Grappling and swearing, they fell to the floor, struggling for advantage in their wrestling match. Von Faber, growling, tried to bite Nutall. They rolled this way and that, knocking the spittoon into the far corner.

Thalia stepped away from the wall, judging the angles as the fight continued. If the opportunity came, she would take a swing at Von Faber herself.

A gunshot froze them, and all eyes turned to the inner door. Madame Sophia Ostrova stood scowling at them, with what closely resembled a Colt .45 in her hand. Thalia glanced at the tin ceiling. It was unmarred. Behind Madame Ostrova, the elegant Mr. Ryker looked on, obviously fascinated.

"Was a blank," Madame Ostrova informed them. Her thickened voice betrayed the fact that she was suffering from a head cold. "Next one is not."

Nutall released Von Faber, got to his feet, and gave Madame Ostrova a courtly bow. "Good morning, Madame Ostrova. So sorry we disturbed you. I think you remember Miss Thalia Cutler."

Von Faber struggled to his feet. "You are my witness, Madame Ostrova. This man attacked me. I think he is crazy."

Madame Ostrova glared at all of them. "Whatever this is about, you're all wrong. This is my place. No call to settle things here."

Nutall inclined his head. "My apologies for the disturbance. I assure you it was not unprovoked."

Madame Ostrova's grimness eased. She gave Nutall a nod. His apology had been accepted. She turned her glare to Von Faber.

Unwillingly, Von Faber muttered the apology Madame Ostrova was so obviously waiting for. She gave him a nod of his own.

Calmed by this, Von Faber put his silk top hat back on,

straightened the diamond stickpin in his cravat, and gave Thalia a crooked half smile. "My offer stands, girl. I'll pay top dollar for your father's old-fashioned tricks. You'll have steady work as my assistant. I can promise you good working conditions as long as you . . . cooperate."

His dirty little smile made Thalia want to kick him in the face, throw her shoe away, and scrub her foot raw. She did her best not to let any of that show. She could tell she wasn't fooling Nutall. With great difficulty she limited herself to a curled lip and the words "Go to hell."

Mr. Ryker, still watching from the doorway, gave Thalia a bit of applause. "Miss Cutler, I admire a woman of spirit."

Thalia ignored him.

Von Faber said to Nutall, "Some *lady* you've got there. I see you've made a silk purse into a sow's ear."

Madame Ostrova cocked her gun. She was still pointing it at the ceiling, not at Von Faber, but her scowl had returned. "Go."

"Gladly." When Von Faber left, he slammed the door so hard the bell almost jangled off its chain.

When the chime of the bell had died away entirely Madame Ostrova said, "An ugly man. Trouble is coming to him. He knows it. What does he do? He runs to meet it."

Madame Ostrova raised her voice. "Anton! Freddie! Cleanup duty. Bring a mop!"

Anton came bearing a mop and Freddie a bucket. Madame Ostrova pointed to the mess made by the overturned spittoon, and they set to work.

To Mr. Ryker, Madame Ostrova said, "Good day, young man. Sorry I cannot help you."

Mr. Ryker took his leave of her, but paused on his way out the

door to give Nutall and Thalia a sweet smile and a farewell bow of
their very own. Thalia, although she tried hard, could not think of
a single farewell remark for him.

When the outer door had shut, Madame Ostrova shook her
head sadly. "How I hate to pass up easy money." After a pause
in which she sneezed twice into her crisp white handkerchief, she
held the bead curtain aside. "Come to my office. Do you have time
for tea and cake?"

"We do." Nutall added, "Perhaps you'd care to do something
about your weapon now?"

Madame Ostrova tucked her handkerchief into her cuff and
devoted both hands to disarming and unloading the Colt revolver.
"There. No weaponry. You feel safe enough to take tea with me
now?"

Nutall offered her his arm. "You are graciousness itself, Madame Ostrova. We will take tea with you happily. But I fear we
have come at a bad time. Surely you are indisposed."

"A sniffle. It's nothing." Madame Ostrova patted Nutall's
sleeve as she drew him onward. To Thalia, she added, "It's a good
cake. Dried cherries in it."

In the years since Thalia had last been here, Madame Ostrova
had changed very little. She was a plump Romani Solitaire lady
who always wore black with a touch of scarlet somewhere. She had
olive skin and long braids, now gray, worn in a coronet.

As Thalia brought up the rear of their little procession, she
glanced back. Anton and Freddie had made short work of the spittoon and its spill. They were now standing behind the counter
with a deck of cards, taking turns to show off their card passes.

The whole place smelled right, Thalia reflected. With the
other visitors gone, it felt right. Stage magic was hard work. The

Ostrova clan took it seriously. In this place, Thalia didn't have to explain anything to anybody. She didn't have to fool anyone. She only had to take care of business.

Madame Ostrova led the way to her office. From either side of the corridor opened workrooms. The very air smelled exciting. Wet shellac, fresh-cut lumber, and the tang of turpentine hinted at the industry all around them. It smelled like backstage at a theater. Thalia wondered if that was why she felt so much at home.

Once they were in her office, Madame Ostrova seated them and went to arrange for tea and cake. Nutall checked the view from the window, intent on the weather. "It's stopped raining. Looks as if it is clearing off."

Thalia appreciated the chance to inspect the array of framed photographs, letters, and news clippings that lined the office walls. The names were legion: Ivan Sandusky; Thalia's favorite, Adelaide Herrmann; Mikhail the Magnificent; and more. In short, every stage magician Thalia had ever heard of, and dozens she hadn't, had done business with the Ostrova Magic Company. Not magicians themselves, the Ostrovas helped make elaborate illusions, but only for those they deemed worthy of their help. It was a source of great pride to Thalia that Madame Ostrova had respected her father. She hoped one day that she would be as respected herself.

Nutall continued his survey from the window. "If it is sunny later, once we've made a plan of action, we ought to take advantage of it. Do what ordinary people do on their days off."

Almost any other Wednesday of her life, Thalia would have been preparing for her afternoon matinee. She'd never given a thought to what the audience did outside the theater. "What do ordinary people do?"

"Walk in the park?" Nutall sounded dubious. "Go to the zoo?"

Thalia couldn't help laughing. "You don't know either."

"I'm not going to someone else's matinee, I can promise you that."

Madame Ostrova rejoined them. Nutall and Thalia took their seats as Madame Ostrova directed a girl about Freddie's age as she brought in a well-furnished tea tray. The small talk grew smaller and smaller as the refreshments were distributed.

The cake plate held only crumbs by the time Madame Ostrova sat back and eyed Nutall and Thalia keenly. "This is all very nice, a pleasant interlude. You came for a reason. What is it?"

"Von Faber does the Bullet Catch." Nutall put his cup and saucer down. "Jack Cutler did the Bullet Catch. Now Thalia does it too."

Madame Ostrova considered her guests. "What would stage magic be if magicians did not learn tricks from one another?"

"As well try to stop the spread of a popular song as the interpretation of a good trick, I agree." Nutall leaned forward as he lowered his voice. "The Cadwallader Syndicate, for some reason, has chosen to grant our friend a noncompete clause. His contract keeps our Bullet Catch out of any syndicate theater."

Madame Ostrova gave a minute shrug of her narrow shoulders. "Lawyers ruin this world. May they all eat each other. I'm sorry for your misfortune, very sorry. Understand. Von Faber is a client here, just like you. We're building a new trick for him, a mirror box. I won't take your side against his."

"Nor would we expect it of you," Nutall said smoothly. "I've brought the inventory of tricks we have in storage here. We've been told that Von Faber's Bullet Catch is identical to ours. I wonder how that came to happen. I know from firsthand experience that Von Faber has stolen props before."

"Stop." Madame Ostrova held up one many-ringed hand. "Do you suggest that tricks and props you pay to store here are less than safe and secure?"

"Certainly not." Nutall's air of injured innocence was perfect. "I do, however, suggest that we compare this inventory to the tricks in storage here."

"Another reason to check the inventory," Thalia offered, "is to see what other tricks we might use in the act. There must be something that doesn't duplicate Von Faber's routine."

Madame Ostrova opened a drawer of her desk and produced a massive ring of keys. "We go look."

Again, Thalia trailed after Madame Ostrova and Nutall, this time through the tidy bustle of the shipping area, where mail orders were packed. The corridor turned again, taking them past the door to the Palace of Mystery, the Ostrova Magic Company's private theater, used for demonstrations and rehearsals. Beyond that, they came to a locked door. Madame Ostrova opened it to reveal a flight of steps that led down to the cellar.

"Down there?" Nutall looked surprised. "When this inventory was made, all the Cutler tricks were stored on this floor."

"Down there is the safest storage we have." Madame Ostrova coughed a little as she punched the button of the electric-light switch and led them down the steep steps. "This is most secure."

"A bit damp, isn't it?" Nutall ventured.

"Perhaps." Madame Ostrova turned to fix him with a pointed stare. "Cheaper, though. How far behind on storage fees are you now? Fifteen dollars?"

"Madame Ostrova, I distinctly recall that we settled the outstanding balance on our account the last time we were here," Nutall countered.

"Two years ago. When account was ninety days overdue, we moved your stuff down here. We keep a copy of the inventory too. I checked. It is all here."

"Has it truly been that long?" Nutall murmured. "Oh, so it has."

Even with both the electric lights on, the cellar was full of shadows. The space had been divided into two rows of storage units divided with rough-cut boards and wire fencing material.

Three cages along, Madame Ostrova paused to open the lock on the door marked "C." "We conduct inventory, then you pay us so your account is up to date."

"Naturally we will pay," agreed Nutall. "Plus a little something on account, hm?"

"Twenty percent," Madame Ostrova stated.

Nutall was the picture of wounded surprise. "That's a bit stiff, isn't it?"

Madame Ostrova smiled at him. "Punishment. Next time, no waiting two years before you come back here for tea and cake."

Nutall smiled back. "Agreed."

Chapter Five

The inventory nearly checked out. Only one item was missing. The original Bullet Catch, as Thalia's father had performed it, had used a "volunteer" firing squad. In its fullest form, the trick involved catching bullets from six specially adapted muzzle-loading rifles. One had been sold to a collector. Soon enough the difficulty of finding and discreetly paying five suitable volunteers had brought the number of muzzle-loaders used onstage down to three. Then two. Finally, one bullet was all the magician caught.

When Thalia had performed the trick, she'd done it with the weapon her father had favored. The other four rifles had remained in storage, safely locked away. Both the inventories verified that fact.

Now there were only three. Since the last inventory had been taken, one of the Cutler muzzle-loaders was missing.

"Isn't that interesting?" Nutall stroked his pencil-thin mustache thoughtfully.

It was a grimy business, taking inventory of every prop and trick in storage cage C. Although everything the Great Cutler had in storage was still functional, none of it inspired any brilliant ideas for a new routine. By the time they had finished, both Thalia and Nutall needed soap and hot water.

"You think Von Faber got the rifle from us?" Even as Madame Ostrova blazed with indignation, she took them back upstairs to scrub off their accumulated grime in the washroom. Once they were back in her office, she told them, "The Ostrova Magic Company does not make this kind of mistake. I will find out who is responsible. I will find out how this happened."

"We know you will," Thalia assured her. "We trust you."

"I need to talk to the children."

"You missed a spot." As Madame Ostrova left the office, Nutall took out his handkerchief and rubbed at Thalia's chin, leaning close to murmur, "I think I can persuade her to compensate us with a new trick. Make yourself scarce so I can work on her alone."

Thalia thought about the inventory's complete list of distinguishing marks on the guns. If they could prove Von Faber's muzzle-loader had come from the Cutler inventory, they could bring charges against him for theft. What use would his noncompete clause be then? "I'll go around to the Imperial Theater and find out who handles his props for him. I'll ask a few questions."

"Not without me, you won't," muttered Nutall. "I'll tell Madame Ostrova that you have an appointment for a costume fitting. I'll meet you back at the boardinghouse."

"Oh, very well." Thalia looked around for her outdoor things. "If the sun is really out, it's a good day for a stroll. I'll shop a bit."

"Perfect. Just don't talk to any strangers." Smiling, Nutall tapped his nose and waved Thalia off as Madame Ostrova returned. "Now, about that rifle."

Thalia emerged into brilliant daylight. While she had been indoors, the weather had well and truly cleared. The streets were still busy, but the morning press of activity had passed. As she set out, she minutely adjusted the brim of her hat to account for the sun. Time to study the finer points of the coming season's fashions. The windows at Stern Brothers were on her way. She could see what people were really wearing while she walked there, considering the next move.

Deploying lawyers against Von Faber would be expensive. Deploying a charge of theft might actually get them somewhere. Thalia trusted Nutall to speak with Madame Ostrova. Once he'd finished, they would discuss what to do next.

"Ah, Miss Cutler. Forgive the intrusion." Thalia turned to discover Mr. Nathaniel Ryker at her side, spectacles glinting in the sun. "I know your time is valuable, but I beg you will spare me a few minutes." He gave her his flicker of a smile. "As I said, I was lucky enough to see you perform last night. A friend insisted I accompany him to the Majestic. I am so glad I did. You were, um, spellbinding."

"Thank you." Thalia was acutely aware that for someone to tell her she had been, um, spellbinding was not quite the same as telling her she'd been good. At Madame Ostrova's, the man had been in unfamiliar territory. His diffidence had been charming. Now, he seemed to own the street. Diffidence was gone, replaced by the smug self-assurance of a Trader. "You are too kind."

"I hope you and your associate Mr. Nutall will accept my escort home." Ryker pushed his spectacles firmly in place as he gestured toward a waiting carriage, complete with liveried coachman. "Permit me to share my resources."

Nutall's words came back to Thalia. *Don't talk to any strangers.* She was wary, but she could not resist the chance to really look at the man. So this was what a polite Trader looked like. Had her mother's parents been like this? Had her mother? Thalia scolded herself. How had she ever wasted a moment believing she was a Trader?

Ryker's wealth was written in not only the quality of his clothing but the care with which it was kept. His boots were glossy. His hat was glossy. Thalia decided his glossy wire-rimmed spectacles made his brown eyes seem larger than they actually were.

Ryker had taken note of Thalia's scrutiny. He gave her another flickering smile. "I wouldn't have offered to wait for your chaperone to join us if my intentions weren't of the purest. They are, though. I have a proposal to make."

"A proposal?" Thalia was proud of her deadpan. "Mr. Ryker, this is so sudden."

Ryker chuckled, a delightful burst of amusement that made him look as young as Thalia. "That's funny. You're funny, Miss Cutler."

This observation did nothing to endear him to her, so she said nothing. In Thalia's experience, people who said things like "You're funny" were seldom good judges of what was actually amusing.

"I have a business proposal," Ryker continued.

"I will do my utmost to conceal my disappointment," Thalia assured him.

"You aren't disappointed at all."

"Well spotted." Thalia took another look at the carriage and its coachman. "You've been waiting all this time."

"I have, yes. Would you care to wait for your companion inside the carriage?"

"How thoughtful of you, sir. That's not necessary. I won't accept your kind offer. I prefer to walk." Thalia gripped her furled umbrella like a walking stick and set off toward Sixth Avenue. Window-shopping would just have to wait.

"Excellent. I'll walk with you." Ryker matched her pace exactly.

"Oh? What about Mr. Nutall?" Thalia stopped for a meaningful look back at the elegant carriage. "I'm sure he will appreciate your resources more than I do. He's much older than he looks, you know."

Ryker grew serious. "But I prefer your company."

"What a shame, for I prefer solitude." Thalia turned her back on him to cross the street.

"That is a pity." Ryker, impervious to the snub, came with her. "You've come to quite the wrong place. New York is a city full of possibility, but solitude is not easy to come by." He took her arm, but only to hurry them both out of the path of an oncoming horse-drawn bus.

"So it seems." Safe on the far side of the intersection, Thalia gave Ryker a meaningful look but his grip on her arm remained. She turned the meaningful look into a cold stare. "Let me go."

Begging her pardon, Ryker released her and took a step back. As he did so, Thalia sidestepped to use a passing pushcart as cover and left him behind, lost in the crowd. She doubled back a block before she crossed the street, taking care to keep as many shoeshine boys, street vendors, and pedestrians between them as possible.

Thalia turned down Sixth Avenue and made for Twenty-Third Street, the nearest El stop. The train would cost a whole nickel, but the speed would be worth it. Briefly she toyed with the notion of cutting across Madison Square to Fourth Avenue. The Rapid Transit subway was new since her last stay in the city. She had wondered what it would be like to travel underground, but her curiosity would have to wait. For the moment, Thalia focused on eluding Ryker.

Traders were more fun to talk to than Thalia had expected, but distressingly slow to take a hint. Such a pity. Ryker was the best-looking man she'd seen in ages, and she was running away from him. Still, it was hardly the first time a personable young man had believed that expressing his admiration for her earned him the right to impose on Thalia's time and person.

Ryker had waited outside the Ostrova Magic Company while Thalia and Nutall had inventoried the Cutler storage unit. That had not been a short period of time. Thalia found that level of interest from him alarming. Ryker was too rich for the likes of Thalia, rich in every sense of the word. Ryker was like an elaborate dessert. Tempting to risk a taste, but how much would it take to make her sick? Not much.

At Twenty-Third Street, Thalia crossed into the chilly shade cast by the tracks on the east side of Sixth Avenue. She climbed the iron staircase to the uptown ticket booth. The harried-looking white Solitaire woman in front of her had four children in tow. Once Thalia paid for her ticket and dropped it into the platform chopper box, she pretended to be part of the little group. She carried it off well enough to earn a tired smile from the woman to acknowledge Thalia's help in herding the children.

Slowly, the bustle of the city restored Thalia's good temper. She was able to ignore the encounter with Ryker and focus on her own situation. She was out of work, yes. But she was not out of opportunities. At that very moment, Nutall was working some angle with Madame Ostrova. Things were sure to improve.

Thalia didn't even have to crane her neck to look for the next train. It was already in view and coming in fast, making a racket like a million saucepans rattling at once.

The oldest of the four children, a boy of about six, was watching her wide-eyed. "Are you a nice lady?"

"No." Thalia believed if one absolutely had to deal with children, it was vital to be honest. "I'm a stage magician." To prove it, she did a French drop, concealing the coin in her hand until she reached in to pull a penny out of the boy's ear. She handed the coin to him as the train drew up.

"You can't be a magician." As he gazed at the coin, the boy was a picture of scandalized delight. "You're a *lady*."

"Don't be so sure about who can do what." As the carriage doors opened and passengers emerged, Thalia reached out and extracted her penny from his sticky hand.

"Hey!" The boy's face puckered in dismay.

"I am not a *nice* lady." Thalia tossed the coin back to him. As she turned to board the last car in the train, she called back to him, "The moral of this story is *don't talk to strangers*."

Back at the boardinghouse, Thalia just had time to take care of the doves, confirm the snake was still alive and not yet ready for its next meal, and get in a bit of practice before Nutall tapped at her door to signal his return.

"Walk with me," Nutall said. "Not far. We're only going around the block."

Thalia put on her hat and gloves and followed him out, ostensibly for a pleasant afternoon stroll. In truth, the walls of the boardinghouse were thin. If one wished to speak privately, it made sense to go elsewhere.

The day was still pleasantly sunny and relatively calm and uncrowded. When they reached a stretch of sidewalk with no one in earshot, Thalia spoke. "Thanks for cutting me loose. What did you and Madame Ostrova have to discuss that you couldn't talk about with me there?"

"Madame Ostrova would never compromise her professional ethics by discussing one magician in the presence of another. She disapproves of Von Faber but he is still a stage magician, and so are you."

"But she talked to you." Thalia lifted her skirts and took a long step to avoid a puddle on the pavement.

"I may be your stage manager, but I am not a stage magician and never will be. Madame Ostrova was willing to speak frankly to me."

"And?"

Nutall was silent as they walked past a newsstand. In the clear space beyond, he stepped to the edge of the sidewalk and looked up at the sky as if judging the weather. "In Madame Ostrova's opinion, legal recourse would be a waste of time and money."

"But the rifle! What if we can prove he stole the Bullet Catch from us?"

"Madame Ostrova says that Von Faber has something on the head of the Cadwallader Syndicate. That's why he has a noncompete clause. It actually costs the syndicate money, shutting down acts that Von Faber says are copying him. They wouldn't do that unless he knows something the head of the syndicate wants to keep a secret."

"But—that's blackmail."

"It is," Nutall agreed. "But Madame Ostrova seemed quite sure of her facts."

"Right. Good." Thalia set forth walking again, this time at a faster pace. "There are other syndicates. We'll get a contract with one of them."

"We could do that." Calmly, Nutall kept up with Thalia. "In Madame Ostrova's opinion, however, we should simply change our act so that it doesn't have anything in common with Von Faber's."

"How will we know what Von Faber's act is going to be? All he has to do is copy us again, and we're back where we started."

"We will go see Von Faber's famous headlining act," Nutall said soothingly. "If necessary, we will use some of the tricks in storage to mount an act that doesn't use any of Von Faber's current tricks. In the unlikely event Von Faber decides to change his act to copy us, then we will go to the authorities and charge him with stealing our rifle."

The tricks in storage had not inspired Thalia. "What about your idea that Madame Ostrova will give us credit for a new trick to make up for the theft from our inventory?"

Nutall looked chagrined. "I didn't get as far with that as I'd hoped. If we had the money to commission a new trick, she agreed to give us ten percent off the cost. That's the best I could do."

"Ten percent." Thalia shook her head. "Even if we had the plans for a new trick today, which we don't, that's a lot of money to tie up when we're out of work."

"Not to mention the time it would take," said Nutall. "The Ostrovas cut no corners."

Thalia uttered a heartfelt sigh. "So we need money."

"As usual," Nutall agreed.

"But we need tickets to see Von Faber's act at the Imperial."

"We need to see Von Faber's act," agreed Nutall. "Under no circumstances will we pay for tickets. I have a friend who works at the Imperial. I'll see if he can provide us with passes."

"Do you think we can go tonight?"

"It might be rather short notice."

In fact, the projected trip to the Imperial Theater had to be delayed. When Nutall and Thalia returned to the boardinghouse, Mrs. Morris told them that a message had arrived for Thalia. "The messenger is in the front room, waiting for a reply."

Addressed to "the elusive Miss Cutler," the message proved to be from Nathaniel Ryker.

"How does he know where I'm staying?" wondered Thalia.

"I imagine that has something to do with the fact that he gave me a lift back here from Ostrova's." Nutall watched with interest as Thalia read the letter. "Not to be inquisitive, my dear, but what does the Trader have to say for himself?"

Thalia frowned at Nutall. "Didn't you warn me about strangers?"

"As if you ever pay the slightest attention to the advice I give you. What does Mr. Ryker say?"

"See for yourself." Thalia handed over the expensive sheet of paper.

"An invitation—extended to both of us—very proper of the lad—to dine with him this evening. At Delmonico's. I like this young man, Thalia. He knows the way to an old showman's heart." He folded the letter and handed it back.

"Which lies through his stomach," Thalia finished. "I thought we were going to the Imperial tonight."

"We may certainly do so if you insist."

"But you're saying that you want me to accept this invitation." Thalia tapped Nutall's chest with the letter. "You think we could enlist Ryker as a backer, don't you?"

"All I am saying is, *dinner at Delmonico's.*"

Thalia turned the letter over, ready to write her acceptance on the back. "To which I say, lend me your pencil."

Chapter Six

Thalia suspected that going somewhere as fancy as Delmonico's in her Lady of the Lake gown could make it look as if she'd wandered in wearing her stage costume. Still, the white brocade gown was the closest thing to a formal evening gown Thalia owned, and she knew it suited her to perfection.

Its hanging sleeves were tight from shoulder to elbow, then fell free past her knees, points swaying dramatically thanks to a tiny lead drapery weight sewn into the hem of each sleeve. Without her hidden dove cage, Thalia had laced the sides of her gown tightly to show off her corseted figure, then accentuated her small waistline with the gold brocade sash that tied in front and then fell nearly to the floor. The crown she wore onstage would have looked absurd, so she wore a fine lace shawl, another expensive thing she'd inherited from her mother, instead.

In the high style of Delmonico's, Thalia's medieval stage splendor didn't seem unusual. Still, she took great care as she walked. Those weighted sleeves wanted to swing and sway as she moved. They could easily catch small unmoored objects and knock them to the floor. Thalia wanted to make a grand entrance, not to destroy property.

Mr. Nathaniel Ryker and Delmonico's majordomo led the way into the main dining room, en route to the private dining room their Trader host had engaged for the meal. Nutall was Thalia's escort. She held his arm and let him steer while she kept her treacherous sleeves out of trouble.

Despite her concentration, Thalia took note of those already in the main dining room. She recognized people she'd read about in Scene about Town, the Solitaire gossip column in *The New York Herald*. The bored white Trader lady in pink silk had to be Miss Onderdonk, heiress to the Onderdonk family trust and publishing fortune. She had two worried-looking chaperones and three attentive young Trader gentlemen at the table with her.

Thalia noted a young black man as he brushed past her leaving the main dining room. He was a Solitaire, she thought. He wore a well-cut dark suit and carried a black slouch hat as if he'd taken it off only out of courtesy and was going to put it back on the moment he was clear of the place. He was clean-shaven, and Thalia noted a scar on his chin that must have been a serious injury at the time it had been made. He had wide-set eyes bright with mockery, and the look he gave Thalia summed her up and dismissed her. *You're one of them,* that look said. His obvious dismissal of her piqued Thalia. She turned her head for a second glance at him, but he was already out the door.

If that brisk young man had considered Thalia to be *one of them,* whoever that was, she told herself she must be doing well at fitting in with her plush surroundings. She put the stranger out of her mind and took another quick look around the room. Her interest was rewarded at once.

Miss Lillian Russell herself, Solitaire of white Solitaires, majestically beautiful and corseted like the figurehead of a ship, dined at the next table. The man gazing adoringly at her from the other side of the candlesticks was Mr. Cornelius Cadwallader, white Solitaire head of his own theatrical syndicate, with a cigar in one hand and a glass of champagne in the other.

Nearby, at the best table in the room, sat the Italian Trader opera singer Enrico Caruso, happily eating oysters amid a throng of admirers. Thalia knew from the magazines her landlady read that Traders very seldom chose a life in show business or the arts. Only when the need to perfect their artistic gifts drove them to it, only then, would a Trader turn away from the luxuries of Trader society. Hard work and discipline were required to excel. Caruso's voice was his gift to the world.

Thalia soaked in every detail. This was the high life. Mrs. Morris would be eager to hear about her famous fellow diners. Thalia's delight in seeing and being seen was short-lived, however. They were shown into the private dining room Ryker had engaged.

Old money, Trader and Solitaire alike, seemed to prefer showing off in private. Thalia knew she would never be content with such discretion. Ryker, looking right at home amid all this luxury, inspected the preparations and gave the majordomo a nod of approval.

The table was lavishly set with silver, crystal, and porcelain on spotless white linen. The centerpiece was a silver cornucopia propped up to balance on its curving tip by three tipsy-looking silver cupids. The open mouth of the horn of plenty was heaped with real fruit and flowers, purple grapes and pink roses, both wildly out of season. In the warmth of the room the hothouse grapes and roses gave off a scent that mingled with something in the very air of Delmonico's.

"Smells like money." The words escaped Thalia despite herself.

Her bluntness earned her one of Ryker's flickering smiles. "Do you object?" He held Thalia's chair for her. Thalia accepted his help.

"On the contrary." Nutall seated himself. "We share the position of many unfortunates. Money is an absolute requirement for our existence. Our means of earning it has recently been curtailed."

"Unfortunate." Ryker, now seated, shook out his napkin. "Yet isn't money an absolute requirement for everyone's existence?" The waiters brought in the first course. A small amount of champagne was poured for Ryker's approval.

"Not at all." Nutall arranged his own napkin across his lap. "There remain a few places in this world where no currency exists because none is required."

Ryker nodded to the wine waiter, and champagne was poured for Nutall and Thalia, then Ryker's glass was filled. "Let me guess. These places are uninhabited."

"He means Sylvestri places," Thalia said. Nutall had long since drilled Thalia's table manners into her like military maneuvers, but no boardinghouse had ever presented her with the choices she now encountered. On either side of the plate and above it, her place setting was fortified by ranks of gleaming silverware. She worked out which fork to use by watching Nutall and Ryker. "He used to tell me the best bedtime stories, all about people who live in a forest and make their own everything."

"Indeed?" Ryker regarded Nutall with interest.

"I read about it in a book once." Except for a single sip to acknowledge his host's toast, Nutall did not drink his champagne. However, Nutall showed no hesitation in choosing among the fruit knives and the orange spoons. He seemed not at all impressed by the splendor of Delmonico's. "Unfortunately, we live here and now, not in Arcadia."

"And that takes money," Thalia agreed.

"Money definitely has its uses," Ryker agreed. The small talk went on as they enjoyed their food.

Lobster Newburg, Thalia discovered, tasted like lobster, butter, and cream. There was an edge of cayenne pepper over a treacherous undercurrent of sherry and cognac. Just as the private dining room had smelled like money, lobster Newburg tasted like money, smooth and comforting, with an exciting edge of possibility.

Thalia ate slowly, not only to memorize the tastes and textures, but to be absolutely certain nothing spilled on her gown. Emulating Nutall, she took just one sip of champagne, purely in the interest of exploration. It was good to know how really excellent champagne tasted, but on this of all evenings, Thalia wanted to have all her wits about her. It was no time to get fuddled on fizz, however excellent.

Nutall and Ryker discussed the horse-racing season to come at Keeneland and Saratoga Springs. Then they talked about the merits of fly-fishing. Thalia kept her place in the discussion with a question now and then, but mostly she watched Ryker.

Lobster Newburg was nothing special to Mr. Nathaniel Ryker. Thalia could see that in the methodical neatness with which he

ate each course of his meal. Nothing distracted him from his talk
with Nutall.

Lobster Newburg gave way to white asparagus, which gave
way to steak and mushrooms, which gave way eventually to strawberries in cream. Strawberries in April. Thalia had all she could
do to keep her astonishment to herself. She did not want to betray
how impressed she was.

Thalia knew this might be the best meal she would ever eat.
She devoted herself to it with passionate attention and a complete
disregard to the tightness of her stays.

There had been some very hungry nights in Thalia's life, and
she knew there would be hungry nights yet to come. That was the
price one paid for the freedom of a career in show business. Let
this meal, this whole splendid night, be caught in her recollection
forever, so there would always be a memory of warmth and light
and the scent of grapes and roses to remind her of dinner at
Delmonico's.

Her first dinner at Delmonico's, Thalia promised herself. Her
first, but not her last. Someday, somehow, she would find her way
here again, and not as anyone's grateful guest, either. Thalia would
come as a star in her own right, able to pay for such luxuries on her
own behalf. Able to invite guests of her own. Able to delight them
with the splendor of Delmonico's hospitality without counting the
prodigious cost.

Ryker laughed with Nutall. Thalia watched them and resolved that her next meal at Delmonico's would be in the main
dining room, where the whole point of the place was to see and
be seen.

Ryker caught her eye. "Sorry to bore you, Miss Cutler."

"Oh, I'm never bored," said Thalia. "It's not in my nature."

"That's true." Nutall backed her up. "You have the rare ability to entertain yourself at all times. At your age, I risked death by ennui on a daily basis, but you seem entirely immune." He turned to Ryker. "What about you, sir? When you were Thalia's age, were you boisterous or bored? Or can't you remember?"

"It wasn't so long ago as all that," Ryker protested. "Once I satisfied the Board of Trade—that is, once I came out in society—I was able to complete my education at college. I considered it a grand waste of time at the age of nineteen, but now I'm glad I did it. Education is important. I trust you agree, Miss Cutler?"

"In theory, I do. In practice, my father taught me his profession. Mr. Nutall has been kind enough to tutor me in everything else. I have no formal schooling."

"Show business requires one to live on the wing." Nutall made a minute adjustment to the angle of his fork. "No schoolroom could keep up. I've done my best. Where I had no knowledge, for example in music, I was able to enlist the occasional tutor. Fortunately, Thalia has always been an apt pupil."

"Have you ever considered becoming a tutor yourself?" Ryker asked Thalia. "My sister Nell has many interests. As the Board of Trade has yet to set her ordeal, she hasn't come out in society, so she is confined to our family home. I fear she finds that dreadfully flat. As a result, she has conceived a desire to go into show business, specifically as a stage magician."

"Dear me," said Nutall.

"Precisely." Ryker continued. "Miss Cutler, I would pay handsomely to enlist your services as tutor for a day. To be candid, I suspect an hour would suffice."

Thalia frowned. "Stage magic takes more than an hour to learn."

"No doubt it does, but I don't wish you to teach her any. I want you to give her a clear idea of what life in show business is like for a young woman of character. Tell her what it truly entails."

"She can't leave the house," Thalia pointed out. "How could she possibly go into vaudeville?" Not that Traders had any right to poke their noses into Solitaire professions like show business, she carefully did not add.

Ryker looked thoughtful. "Perhaps because Nell cannot yet leave the house, the idea of traveling from city to city on the vaudeville circuit appeals to her romantic nature. Soon the Board of Trade will set her ordeal. Given Nell's character, I am sure she will succeed. Once she is mistress of her ability to Trade, she will be free to go wherever she wishes. I dearly hope she has changed her mind by then. She often does."

"What level of compensation did you have in mind?" Nutall sipped his champagne.

"I would gladly pay Miss Cutler twenty dollars for her time, even if she is finished in half an hour," said Ryker. "With a bonus of another twenty dollars if Nell takes your advice."

"Thalia?" Nutall regarded Thalia with kindly interest. That meant the decision was up to her. He thought it was a good idea. Since twenty dollars would pay for a month at Mrs. Morris's boardinghouse, Thalia thought so too.

Thalia put her fork down. "I'll do it."

"Wonderful." Ryker beamed at her. "I'll send a driver for you at four o'clock tomorrow afternoon."

"Why not first thing in the morning?" Thalia asked.

"I want my sister to listen to your advice. Nell is not at her best first thing in the morning. She will be in a much more charitable frame of mind if we wait until teatime."

After Delmonico's, Ryker returned Thalia and Nutall to their boardinghouse with as much pomp as if they had been staying at the Astor. Ryker kissed Thalia's hand and took his leave. Nutall held the door and Thalia entered the foyer to find their landlady gazing after Ryker's carriage with awe.

"Well?" Mrs. Morris prompted. "Tell me all."

"I saw Miss Lillian Russell." Thalia knew Mrs. Morris was a devotee of the illustrated papers, Solitaire and Trader alike. "She was letting Mr. Cornelius Cadwallader admire her front."

"That is not what I meant and you know it." Mrs. Morris managed to look delighted and scandalized at the same time.

"We ate lobster Newburg and white asparagus," Thalia offered.

"It's the plain truth. Youth is wasted on the young." Mrs. Morris gave Thalia's shoulder a friendly swat. "You didn't really waste your one night at Delmonico's worrying about what you were eating, did you?"

"Who says it is my one night?" Thalia countered. "I'll go back there when I'm a headliner. Tonight was more of an audition."

"Then I hope you did well." Mrs. Morris turned from Thalia to Nutall. "How was it really?"

"Oh, very glamorous." Nutall hung up his coat. "Miss Russell was there, and the great Caruso too. I even saw the Skinner of New York, although he was just passing through."

"Which one was he?" Thalia had a vague idea that Skinners were a kind of bodyguard, something to do with Traders and their natural enemies, and until now, Thalia had never given them a thought.

"The man with the big black hat," Nutall replied.

The man whose glance had dismissed her as *one of them.* "Oh. Him."

"You must think me a ninny," Mrs. Morris said. "I meant what did your handsome young Trader want to discuss?"

"Mr. Ryker has engaged me as a tutor for his sister. Short-term employment at a reasonable rate." No sense in telling their landlady exactly how generous Ryker's terms were. Their daily rent might go up accordingly.

Nutall swept Mrs. Morris into an impromptu waltz step across the foyer and back, endangering a potted rubber plant as they went. "It was brilliant." He released Mrs. Morris and bowed deeply, first to her, then to Thalia. "You were perfect. Tomorrow you will deal with his sister."

Thalia bade Nutall and Mrs. Morris good night and went up to her room to think matters over. It had been an exceedingly long day.

Once Thalia had checked on the doves and the snake, once she was out of her stays and comfortable enough to think straight, she let down her hair and gave it her usual one hundred strokes of the hairbrush. As she brushed, she mused. If Ryker had only wanted someone to tell his sister the facts of life about show business, why had he taken them to Delmonico's to ask for her help? He could have done it when he stopped her on the street outside the Ostrova Magic Company.

Perhaps his sister wasn't quite right. Perhaps there was something more Ryker hadn't seen fit to mention. There was really no telling with Traders. Thalia mocked herself again for ever believing she was like them.

If buying an hour of Thalia's time was worth twenty dollars to Mr. Ryker, Thalia would oblige him. Money was going to be hard to come by until she and Nutall made their next move. A new act, one that didn't compete with the odious Von Faber, was bound to cost money.

In a way, the distance between Mrs. Morris's boardinghouse at Forty-Ninth and Ninth and the Ryker mansion on Riverside Drive was far greater than forty city blocks. Thalia, clad in her brown tweed suit with velvet lapels and a vaguely military hat with a touch of gold braid, could not have felt the sensation of going up in the world more vividly if she had been riding in an Otis elevator.

Ryker was as good as his word. At four o'clock sharp, his motorcar—to the delight of Mrs. Morris and her lodgers—had arrived to collect Thalia. The uniformed driver left the wheel to escort Thalia from the curb to the glassed-in passenger compartment, saw her seated comfortably, and tucked a fur lap robe over her knees as if he were driving a one-horse open sleigh instead of the latest in Pierce-Arrows. The vehicle pulled out with due ceremony and left the boardinghouse behind.

Thalia marveled at the smoothness of the motorcar's passage. There was much more room in the passenger compartment than in a hansom cab. Fitted into the barrier between the passenger compartment and the driver was an intriguing set of brass-trimmed wooden panels. Behind them, Thalia found an inkwell, an ashtray, a humidor with two cigars in it, a drop-down writing surface complete with blotter, a pen with a golden nib, and a silver penknife.

Before Thalia had fully explored the possibilities of the passenger compartment, the driver turned off Forty-Ninth and headed north. Theaters, boardinghouses, and hotels were left behind for cleaner streets and newer buildings. When they reached Riverside Drive, a few turns later, the splendor increased. To the left, the world opened out into a vista of grass, trees, and the gleaming Hudson River beyond. To the right, the row of fancy new apartment buildings gave way to even fancier town houses and mansions. It was like driving past a wall of money.

What would it have been like to grow up used to such wealth, Thalia wondered. Would it eventually get boring? Thalia couldn't conceive of such a thing.

At last, the Pierce-Arrow drew up at a stately building that could have doubled as a small palace, turned sharply, and drove between gates of spiked wrought iron into a small courtyard. As Thalia watched out of the back of the automobile, the gates swung shut after them. A metal bar, apparently magnetized, dropped into place, locking the gates securely. Only by looking closely did Thalia spot the clockwork gears that governed the mechanism. Clearly the Ryker family spared no expense when it came to protecting itself.

The driver opened the door for Thalia, removed the lap robe, and helped her emerge. Thalia shook out her skirts and patted a hatpin firmly back in place as she looked around. Every window gleamed. Every stone was scrubbed. The Ryker mansion was like a little city of its own, bustling with activity, fortified against the outer world.

The servants, Thalia judged, were ordinary Solitaires like her. No Trader would serve another. No Sylvestri would be engaged as servants, even if they took it into their heads to apply for positions so ill-suited to them. They were too different from Traders, too unpredictable in their behavior. Sylvestri cared more for a flowering tree than they did for any human's comfort, even their own.

Once inside the great house, Thalia was intercepted by the

butler, who had the long bony face and bright red hair she associated with the Scottish. He relieved her of her umbrella. "Mr. Ryker will join you shortly, Miss Cutler. He has gone for a swim."

"A swim." Thalia couldn't keep the words back. "In April?"

"Indeed." The butler showed her into a mirrored music room with a grand piano and many enormous potted plants. "It is Mr. Ryker's daily custom to swim in the Hudson. Please wait here, Miss Cutler. Miss Ryker is not at home, but Mr. Ryker asked me to assure you he will not be long."

Once she was alone, Thalia took a wary look around the music room. The grand piano, a Bechstein, fall board folded back to reveal the gleaming keys, was the heart of the lovely room. Perched on the bench, Thalia could see Riverside Park and the river beyond through the windows, open yet barred. Despite the river traffic that plied the Hudson, this place seemed very remote from the city. It felt like a castle in one of Nutall's stories.

The breeze through the open window, although chilly, brought a delicious scent of fresh water and blossoming trees. The river water must still be freezing cold. Thalia was confident that Ryker wasn't swimming in his human shape. He must have Traded. Would he come back smelling of fish?

Thalia touched middle C on the Bechstein's keyboard.

Miss Ryker was not at home. Nonsense. She was under what amounted to house arrest. If she'd ordered her staff to tell people she was not at home, that meant Thalia was wasting her time. She didn't count on Ryker compensating her for the visit if she never laid eyes on his sister.

Middle C, Thalia reflected, had filled the empty music room the way water fills a glass. She took off her gloves and played a scale. The Bechstein lured her on. She began one of the études she'd learned as a girl, when finger-dexterity exercises were far more important than musical training.

The Bechstein made it a pleasure to play faster, more precisely, moving from the simplicity of the étude to the pieces she'd learned from Milo. Thalia's fingers had not forgotten. From nursery rhymes and hymns, she moved to her favorite piece, a Chopin nocturne.

"Dear lord, woman. Stop!" Ryker was standing immediately behind Thalia. "For the love you bear your own ears, if not mine, stop that row at once!"

Embarrassed, Thalia put her hands in her lap as she turned to face her host. "I didn't hear you come in." It had been rude of her to help herself to that glorious piano. Her face had gone hot. She was certainly blushing as if she'd been boiled.

Ryker, despite his language, did not look angry. He seemed to be suppressing some strong emotion, but Thalia couldn't tell what it was. His spectacles glinted as he regarded her unsmilingly. He was wearing a serge suit in a deep gray that suited him perfectly, with a faultlessly pressed white shirt and a dark green cravat. His hair was still slightly wet and his face rosy with cold from his swim.

"Move over." Ryker joined her on the piano bench. Thalia could not help noticing that he did not smell like fish. He smelled like fresh air and balsam spruce, probably from the pomade in his hair. It became clear to Thalia that the emotion he was fighting to hide was amusement. "Have you no heart, woman? It goes like this."

Slowly, meltingly, the nocturne resumed. Thalia knew the notes. Clearly, Ryker did too. He drew the music forth much more slowly than Thalia would have done, as if it were a series of sighs. The music surrounded them, another glory of the Trader mansion.

A thought came to Thalia from nowhere. If Ryker's hands could do that to the Bechstein, what could they do to her?

The last chord had faded before Thalia noted that Ryker had finished and turned his attention to her. She brought her thoughts firmly back under control. "Beautiful."

"It's called phrasing. You might try it sometime." Ryker shook his head, marveling. "Where did you learn to play? On a mechanical piano?"

Thalia met his gaze with a marveling look of her own. "Mocking your guests. Is that the Trader way? Who taught you your manners?"

"I'm not mocking you." Ryker's smile reappeared, then vanished again. "My sister tells me that when I address a modern woman, frank honesty is the best way to show my respect. I'm doing you the honor of speaking to you as an equal."

"Frank honesty, eh?" Thalia accepted the challenge. "My turn. My piano lessons were with Milo the Strongman. My father paid him a nickel for each lesson."

"He earned every penny, then. What became of him?" Ryker asked.

"My father or Milo?"

"Either. Both."

"My father died three years ago."

"I'm sorry."

After they shared a moment of silence, Thalia continued. "Milo went west to seek his fortune in the Klondike gold rush. That's when I had my last lesson."

"If it's been that long since your last lesson," Ryker conceded, "I suppose you actually play quite adequately."

"Where *did* you learn your manners? By correspondence course?"

"Frank honesty, remember? For someone in your profession, surely piano lessons would be a great luxury."

"Music lessons were good memory practice. More than that, playing the piano is good for strength and dexterity." From her little drawstring purse, Thalia drew out a silver dollar and made it run like a cascade of silver, first down the knuckles of her left hand, then down her right. "See?"

"I do see." Ryker drew an inch closer on the bench. "I suppose you must play to your strengths. There's a composer newly rediscovered who might suit you well. J. S. Bach. Look into him sometime."

Thalia still had the sense she was being laughed at, and she didn't like it. "Your sister is not at home. That's a neat trick for someone who's not allowed to leave the house. So why have you issued this invitation?"

"Frank honesty," Ryker assured her. "My sister can be moody. I apologize for that. Give me time. I hope to persuade her to meet you after all. Don't worry about the money. I'll pay you either way." He broke off to move six inches farther away on the piano bench, but he held her gaze. "I confess, this is rather awkward."

Thalia surprised herself with how willing she was to take what she thought was a rather obvious clue. Ryker's expression was now one of intense interest. "It doesn't need to be awkward." She leaned toward him and let her lashes flutter once as she closed her eyes, waiting for the kiss. "Frank honesty," she reminded him.

The kiss did not come. Ryker sprang to his feet as Thalia opened her eyes. He had turned red. All his interest and amusement had disappeared behind a stiff facade of propriety. "My sister," Ryker choked. "I have expressed myself poorly. I apologize for that."

"It is forgotten." If only that were true. Thalia was blushing so hard she felt dizzy.

"Certainly." Ryker started again. "My sister is determined to go on the stage."

"Yes, so you said," Thalia responded crisply.

"Nell has sworn herself to a career treading the boards," Ryker continued. "It was no difficulty when she wanted to play Shakespeare. Amateur theatricals are rather amusing. We were in no danger that any theater management would confuse Nell with the Great Bernhardt."

Amateur theatricals were never *rather amusing*. More like excruciating. Thalia had been preparing to say something scathing about Traders in show business, but the reference to Sarah Bernhardt, the artist who Traded between her identities as a tigress and as the greatest actress in the world, stopped her. Caruso was a Trader too, she remembered belatedly. Never mind, plenty of other reasons for a Trader to avoid the profession. "I imagine not."

"For a friend's recent birthday party, bodyguards were engaged and Nell and her friends attended Von Faber's show. Now Nell is determined to become a stage magician instead." Ryker's disgust was unmistakable. "Nell doesn't just want me to pick a card. That's not good enough. She wants to go onstage to do her tricks. Next she'll want one of my top hats to put a rabbit in."

"Dear me," said Thalia, in her best imitation of Nutall's tone. "How distressing."

Ryker missed her sarcasm completely. "It is! You'll make her see sense, won't you? You'll make her understand what it means to live among Solitaires, to be a woman in *show business*." Ryker all but spat the words. "No reputation, no morals, no future—"

"No more talk." Thalia rose from the piano bench and paused to put her gloves on. Smoothing the seams with care soothed her and gave her something to look at besides Ryker. So much for wondering what his expressions meant. So much for guessing at his stupid moods. She had been brought here as a cautionary tale, a horrible example for a spoiled little Trader girl to learn from. Nothing more. "Your sister wants to do something with herself. How can you blame her?"

"I don't. I am the Ryker, the head of the family trust. I have the family business to run. It's only fair she should have interests of her own." Ryker ran both hands through his hair. "She's always been adorable. But Nell isn't twelve anymore. She'll destroy her reputation before she's even attempted her ordeal."

With his hair on end and his eyes hollow at the thought of his sister's wayward behavior, Ryker actually looked better to Thalia than he had before. What a shame he was disgusted by Thalia's very existence. What a shame that Thalia had been too stupid to notice his innate distaste for her, too drawn to him to read him accurately. "Why are you so concerned with reputation and morals? Hiding some interests of your own? Never mind. I don't care. I've had quite enough frank honesty." Thalia turned for the door.

Ryker was quick. He edged between two enormous potted plants as he came around the grand piano and reached her as she opened the door. As his fingers brushed her shoulder, Thalia drew her elbow back hard and caught him in the solar plexus. "Get off me!"

"Oof—" Ryker stumbled backward. "Wait!"

Thalia stormed her way into the foyer. The butler loomed up, Thalia's umbrella in hand. "Here you are, miss."

"Rogers, stop her!" Ryker ordered.

"I said." Thalia took the umbrella and whirled to place its point against Ryker's top waistcoat button. "Get off."

From the other side of the foyer, a girl called out joyously. "The Lady of the Lake!" Nell Ryker, all shining black ringlets, rosy cheeks, and merry laughter, came dancing forward with a little handclap of appreciation. "Oh, Nat! You are the best brother in the world."

Thalia held the umbrella steady as she turned to address the brat. The brat paid no attention. She tossed her curls fetchingly as she came to a halt so close that Thalia could see her every eyelash.

"Just play along," the girl murmured, scarcely moving her lips. Thalia was startled by the gleam of malice beneath the brat's sunniness as she addressed her brother. "You've brought me the Lady of the Lake for my birthday!"

All frank friendliness, the girl held out her hand to Thalia. "I am Eleanor Ryker. You must call me Nell. I am sure we shall become great friends."

"No, you won't." Ryker made a fizzing sound of pure disapproval. "That is not why she is here. Nell, don't do this."

Anything that made Ryker make a noise like that was fine with Thalia. She had to lower her umbrella and shift it to her left hand to accept Miss Ryker's offered handshake. To her surprise, Miss Ryker's grip was firm enough to make her hand twinge painfully. "I am Thalia Cutler. I'm pleased to make your acquaintance."

"Delighted to meet you, Miss Cutler." Nell Ryker turned to her brother. "Go away, Nat. I want to speak with Miss Cutler in private. Just us modern women."

"Nell, please behave yourself." Ryker adjusted his spectacles. "Miss Cutler, however low your opinion of me might be, while you are under this roof, I trust you will behave responsibly."

"Mr. Ryker." Thalia searched for words sharp enough to cut him down to size. In the end, she had to settle for a feeble "Never speak to me again."

Ryker bowed stiffly and left them. A moment later, entirely impassive, Rogers followed in his wake. Thalia was alone with Miss Eleanor Ryker.

Chapter Seven

Nell Ryker bounced with glee as she seized Thalia's umbrella. "Let me take this. Come up to my workroom so we can have some privacy. If we stay down here, Rogers will listen at the keyhole. Won't you, Rogers?"

Thalia followed her hostess. Nell Ryker was quick and graceful. They climbed flight after flight of stairs. Thalia marveled at the size and splendor of the house, but she said nothing to Miss Ryker.

At the top of the house, Nell Ryker stopped, her hand on the ornate handle of a door with a pointed arch like something from an illustrated storybook. Thalia had never seen such a door in her life.

"My inner sanctum," Nell Ryker told Thalia solemnly. "We will be safe here."

Thalia let her hostess lead her into the slant-ceilinged room beyond. At one time, it had clearly been a playroom or nursery. There were toys still on the shelves, and a rocking horse of un-usual beauty in the corner. Now it was a workroom. The table by the window was littered with stacks of coins, decks of cards, and handcrafted tricks of the sort the Ostrova Magic Company sold to children. Alongside lay sheets of paper covered with notes and diagrams.

Nell Ryker showed Thalia everything, her pride and ambition unmistakable. Thalia felt her throat growing a bit tight with emo-tion. Despite her years, however many they might be, Nell was little more than an enthusiastic child. No wonder her odious brother wished to protect her, however clumsily he went about it. Thalia considered what the theater folk she knew would make of Nell Ryker's artless Trader charm. Not everyone found such vivacity appealing, and some would make it their business to address Miss Ryker with such blunt honesty that she would be reduced to tears. It didn't bear thinking of.

"Nat tells everyone I've gone mad, of course," Nell Ryker said, ushering Thalia to a slightly battered yet surprisingly comfortable chair. "He doesn't understand. If one is given a gift, one must use it."

Thalia thought about trying to explain the difference between a voice like Caruso's and an ability to use an Ostrova Magic Com-pany trick. She chose to refrain from comparisons, at least for now. "You believe you have a gift for stage magic?"

"Believe? I know I have!" Nell Ryker's sweeping gesture offered herself as evidence. "Look at me!"

"You're a Trader."

"Yes, thanks." Nell Ryker dropped into a chair across the table from Thalia's. Her dark eyes were like her brother's, their expres-sion even more intense. "I know that."

"With all your advantages," Thalia asked, as diplomatically as she could, "why do you care about stage magic?"

The answer came promptly. "Why do you?"

"It's my family business." Thalia didn't waste any breath trying to remind Miss Eleanor Ryker that frivolous young Traders were ordinarily much too busy being rich to go in for hard work. They both knew that much. "Your brother says the Rykers have a family business too. Don't you care about that?"

"We have ships." Nell Ryker wrinkled her nose. "I'm not interested in ships anymore. I used to be, when I was just a young girl. Then I realized they'd never let me sail one by myself. Do you mean to tell me that the only reason you do stage magic is that you were brought up to do it? That's disappointing."

Thalia thought about the joy of performance, of taking her place in the spotlight, of using her powers of mind and body to their fullest extent to make an audience see what she wanted them to see. "I trained for it all my life. It's what I do best. I love it, I'll admit. But I still trained for it."

"I understand about training and hard work." Nell Ryker had her brother's smile too, and no flickering. It was a pure beam of happiness. "I can work hard."

Thalia smiled back. "Why? Money's no object to you. You have no need to go on the stage."

"No financial need," Nell Ryker conceded. "There are other needs. Pressing needs. Artistic needs."

"Artistic needs, eh?" Maybe the kid had it worse than Thalia had thought. "Name one."

"The need to improve." Nell Ryker held up a deck of cards. "I know the stage magicians' code forbids you to give away your professional secrets. I don't expect you to share your tricks with me.

I just want you to critique my work and help me polish what I've learned so far. Let me show you a simple card pass."

Before Thalia could protest, Nell shuffled the deck and began methodically to move cards from the top of the deck to the bottom, using only one hand. It wasn't smooth enough for the stage, but it was approximately three hundred times better than Thalia had expected. "Okay. Where did you learn that?"

Nell Ryker kept doggedly on with the card pass. "Promise me you won't tell Nat."

"I don't plan ever to speak to your brother again in my life, so yes. I promise." Thalia took the deck of cards away from Nell. "You didn't pick that up playing solitaire. Tell me."

"Rogers wasn't always a butler. He's gone straight, truly. He's been on the staff here ever since I was a baby and we've never had so much as a teaspoon go missing."

"What was he before, a cardsharp?" Thalia took off her gloves and began to shuffle the deck herself.

"A burglar too." Nell Ryker confided, "I can pick every lock in this house."

"Dear me." Thalia moved the freshly shuffled deck into a card-pass drill. "Why waste your time in show business? If your family trust ever runs out of money, you could crack safes for a living."

"Oh, don't keep harping on about how to make a living. There's more to life than money. I want to express myself."

"Oh, yes. Artistic needs. I'd forgotten." Thalia, still absently drilling herself with the cards, spoke honestly. "If you think you need to get up in front of people onstage to have everyone's attention, you're wrong. You're a debutante, aren't you? You'll have plenty of attention. The good kind. In show business sometimes it's the bad kind."

"Fine!" Nell Ryker rummaged among the stacks of coins and decks of cards on the table. "Save your breath. Nat has told me a thousand times about how I'll be ruined if I go onstage."

Thalia finished her card pass. "I don't think you have any idea how much I hate to say this, but you should listen to your brother."

"Oh, please don't say things like that." Nell Ryker found what she was looking for, another deck of cards. "I want lessons. Cut you for it."

Thalia couldn't help laughing. "Don't be silly."

"You win, I'll do as Nat tells me. I win, you teach me what I need to know to go on the stage. As a magician, mind you. No featherheaded-assistant jobs for me."

"You have no idea what those so-called featherheaded assistants really do. Don't sell them short."

"Teach me what they do, then," Nell Ryker begged. "That's all I want. Someone to teach me. You said yourself that money is no object for me. I'll pay you."

"Oh, really? Your brother said he'd pay me twenty dollars," Thalia said. "Although I'll admit he only expected there to be one lesson."

Nell Ryker beamed. "That's fair. I'll pay you twenty dollars for each lesson, as many lessons as you're willing to give me."

"Your brother wouldn't permit it," Thalia reminded her. "I'm not interested in making a business agreement just to have your brother cancel it."

Nell Ryker's smile faded slightly but it did not vanish completely. "Cut for it. Aces high. You win and we're done here. I win, and I'll talk Nat round."

"Suppose you got your way. What would you want me to teach you first? Coin passes?"

"When I get my way," said Nell Ryker cheerfully, "I want your honest opinion of my card pass. I want a lesson from you right now, and for you to come back here tomorrow and as many days after as you need to until I'm perfect."

Thalia kept her face straight, but not without difficulty. The Trader girl was better than she'd expected, but she wasn't days or weeks away from the professional level. More like years. Nell Ryker was sure to lose interest long before she was truly proficient. Thalia took her time and thought it over. "It's a deal."

In her delight, Nell Ryker bounced up and down in her chair twice as they shook hands on the agreement. "We'll use this deck. I'll shuffle, Miss Cutler. You cut."

Thalia laughed aloud. "Nerve like that will take you far, Miss Ryker."

"Please, call me Nell."

"All right, Nell. You may call me Thalia. Now, I'll shuffle. You cut."

They both drew the ace of spades. Thalia's opinion of Nell went up a notch, but she didn't let it show. "Look at that. A draw."

"Flip a coin?" Nell offered hopefully.

"Sure." Thalia brought out her pet silver dollar. "My coin. Heads we start with coin passes today. Tails we talk about your card pass."

Nell's smile blazed forth. "You're on."

Thalia made certain that the silver dollar came up heads.

Nell clapped her hands together in delight. "Splendid. Let's start at once."

"Payment in advance," Thalia countered.

Nell produced a twenty-dollar gold piece from what she plainly considered to be thin air. She held it up triumphantly, turning it this way and that. "Voilà!"

Thalia stowed the coin safely away in her purse. "Next time, turn your wrist a little more when you switch, and keep your hand steady on the reveal. It's gold. We can see it fine without you waving it around the room."

Nell bounced in her chair. "Oh, this is exactly what I wanted! Nat said he was going to invite you for tea. Do you mind having it up here?"

Thalia thought about Ryker's probable reaction to his sister's business deal. "I'd prefer it, actually."

Nell rang for a maid and ordered tea be served on her worktable. "Indian tea, not China. Cake if it's chocolate. Salmon sandwiches, if there's any salmon left. Lots of sandwiches, no matter what."

While they waited for tea to be brought up, Thalia began lesson one. "You have a beginner's grasp of palming and stealing. How are you at ditching and loading?"

Nell was intrigued. "I've never heard of them, so I think I'm probably dreadful. Do show me!"

Thalia left the twenty-dollar gold piece safely in her purse and brought out a silver dollar instead. "Palming." Thalia made the coin disappear and then turned her hand to show Nell where she'd hidden it with her fingers. "Stealing." With a smooth gesture, she produced her original silver dollar from a fold in the cuff of her left sleeve. "Ditching." She tucked it into her right cuff. "Loading." A silver dollar returned, doubled itself, and disappeared again.

Nell's eyes had gone wide and bright. "Show me again."

Thalia held out her purse. "Take two pennies and run through it with me. Ready?"

They worked on hand positions. "No, lift your hand more. Show the marks what they're supposed to be looking for. If you can get the coin to catch the light that's great, but don't wave it around. You have to look completely natural on the outside while you're completely artificial on the inside."

"This *is* natural," Nell protested.

The lesson was suspended when the tea tray arrived, a glorious array of cake and sandwiches on a tiered stand, a silver teapot, two china cups, and two saucers. Nell poured out tea and offered Thalia a plate of finger sandwiches and slices of two kinds of chocolate cake.

Watching Nell, Thalia concluded that the Trader girl's every gesture was indeed naturally theatrical, as if she'd been raised by an actress. Thalia wondered if had something to do with being a Trader. "If you scale it back a little, you'll have better luck. Right now, the marks will be watching you instead of what you're doing."

By the time the last of the tea had gone cold, all the cake and most of the sandwiches were gone, and Nell was losing her ability to concentrate.

Thalia wondered how the Great Cutler had ever had the patience to teach her. She couldn't remember a time when these elementary moves hadn't been second nature. It frayed her patience, trying to find simpler ways to explain technique to Nell. Better to stop now and resume fresh the next day. That would give Nell time to practice and Thalia time to think up new explanations. "That's enough for today."

With visible relief, Nell put her coins away. "Let's go find Nat. I need to tell him about our agreement."

"Good idea."

"I'll also need to tell Rogers to let you in from now on, no matter what silly orders Nat issues."

"Right. Good. Remember ditching and loading. Practice it more tonight."

"Magic lessons?" Ryker brought both hands crashing down discordantly on the piano keyboard. "Out of the question!"

"Oh, Nat!" Nell clapped her hands in delight. "You sounded just like Mama then. Do it again!"

Ryker looked as if he'd bitten a lemon. "I said no."

Nell shook her head. "Close, but not quite as good."

Ryker ignored his sister in favor of giving Thalia an absolutely baleful stare. "Miss Cutler. I don't care what kind of arrangement you think you've made with my sister. It's off. Do you understand me?"

Silent, Thalia stared right back. This was between brother and sister.

"Nell, you are making yourself ridiculous. You haven't passed your ordeal, therefore you are not a full member of society. You cannot enter into a legally binding contract until you are."

Nell laughed merrily. "Just listen to yourself!"

Thalia found the most comfortable chair in the music room and seated herself. Ryker's true opinion of women in show business had been a blow. Watching his sister win an argument with him seemed like fine entertainment to her.

"Don't let this woman's refined looks fool you. She had her piano lessons from a circus strongman," said Ryker. "She's spent her entire life at the circus. You don't want to end up like her."

Nell gave him both dimples. "Yes, I do."

Thalia was happy she hadn't told Ryker more about her music lessons. When the pit orchestra had been busy rehearsing, Milo had given her lessons at the piano in the nearest whorehouse instead. It had never occurred to Thalia to wonder, although now she could make a shrewd guess, exactly how Milo had accessed the piano for a lesson. None of that was any business of Ryker's. "Vaudeville, not circus," she called, but Ryker paid her no attention.

Nell retorted, "I don't care what you think of her. I've paid her in advance and had my first lesson. So there. She's coming back tomorrow for the next one."

"No, she is not."

"She is."

It went on that way. Ryker lasted ten minutes, then left the room growling under his breath.

When he was gone, Nell took his place at the piano and began to pick out a wandering little tune on the keys with only the tip of her left index finger. "Any minute now, it will occur to Nat that spending time with you is a sure way for me to learn how terrible a career in show business really is. He'll change his mind about you tutoring me in about two hours."

Thalia concealed an inward sigh. "Should I stay until then?"

"No need. I'll tell Rogers to get the car for you."

Before Nell could leave the piano, the door opened and Ryker rejoined them, looking uncomfortable. He came to stand directly before Thalia. "Miss Cutler."

"Mr. Ryker." Thalia looked up at him with distaste. "Don't you know it is rude to loom?"

Ryker continued to stand too close. "I owe you an apology. You are my guest. I was wrong to generalize about the role of women in show business, and in particular, I was wrong to insult a guest."

Thalia waited a moment to reply, enjoying his obvious discomfort. "You were rude about my piano playing too."

A spark of indignation spoiled Ryker's gravity. "I have no intention of apologizing for that. I speak to you as an equal. To pretend to accept your mechanical choice of tempo would be patronizing and wrong."

Thalia remembered several true but unkind remarks she had just made about Nell's technique and relented. "Fair enough. So long as you show me and my profession your respect, I accept your misshapen and ill-conceived apology."

Ryker took her hand as if he meant to kiss it, but when Thalia arched an eyebrow at him, he changed course and shook it firmly instead. "Understood. Thank you."

Nell, who had been practicing with her coins again, stopped to clap her hands approvingly. "That's more like it. Miss Cutler, what time will you return tomorrow?"

Thalia wondered what progress Nutall had made on finding a pair of passes to see Von Faber's performance at the Imperial Theater. Unless she somehow grew wings and flew downtown, she would be too late arriving back at the boardinghouse to see it tonight. Tomorrow night? "Perhaps it would be best to begin earlier. Three o'clock? We can work on switches."

"Perfect." Nell glowed with anticipation. Ryker merely looked resigned.

"Practice," Thalia ordered.

"I will!"

"I'll send my car for you," said Ryker grudgingly.

Ryker's Pierce-Arrow brought Thalia back to Mrs. Morris's boardinghouse at six o'clock. The driver lingered in the street until Thalia was safely inside; then the car purred off around the corner.

Mrs. Morris, never busy with dinner preparations when there was curiosity to be satisfied, emerged from the kitchen to greet Thalia. "How was it, dear?"

"The Pierce-Arrow was a wonder." Thalia handed Mrs. Morris Nell's twenty-dollar gold piece. "Have this on account. Is Nutall here?"

"I don't know where he's got to." Mrs. Morris pocketed the coin and turned back to the kitchen. "I'll give you a receipt after dinner."

Thalia had chores of her own to do. She changed into a dress that was less than impressive but easy to clean, put on an apron, and took care of her doves and the snake. Nat and Nell Ryker had provided an admirable distraction, as well as a generous amount of money, but the distraction was, temporarily at least, over. Thalia considered her options as she worked. Leaving Von Faber out of things, what would she like her new act to include? Some might have called it daydreaming. Thalia considered it to be vital planning.

Thalia was at the dinner table when Nutall returned looking flushed and pleased with himself. He pulled up a chair next to Thalia. "Inigo paid for my dinner, but I could never say no to a slice of Mrs. Morris's excellent pie."

Thalia passed along the slice Mrs. Morris cut for Nutall. "What about tickets?"

Nutall plied his fork nimbly. When he'd finished chewing, he used his napkin. "Inigo came up trumps. We have two passes to the performance tomorrow night." When Nutall finished his second bite of pie, he countered, "Are you enthralled with Mr. Ryker yet? He seemed bent on making a good impression. I believe Traders consider it great sport to enthrall comely young Solitaires."

"You've warned me before." Thalia put her fork down. "I am far from enthralled with Mr. Nathaniel Ryker. If Miss Ryker is enthralled with anything, it is the notion of going onstage. Both of them are generous, I'll grant them that." Thalia told Nutall about her afternoon in detail. "I've accepted his apology, so I'm going to be polite to him, but the next crack he makes about my lack of reputation, I'm going to punch his nose."

"If you must." Nutall looked thoughtful. "Rogers sounds like someone it might be useful to know. Watch out for him. You're going back tomorrow?"

"Three o'clock," Thalia said. "Sharp."

"Keep your temper in check," Nutall advised. "Try not to punch the goose who lays the golden eggs. This gig of yours is a great piece of luck. Come back from tutoring your Trader as soon as you can. By the time we leave for the Imperial, I want neither of us looking anything like our usual self. Wear something appropriate yet unrecognizable. I won't give that weasel Von Faber the satisfaction of knowing we're in the house."

Thalia ran a swift mental inventory of her wardrobe. "Er."

"Ask Mrs. Morris for advice." Nutall resumed his attack on the slice of pie before him. "But don't stay up all night sewing your disguise."

Thalia couldn't help laughing. "I'm no seamstress."

"Don't I know it. Try not to get carried away."

Thalia waited until dinner had been cleared up and the evening chores finished before she asked Mrs. Morris for advice on her disguise.

"Bless you, I'll be happy to lend you my sister's Sunday hat. Put the veil down and you'll look older than I do." Mrs. Morris, delighted to consult, gave Thalia advice on how to move as if she were three times her true age.

"Now, what was it like at the Trader mansion you visited this afternoon?" Mrs. Morris was clearly bursting with curiosity. "Lots of servants?"

"An army," Thalia assured her, "so well-trained, I only saw four altogether the whole time I was there. But the place is huge. They must have dozens of Solitaires to help."

"I suppose that's one thing Traders are good for," Mrs. Morris said. "They do give a lot of people work."

In the morning, Mrs. Morris presented Thalia with the receipt she'd written for the twenty dollars she'd received on account. "Where did Mr. Nutall go last night? I would ask him myself, only he's gone out already. I remembered your payment on account quite late last night. I wanted to tell him you'd paid, but when I knocked on his door, he didn't answer."

Thalia frowned. "How late is quite late?" Nutall had come in during dessert, but he'd stayed in for the rest of the night. Hadn't he?

"Oh, well past one in the morning." Mrs. Morris sounded sheepish. "I know it was rather late to disturb a paying guest, but Mr. Nutall has always been so friendly. I thought I would just try on the off chance he was still awake."

"He must have been asleep."

"That's what I thought, but then it struck me that I didn't hear anything. Not a snore. Nothing. I wondered if he was all right. I opened the door." At Thalia's expression, Mrs. Morris added hastily, "It was quite unlocked."

"Of course it was," Thalia said. "Go on."

"Everything was in perfect order, but Mr. Nutall wasn't there. He's come in since then," Mrs. Morris assured Thalia. "When I checked a few minutes ago, his bed had been slept in, but he's gone out again already."

"I'll ask Nutall about it when I see him."

"It's just that it was quite late to be out," Mrs. Morris explained.

"You keep a sharp eye on us, don't you?"

Mrs. Morris gave Thalia a penetrating look. "If you knew the world the way I do, Miss Thalia Cutler, you'd keep a sharp eye too."

"I wasn't criticizing."

"Yes, you were."

"I'll ask Nutall about it. I'd like to know where he was myself. I thought he was in for the night."

Nutall still wasn't back by the time the Ryker automobile arrived to collect Thalia. She scratched out a note to remind him where she would be and for how long, and then went out to the car. She'd worn her best suit the day before, so she was back in the clothes she'd worn to visit Madame Ostrova on Wednesday. She chose a less imposing hat and her best gloves. She felt smart enough to do justice to the Pierce-Arrow.

This time the car created an even greater sensation among Thalia's fellow lodgers than it had the day before. Once aboard, Thalia spent less time fiddling with the luxurious fittings in the passenger compartment and more time paying attention to the route the driver took. It was a windy, overcast day. Street-corner newsstands were hawking Trader papers, with "Manticore in Manhattan!" and "Send for the Skinner!" in the headlines chalked on the notice boards out front.

Thalia thought about her meeting with Professor Evans. If she'd truly been a Trader, those headlines would freeze her with fear. As it was, she felt nothing more than mild interest. She wondered how the Ryker siblings would respond to the news.

On Thalia's arrival, Nell Ryker met her in the courtyard, newspaper in hand. "Isn't it terrible?"

Thalia extricated herself from the backseat of the automobile and brushed imaginary creases out of her skirt. "What's happened?"

"Last night a manticore was sighted in Central Park. It ran away before anyone was hurt." Nell added, "They haven't seen one in Manhattan in more than two years."

"That is bad." Thalia looked around at the splendors of the Ryker mansion. "You and your brother should be safe from it here, though?"

"Oh, Nat's in no danger. He passed his ordeal when he was seventeen. But he's not going to let me out of his sight until I pass mine," Nell explained. "With a manticore near, the Board of Trade will suspend setting all ordeals until the Skinner has killed it."

"That's good, isn't it?" Thalia followed Nell as she led the way indoors and up to her workroom.

"I suppose so." Nell folded the paper and tucked it under her arm. "But until I pass my ordeal and come out in society, I'm stuck here even though I can already Trade perfectly well. With a manticore in town, there's no chance Nat will hire a bodyguard for me so I can visit friends or go to the theater. I'm confined to quarters until the Skinner does his job."

"How does it work?" asked Thalia. "How do you Trade? What animal do you turn into?"

"I don't turn into an animal." Nell sounded repulsed by the very thought. "I am one person in two forms. One is the form you see when you look at me now. The other is the form I Trade into."

"Why is it like that?"

Nell rolled her eyes. "I don't know. Why are you Solitaires so small you fit into one form? It takes both sides to contain a Trader soul. Our souls are that big. If I Traded, you'd see me as an otter. But there's no . . . intermission. It's not like ice melting into water. It's a Trade."

"Oh." Thalia thought it over and repeated her earlier question. "How do you do it?"

"I just . . . find the common thread." Nell broke off and gave a little shrug of her shoulders. "I don't know if I could explain it properly even to another Trader. They say it's different for everyone. Practice is important. We have the Changing room here, but there's nothing like fresh air and sunlight. It's lovely to be so close to the Hudson. Nat swims almost every day, and so will I once I've passed my ordeal and come out in society."

"What's the common thread?" Thalia asked.

A thoughtful pucker appeared between Nell's elegant eyebrows. "It's the same deep down. Both forms are the same. I learned to find what my forms had in common, the otter and the human, where they are both the same. Then I could Trade." Nell smiled and the pucker cleared. "I haven't been able to Trade properly for very long. Only a month or so. That's why Nat hasn't had time to set up my ordeal. Now I don't know how long I'm going to have to wait."

"But you don't mind waiting if it means you're safe from the manticore," Thalia ventured.

"I don't," Nell conceded, "but then again, I do. Once I'm out in society, I'll be a legal adult. I can sign a contract to perform onstage."

"We should make sure you have something to perform, then, shouldn't we?" Thalia asked rather pointedly.

Nell was delighted by the thought. She demonstrated how she'd been practicing palming and stealing. Thalia showed her a few of the finer points, corrected one or two incipient bad habits, and moved on to ditching and loading. She was sure that Nell bored easily. There was a lot of material to cover, luckily, and plenty to practice.

Thalia was back at the boardinghouse and had changed into her disguise by the time Nutall returned. Mrs. Morris had been as good as her word. Thalia was wearing her landlady's sister's broadbrimmed black hat with a heavy black veil, and she had added a Persian lamb stole over her shoulders. She looked at least twice her actual age and twenty years out of fashion.

Nutall looked different too. His customary tailored neatness had been discarded for a baggy brown plaid suit with a mustard-colored waistcoat. Instead of his usual black top hat, he wore a brown bowler. A bushy false mustache concealed his own pencil-neat one.

Thalia stared at him, lost for words.

Nutall beamed. "That's precisely the effect I was hoping to achieve. You look rather ghastly yourself, I must say."

Thalia dropped him a curtsy at the compliment. "Should we use false names?"

"Good idea." Nutall thought it over. "You're my spinster niece Jenny and I'm your uncle Jonathan."

"Surname?" Thalia prompted.

Nutall looked around the parlor for inspiration. "Brown settee, black bench, green aspidistra. Brown, Black, or Green. Take your pick."

"Call the settee a davenport instead," Thalia suggested. "Jonathan and Jenny Davenport."

"Jenny Davenport, it is an honor to accompany you to the theater." Nutall offered her his arm. "Let's go criticize Von Faber's shoddy technique. After the show, we'll treat ourselves to a late supper to celebrate."

"It will be a pleasure." Thalia took Nutall's arm. As they reached the street, she asked, "Where did you go?"

"I had lunch with Inigo and his friends," Nutall replied. "We were talking over old times."

"Not today. Last night." Thalia matched her stride to Nutall's. "Mrs. Morris went to your room quite late and she said you weren't in."

"I didn't answer." Nutall dropped his voice to a murmur.

"Between ourselves, Jenny, a man does not invariably wish to speak to his landlady à deux, particularly not in the middle of the night."

Thalia started to tell him that Mrs. Morris had checked his room, but broke off when instinct told her to leave the words unsaid. It wasn't like Nutall to lie to her.

But then, Thalia asked herself, what made her so sure of that? Did she know Nutall as well as she thought she did? Until Philadelphia, he'd never told her that her mother was a Trader. If the cuff hadn't jammed, if they hadn't gone to see Professor Evans, would Nutall have mentioned it at all? Ever?

To be fair, Thalia reflected, her father could have told her she was half Trader years ago. Why had he chosen to keep her ignorant of half her heritage? He had known he was marrying a Trader against her family's will. He had shared that with his friend Nutall, yet he hadn't told his own daughter. It wasn't as if she would have demanded they petition for a share of her mother's family trust. It wasn't as if she would have gone around telling people.

For that matter, what about her father's family? She knew nothing. He had been raised in an orphanage. That was all she knew. If her father had known more, he might have shared it with Nutall. But would Nutall share what he knew with her unless he had to?

Caution warred with curiosity. Caution won. Thalia had many questions for Nutall—but now was not the time to ask them.

Chapter Eight

The Imperial Theater, once Nutall had presented their passes and gained them admission to decent seats in the mezzanine, was far larger than the Majestic. The red plush velvet seat covers and stage curtain were almost new. The Cadwallader Syndicate had done Von Faber proud.

Von Faber himself held the stage well. Thalia had to grant him that. His first few tricks involved money, first pennies and then nickels and dimes and silver dollars, followed by at least a dozen paper bills, genuine greenbacks, palmed and produced as from thin air, then tossed carelessly out into the delighted audience. As far as Thalia could judge, Von Faber was throwing away as much money as she'd earned teaching Nell Ryker that day.

The audience applauded Von Faber's generosity. He moved on through a standard series of tricks, making it look easy as hoops and ropes and cups and balls did his bidding.

This was the disadvantage of a solo booking, Thalia reflected. In order to make his audience believe they'd had their money's worth, he'd had to pad the program with routine tricks.

As Von Faber took yet another round of applause with a gracious bow, a young white Solitaire woman in a scarlet gown with gold spangles joined him onstage. Her long dark hair fell loose to the small of her back, like a black silk curtain.

"Nora. She calls herself Mrs. Von Faber," Nutall murmured to Thalia. "Her maiden name was Uberti."

With operatic gestures, Von Faber pretended to mesmerize the young woman. Once she was in a trance, he directed her to lie upon a gilt divan brought to them by two stagehands costumed as footmen. Von Faber made dramatic passes over her once she was in position, demonstrating wordlessly that there could be no hidden wires in place. Then, with the orchestra's enthusiastic support, Von Faber gesticulated as if he were commanding the very air beneath her. The girl, apparently lost in Von Faber's trance, rose slowly to float in midair above the divan.

The audience gasped and applauded even as Von Faber produced a gleaming metal hoop and passed it around the girl to prove there were no wires holding her in position.

Nutall sighed and folded his arms.

Thalia tilted her head, admiring the perfection of Mrs. Von Faber's muscular control. Her spine rested on a metal rod set at a right angle to the lift rod, strong but hard to see, that held her full weight, giving the impression she was floating in midair. Her long hair added to the illusion, as did the spangles, each as big as a twenty-dollar gold piece, sparkling bright with every breath she took. It was a good trick, but the skill that made it convincing wasn't Von Faber's, except in the way he'd manipulated the gap in the hoop so it did not catch on the support rod and betray the subterfuge.

Nothing to worry about there. No trick of Thalia's used levitation. She had seen the trick done far less subtly, by assistants who flopped limp as laundry on an ironing board while they were hoisted. Mrs. Von Faber, who was probably a trained dancer, managed to seem as if she truly were entranced, motionless yet pulsing with life.

Thalia remembered Von Faber's disgusting expression as he'd complimented her on the chains she used in her act. Something in his gestures as he moved around the girl made Thalia think of the look in his piggy eyes that day at Madame Ostrova's. If his assistant had been lying in bed, instead of floating in the air, Von Faber's leering manner would have been right at home.

Von Faber stepped back and raised his hands to point at the floating woman. The orchestra took the cue and played her back down to rest again upon the elegant little divan as Von Faber mimed control. She lay there as if asleep, while Von Faber stood gloating over her. The orchestra played a lullaby, softer and softer, while he watched her. The music died away. Von Faber snapped his fingers, breaking the spell.

The girl woke. Von Faber held his position, looming threateningly over her, as she cowered back.

The curtain fell, the orchestra struck up a jolly new tune, and the lights came up for intermission.

Thalia sat back, appalled, as the whole audience came back to life, titillated into shocked whispering. Little by little, as the atmosphere lightened, members of the audience moved toward the doors to spend the interval stretching their legs, attending to calls of nature, smoking, or drinking.

Beside her, Nutall stifled a yawn. "Who on earth would copy that? One wonders why the man ever bothered with a noncompete clause in the first place." He saw Thalia's discomfort. "It's just Von Faber's way. He soils everything he touches. He can't do a coin pass without throwing it into the audience, as if we were beggars awaiting his largesse. The levitation goes well enough, thanks to his assistant, but he turns it into a pantomime of helpless submission."

"Is that what the pantomime was?" Thalia suppressed a shudder.

"His audience is not your audience," Nutall reminded her.

Thalia grimaced. "I guess not. I'm out of work and he's playing to a packed house."

Nutall leaned toward her. "The man's only advantage is his instinct for the lowest common denominator."

"That and his noncompete clause," Thalia countered.

"Yes, I've done a bit of research on that topic." Nutall smiled. "It seems that Cornelius Cadwallader lends Von Faber his assistance in all manner of situations. I'm told he does what Von Faber tells him to do, whether he wants to or not. There is understandable speculation about the reason. Rumor has it, Von Faber knows something about Mr. Cadwallader that he, as the head of the syndicate, wants kept secret."

Thalia felt her eyebrows go up higher than she'd thought they could. "Von Faber is blackmailing Cadwallader?"

"That's pure speculation." Nutall gave her a wink. "Von Faber also has excellent legal advice, which makes it unwise to make such statements."

Intermission ended as the lights went down. Music built.

Thalia barely caught Nutall's final whisper. "Such claims could be considered slander."

The second half of Von Faber's performance left the seaminess of the first behind. Von Faber transformed his assistant into a rabbit and back again and moved her from one cabinet to another, but nothing in his repertoire resembled Thalia's act until he moved at last to his grand finale, the Bullet Catch.

Von Faber the Magnificent announced that he would defy the only thing in the world that could harm him: a silver bullet. His assistant, now in filmy white draperies, brought the rifle ball out on a black velvet pillow. A professional jeweler was called up from the audience to attest that the object was sterling silver.

"Nice touch," Thalia muttered.

"Too flashy," Nutall whispered back, ignoring the glares their words drew from those sitting nearby. "Why use silver? It begs the question, why not gold?"

The jeweler gave the silver bullet to Von Faber, who passed it to his assistant, who loaded the rifle with due ceremony. As the orchestra played, Von Faber took his place, Limoges plate in hand.

The music stopped as a single drumroll began. The assistant put the rifle to her shoulder, took aim, and pulled the trigger. As the shot rang out, Von Faber fell as if poleaxed, the Limoges plate scattered into fragments all around him. The drummer stopped. Silence fell.

"Bit clumsy," Nutall complained, as the audience's gasps and murmurs filled the theater. Then he paused, and added very softly, "Dear me. How distressing."

Thalia discovered that her mouth was hanging open. She closed it with a snap.

The assistant dropped the rifle and rushed to kneel at Von Faber's side. In the brilliant light onstage, the blood on his chest looked too dark to be real. When the girl looked up, her face was a blank, but her voice was shrill, piercing over the audience's confusion. "Is there a doctor in the house? Somebody help me, please!"

One of the audience members, presumably a doctor, made his way to the aisle. An usher led him to the stage and helped him up.

The curtain came down then, concealing the tableau onstage, even as the stage manager stepped out from the wings to address the uneasy audience.

"Traders and Solitaires, ladies and gentlemen, please remain in your seats. The proper authorities have been summoned. Everything is under control."

The audience stirred and grumbled. The murmurs were precisely as Thalia had imagined when she thought about the trick going wrong. Yes, it was dreadful. Yes, they had witnessed disaster. Already they were practicing their stories of the shocking mishap they had witnessed.

The stage manager gestured for silence. "Keep your seats. Everything is under control. Maestro?"

With a flick of his baton, the conductor brought the orchestra back to life with a lighthearted waltz.

Thalia turned to Nutall. "Let's get out of here."

"Keep your seat. They've summoned the police. I expect they will be taking names at the door. If we leave now, we'll only draw the wrong kind of attention to ourselves. Better to look morbidly interested and leave when everyone else does."

"Von Faber has been shot." Thalia found that saying it aloud didn't make it any easier to believe. "What went wrong?"

Nutall closed his eyes as he shook his head. "There's simply no way to tell as yet."

The orchestra played on, waltzes and polkas, while the audience grew more and more restless.

At last the stage manager returned. "Ladies and gentlemen, we thank you for your patience. The authorities are here. We request your further cooperation in one more respect. As you leave the theater, please give your name and address—your real name and your real address—to the officer of the law stationed at your queue."

Hecklers from here and there in the audience demanded the reason for such a request, but the stage manager was firm. "Just do as you are told."

With no further ado, the seats began to empty as the theatergoers were permitted, ever so slowly, to leave. The audience around them rose and shuffled toward the exits in a slow line. Nutall and Thalia remained in their seats, resigned to a long wait and determined to spend it sitting down.

"You'd think the management would promise a few free passes or at least a discount on admission," Nutall observed. "But no. Not even an apology for the interrupted performance."

"No updates on Von Faber's condition either," said Thalia. "Do you suppose they took him straight to the hospital?"

"Thalia." Nutall was taken aback. "I thought you knew. Von Faber's dead."

Thalia frowned at her own stupidity. The bloodstains on the man's broad chest had formed so sluggishly. She ought to have known at once. "They never said."

"Why risk alarming the crowd?" Nutall inspected her. "You've gone pale. You aren't going to faint, are you?"

"Certainly not." Thalia knew what it was to feel faint. This was different. She felt distinctly odd, but it was not an unpleasant oddness. "If he's dead, so is the noncompete clause. I can work again."

"Just so." Nutall looked away. "We might want to keep that to ourselves for a bit, until we find out exactly what went wrong tonight."

Thalia put Nutall's words and the expression on Nutall's face together and felt as if her stomach had dropped away. "It could be considered a motive. If someone made the trick go wrong on purpose, if someone . . ." The enormity of it silenced Thalia.

If someone had spoiled the Bullet Catch on purpose, that was murder. There were many ways to ruin stage magic without meaning to, but not many people knew how to do it on cue. If people found out about the noncompete clause, Thalia herself would be a murder suspect, and Nutall with her. She felt sick. "This is bad." Cattle on the slaughterhouse floor died with as much ceremony as Von Faber had.

"It is." Nutall was still absorbed in the slow progress of the rest of the audience toward the exits. "But we need to focus on our own requirements for the moment. They're taking names and addresses at the door." Cautiously, Nutall drew out his pocketbook and selected a two-and-a-half-dollar gold piece, which he palmed. "Fortunately for us, the police in this city are notoriously susceptible to bribes."

Thalia marveled at the size of the prospective bribe. Nutall was serious. "I'll follow your lead."

"Let us join the press of humanity, shall we?" Nutall rose and helped Thalia toward the aisle. "We don't wish to be the very last to leave. Keep your veil down and remember, I'm your Solitaire uncle. We live in Brooklyn. Let me do the talking."

Nutall was the only person Thalia had ever met who truly did not mind standing in a queue. He waited with her as if no line existed ahead of or behind them, as if he had chosen to stand there purely for his own satisfaction. Thalia tried to do as he did, but she was too much like her father. Any such experience was an invitation for Thalia to notice the people around her and decide precisely why they annoyed her. This response at least had the merit of distracting her from Von Faber's fate. She'd detested the man, yes. But she'd done the Bullet Catch herself. She knew exactly what it felt like to be in his place. She could imagine the final moments of his life all too vividly.

What made Thalia feel worse was that in that narrow moment between learning Von Faber was dead and realizing Von Faber could have been murdered, she'd felt oddly happy. The noncompete clause died with Von Faber. Her stage career was her own again. That fleeting moment of joy now made Thalia feel disgusted with herself. It was mean and low to feel that her relief mattered more than a man's life. Nevertheless, Thalia could not deny that she would benefit from Von Faber's death. She had loathed the man, but Thalia knew it was wrong to rejoice in anyone's death.

Eventually they reached the policeman who was recording names and addresses, his eyes sharp with suspicion. Nutall responded to the policeman's questions with ill-concealed embarrassment. He was Mr. Jonathan Davenport and Thalia was his niece, Miss Jenny Davenport. They lived in Brooklyn. The address he gave sounded convincing but meant nothing to Thalia. She memorized it in case they were questioned separately.

Thalia kept her eyes down and hoped Mrs. Morris's sister's veil concealed her features. She didn't see money change hands but she couldn't miss the policeman's disgust with Nutall. Whoever Nutall said he was, whatever the gear Thalia had borrowed from Mrs. Morris made her seem to be, Nutall was simply far too old for Thalia.

Whatever the policeman wrote down, Nutall and Thalia were waved through soon enough. At last they emerged from the smoky warmth of the theater into the brisk night air beyond.

Despite the late hour, the streets immediately around the Imperial Theater were crowded. There were already reporters there, nagging at the policemen who kept them out of the theater. No photographers yet, but Thalia was glad of her veil all the same. The very last thing in the world Thalia needed was to be identified emerging from a theater where a rival magician performed.

Not a cab to be found, even if they had wanted to waste money on one. Neither of them had any desire for the supper Nutall had originally proposed to end the evening. Thalia fell into step beside Nutall as they walked briskly westward from Times Square back to Mrs. Morris's boardinghouse. The whole way, Thalia had the sense someone was following them. She looked over her shoulder four times and never saw anything.

"What is it?" Nutall asked.

"Is there someone behind us?" Thalia took another look. Still nothing but darkness. "I feel like someone is watching us."

Nutall slowed as they came to a corner and then pulled them both into the shelter of a shuttered newsstand. Together they listened and watched in silence for five minutes, ten minutes.

Thalia watched until her eyes burned and she had to blink repeatedly. There was nothing.

"I don't see anyone." Nutall sounded amused. "Perhaps giving false names to the police is bothering your conscience?"

"No." Thalia was certain the sensation was neither imagination nor conscience, but Nutall's good humor inspired her to ask, "Where were you last night? Don't lie."

Nutall hesitated before he answered, and when he did, his voice was grave. "I went to the Imperial Theater. After the performance, I tried to talk to Von Faber. He wouldn't see me there, so I waited for him outside his hotel. He never came."

Thalia nodded. "You wanted him to drop the noncompete clause."

"I wanted to talk to him, that's all." Nutall cleared his throat. "It occurs to me that perhaps there is good reason this area is deserted at this hour. Perhaps we should go. It is neither a good time nor a good place for a stroll."

Thalia gave it her best effort, but Nutall would say nothing more. Once they were back at the boardinghouse, he went to bed immediately.

Mrs. Morris was waiting for them. Thalia returned the hat, veil, and stole with her thanks.

"Did you have a good evening?" Mrs. Morris asked.

Thalia was tempted to say yes, but she knew the morning papers would be full of Von Faber's death. "Not really. Let me tell you all about it."

Thalia slept surprisingly badly, but eventually morning arrived. She tended to her doves and worried about the snake. At the breakfast table, talk among the other boarders was a debate about the best barber in the immediate vicinity. Ordinarily Nutall would have joined in with enthusiasm, but today he was silent yet nervy and on edge. Watchful, Thalia stayed at the table with him. She kept her hands in her lap and did her finger exercises out of sight beneath the tablecloth.

At last, they were all dislodged by Mrs. Morris clearing the table. Thalia tagged after Nutall into the parlor and cornered him near the potted plant. "I'm teaching Miss Ryker again today. What will you be doing this afternoon?"

"I was planning to make the rounds and see about getting us a gig." Nutall produced a neatly folded newspaper. "Now I'm having second thoughts."

Thalia took the paper from him. The only item on the front page that didn't relate to Von Faber's death was an item about a second manticore sighting in Central Park. The headline screamed MURDER NOT MISADVENTURE. Beneath the headline was a photogravure of a wedding portrait, a much younger Von Faber arm in arm with a plump blond bride. Beneath the picture, the caption read *Grieving Widow Offers Reward.*

"That's not Mrs. Von Faber," Thalia said.

"It is the first Mrs. Von Faber," Nutall replied. "According to local gossip, his assistant didn't know that Von Faber had been married before."

"How typical of him to lie to her about that." Thalia took her time reading. "I see what you mean. But the police might find it just as suspicious if we don't do anything. It's normal to look for work."

Nutall eased the lace curtain back and looked out the front window. "Keep your eyes open. Someone may be watching this place."

Thalia craned her neck to look past him. The street view was precisely as usual, a few pedestrians and hardly any wheeled traffic. The feeling she'd had the night before, that sense she was being followed, was entirely absent. "Why would they do that?"

Nutall let the curtain fall back in place and eased away from the window. "It's possible the police have noticed we used false names. Even if they haven't, it won't be long before it occurs to them to wonder about Von Faber's business rivals. His death was good news for us."

"Good news for other people too," Thalia reminded him. "Mr. Cornelius Cadwallader, for one. I can't imagine he enjoyed letting Von Faber push him and his syndicate around."

"That is a good point." Nutall took a seat on the davenport and unfolded the newspaper again.

Thalia considered reminding Nutall that even if the police found out he'd been at the Imperial Theater the night before Von Faber's demise, he wasn't a murderer. She also considered how well sound carried in the boardinghouse and how nosy her fellow lodgers were. Instead, she said, "Plenty of people hated Von Faber. The police are going to figure that out. They can't find anything against us because we didn't do anything. If someone truly rigged the Bullet Catch to do away with Von Faber, it was neither you nor me."

"Neither you nor I." Nutall corrected her absently from behind the newspaper.

That was much more like the usual Nutall, Thalia decided. "So are you going out to find us a gig? Or will you just sit in here and read the newspapers all day?"

"The latter." Nutall sounded preoccupied. "We can start to look for work properly on Monday."

As before, Ryker's Pierce-Arrow arrived punctually. It collected Thalia promptly at three o'clock. The Ryker servants were already used to her. Thalia was sent upstairs on her own once Rogers informed her that Miss Ryker was in her study.

Thalia knocked gently at the door and entered when Nell called permission. To her dismay, she found that the Trader girl had obviously been crying. "What's wrong? What's happened?"

Nell gestured to the Trader newspapers spread across the worktable. "Another manticore sighting. Even though his family had hired a bodyguard, a fifteen-year-old boy was attacked on his way to the theater last night. The bodyguard drove it off before he was seriously hurt."

"Well, that's lucky, isn't it?" Thalia ventured.

"It is, of course it is." Nell produced an embroidered handkerchief and blew her nose. "Only now Nat is going to keep me locked up here forever. Even if the Skinner gets the manticore today—he's on patrol right now, of course—Nat will say two sightings means two manticores. Nat takes no chances. It's terrible. It's his excuse to keep me locked up here until I'm old and gray."

"Your brother won't keep you locked up here forever, I promise. It's impossible." Thalia investigated a lump beneath the layer of newspapers and found that it was a deck of cards. She began to shuffle them absently. "He wants to make sure you're safe, that's all."

Nell made a noise of barely suppressed anger. "Thank you for these blinding truths. Next you will remind me that I'm lucky to have a brother."

Thalia flinched a little. Once she'd had a brother. He'd died as an infant, when Thalia had been only three years old, and their mother had died the very next day. Thalia couldn't remember any of it happening, and her father had never willingly spoken of it. She only knew that her mother had gone. Grief had been with her ever since, a remote injury, aching like a broken bone that never quite healed. "I would never tell you that."

"You don't have to say it. I know I'm lucky to have Nat. But that doesn't change the fact that I'm practically a prisoner here. I know it's for my own good, but I hate it."

"You really don't need me to have this conversation, do you? You're doing both sides of it all by yourself." Thalia handed Nell the deck of cards. "Show me what you did with the ace of spades when we met, only this time make it look a little more clumsy. Sometimes your trick will be more effective if you look like you're trying hard on the easy part. Your mark won't expect it when you fool them with the hard part."

Nell began to shuffle the cards herself. "It's supposed to look effortless, isn't it?"

"It's supposed to *be* effortless," Thalia agreed, "but you need to have complete control over what your mark sees. For now, make me think you're new at this."

Thalia watched carefully as Nell cut the cards and began to manipulate them. She had to suppress a smile when she saw Nell steal the ace of spades and ditch it in her sleeve, ready to be called back into play at the right moment.

As Thalia had hoped, giving Nell permission to be a bit clumsy prompted her to move more fluidly. The faint stiffness she'd displayed, common to beginners, melted away. Nell fanned the cards and folded them, cut and shuffled and cut again. She finished with a flourish as she set the deck down and flipped the top card faceup: the ace of spades.

"That was all right," said Thalia. "Now make it look easy."

Nell worked through the trick again, still not quite as smoothly as Thalia would have liked, but better than before.

"Good," said Thalia. "Now roll up your sleeves. Let me see your wrists."

Nell straightened indignantly. "That's not fair."

Thalia congratulated herself on distracting Nell entirely from her manticore sightings. She pushed her own cuffs back. "I'll show you."

Thalia ran through the trick again. As she produced the ace of spades on cue, Nell exclaimed, "I wish I had a kinetoscope. You go so fast, I can't see it properly. If I could watch moving pictures of you, I could learn to do it better."

"I don't know what a kinny-whatsit is, but if you practice enough, you won't need one," Thalia advised.

Nell chuckled to herself. "A kinetoscope records pictures of things moving. When the film is developed, it's projected on a white surface. You get moving pictures."

"Sounds expensive," said Thalia. "Show me again."

"My birthday is coming soon." Nell shuffled the cards dreamily. "Maybe I'll ask Nat to get me one."

Thalia was firm. "Just keep practicing."

When the lesson was over for the day, Thalia left Nell still practicing. She let herself out of the workroom and walked alone through the magnificent house. In the courtyard, the chauffeur retrieved the Pierce-Arrow and brought it near the front steps.

The odd feeling Thalia had experienced the night before, that utter certainty that she was being watched, returned in full force. Thalia stood poised on the mansion's wide stone steps, scanning her surroundings warily, while the car idled gently below. There was the courtyard. There were the servants. There was the street, just visible beyond the gates. Thalia's surroundings were not deserted by any means, but she could see no threat, nothing to explain the pins and needles she felt at the back of her neck.

"Coming, ma'am?" called the chauffeur.

Thalia entered the backseat and settled herself comfortably as they moved slowly across the courtyard. Two servants opened the wrought-iron gates, and the car moved through them into the street.

The chauffeur was shifting gears when a man threw himself at the Pierce-Arrow and struck at the window nearest Thalia. She gave a squawk of surprise and shrank back in her seat. The window glass held, but the attacker's intention was unmistakable to Thalia. He was after her. He meant to attack her. Not the chauffeur. Not a random passerby. Her.

The pallid face pressed to the glass was wild-eyed, the mouth agape. He smelled terrible. Even with the windows shut, the attacker's breath was a stomach-turning mix of rotten meat and stale urine. Thalia gagged. The smell of him clogged her nostrils. Thalia remembered how she had felt that night in Philadelphia when everything had gone wrong. There was something she must do. She didn't know what it was, but a strange urgency seized her.

The chauffeur, startled by the attack, ground the Pierce-Arrow's gearbox. The car was just outside the wrought-iron gates, and still moving forward slowly.

The attacker, balancing on the running board and clinging to the roof, raised his hand to strike again. Thalia saw that he was holding a stone, clearly intent upon shattering the glass of the rear passenger window. When he came through the glass, he would try to kill her.

Thalia, her deftness turned clumsy, fumbled with the elaborate fittings designed for a passenger's convenience. She managed to unlatch the panel that dropped to reveal the writing desk. She seized the penknife. In her other hand, she clutched her reticule. The soft cloth of the purse held a handful of coins. It might serve as a makeshift blackjack. Thalia's icy fingers had gone pins and needles.

A second man threw himself at the Pierce-Arrow, this one younger, taller, and much, much cleaner. He grappled with the first. The attacker kicked him, but rather than renew his attack when the cleaner man doubled up in pain, he scrambled beneath the car and emerged on the other side, running away as fast as he could.

Thalia lost sight of her attacker when he rounded the corner of a nearby brownstone mansion. That strange urgency, that drive to do something although she didn't understand what, faded abruptly. Thalia, light-headed with relief, turned her focus back to the clean man. By now, he was back on his feet, wincing as he leaned against the Pierce-Arrow.

Thalia opened the passenger door. The pins and needles were gone. Her hands were her own again. "Are you all right, sir?"

"Yes, I am." To the chauffeur, he called, "Run this beauty back home, will you?" Limping, he moved clear of the car and followed it into the courtyard.

The driver obeyed swiftly. Servants rushed to shut the gates once the car was safely back on the premises.

Thalia's rescuer, whom she now realized was barely her own age, regarded Thalia with disapproval. He was the black Solitaire she'd seen at Delmonico's. His wide-set eyes held a thin layer of brittle courtesy, but mockery still lay beneath. There was no recognition there. Thalia knew him, but he'd not remembered her. He dusted himself off, straightened his black slouch hat, and limped over to lean against the car again. With no ceremony, he opened the rear passenger door and pulled Thalia out. When she was standing, he moved so close his nose nearly touched hers and drew in a deep breath. "I can't smell it but that manticore sure could. Miss, you need to stay in where it's safe until you can control yourself."

Manticore. Thalia stepped back and bumped into the car door. Every fear she'd had about being a Trader came rushing back. That had been a manticore. She'd just been attacked by a manticore. Her knees were trembling.

Summoned by the uproar, Nathaniel and Nell Ryker emerged from the house and ran to Thalia. Thalia's rescuer turned to them. "You'll be the Traders who live here, I expect. I'm Tycho Aristides. I'm the Skinner of New York. You'll want to keep this young Trader lady of yours safe. She's drawing the manticore. You've no doubt heard there was an attack yesterday."

Ryker and his sister looked at each other with identical expressions of amazement. As one, they turned to Thalia. Ryker said, "But you're a Solitaire."

Nell asked hopefully, "You're a Trader?"

"She's a Trader." Aristides shook his head as if he pitied them. "Can't you smell her?"

Both Rykers leaned close and inhaled. This was by no means as rude as the sniff the Skinner had given her, but Thalia bristled anyway.

Ryker sounded accusing. "You're a Trader."

Nell swatted Thalia on the shoulder. "You should have told me!" To the rescuer, she said, "Why didn't you just shoot the monster dead?"

Aristides narrowed his eyes. "That manticore wasn't six inches away from her. I couldn't risk the shot."

Thalia did her best to stay calm. Professor Philander Evans had been wrong. This was no more than she deserved for trusting a professor of literature. Thalia, still trying to absorb this new truth, said the first thing that came into her head. "What do I smell like?"

"You smell normal," Nell assured her kindly.

"It's very faint," said Ryker, but he blushed.

"Going by the manticore, miss, you smell nice and ripe," said Aristides. "You smell the way all you people smell right before a manticore takes your magic and leaves you to die. Which is exactly what would have happened here if I hadn't been tracking the manticore, doing my job." To Ryker, Aristides added dryly, "Any time now, sir, you can say 'Thank you for rescuing my beloved family member.' Any currency will be gratefully accepted, but gold coin is preferred."

Ryker looked like he'd swallowed a frog. "She's not a family member."

Nell gave her brother a most unladylike punch on the shoulder. "Thank you very much for rescuing our friend for us, Mr. Aristides." Nell beamed up at the Skinner. "My brother will gladly reward you for your valor."

Aristides smiled back.

Ryker asked, "Aren't you going to track that manticore?"

"Oh, I will. But there's a protocol to be observed." Aristides indicated Thalia. "First I have to be sure she's safe. Get her back indoors, will you?" To Thalia, he added, "You really need to get your Trades under control, miss. If you draw a manticore, it may end up attacking someone else."

"Miss Cutler is quite safe with us," Ryker stated stiffly. "She is not a member of our family, but as she is Trader enough to draw a manticore to our very doorstep, it is our responsibility to ensure her safety—and everyone else's."

"We'll keep her with us," Nell added. "Don't worry."

"Wait a minute." No one paid any attention to Thalia.

"Thank you, Mr. Aristides." Ryker brought out his pocketbook and gave Aristides a fifty-dollar bill. "Every Trader in Manhattan will owe you thanks when you've disposed of this manticore."

"Thank you kindly, sir." Aristides pocketed the reward. When he was satisfied with Ryker's assurances, he touched the brim of his black slouch hat as he gave Thalia a small bow. Then the Skinner left, no longer limping.

"My goodness," said Nell. "Wasn't that exciting?"

"Indoors, both of you," said Ryker.

Chapter Nine

"What do you mean by *keep her with us,* exactly?" Thalia had followed Nell and her brother back indoors to the music room. Nell settled Thalia in the most comfortable chair and sent Rogers to organize refreshments.

"Hush." Nell put a comforting hand on Thalia's sleeve. "I know I am only your student, but if our situations were reversed, I'm sure you would keep me safe and show exactly the same concern for my welfare that we're obliged to show any Trader in your situation."

Thalia thought Nell was being optimistic, but she'd let it slide since it seemed to be working in her favor. "Okay."

Nell continued. "Nowhere safer for you to learn to control your Trades than right here with us. Our house has sheltered the young Traders of the Ryker family for generations."

"You want me to stay here? Indefinitely?" Thalia remembered her manners. "That is very kind of you, and I thank you. But I can't do that. I have responsibilities."

"No responsibility outweighs your safety and the safety of those around you," Ryker said. His stiffness had been replaced by concern.

"No, really. I can't stay here."

"It isn't up to you," Ryker said.

"And why can't you stay here, I'd like to know," asked Nell.

"I have doves," Thalia admitted.

"Doves!" Nell clapped her hands with delight. "Wonderful."

Thalia played her last bad-houseguest card. "I have a snake."

"Poisonous, no doubt," Ryker muttered. "Some sort of rattle-snake."

With great difficulty, Thalia resisted the urge to lie and agree. "No. It's only a corn snake. It eats mice."

Nell dismissed the snake and its mice with an airy wave of her hand. "You shall be our welcome houseguest, and so shall your doves and your corn snake. I can hardly wait."

"Send for your luggage and your pets and anything else you please, Miss Cutler." Ryker sounded tired. "Nell, when we've had a chance to calm down a bit, put her in the nursery. That room is most convenient for the Changing room."

The tray of refreshments arrived. There were a cut-crystal de-canter of brandy and suitable glasses, a plate of sandwiches, and a teapot flanked by cups and saucers. Ryker poured them each a measure of brandy. Nell distributed sandwiches. Thalia, still slightly light-headed, managed a cup of tea. She declined both the brandy and the sandwich. She didn't trust her stomach yet.

When the refreshments had been cleared away, Nell led Thalia along a ground-floor passage papered in an elaborate wallpaper pattern that made Thalia feel as if she were walking underwater.

"This is the nursery." Nell opened a white-painted door and led Thalia into a whitewashed room with simple furniture and no windows.

Thalia looked around. There was a drab rag rug on the floor beside the iron bedstead. Otherwise the floor was bare wood. There was a wardrobe with no clothing in it. There was a dressing table with a mirror. There was a small writing desk with a simple chair. Counting the door they had come through, there were three doors in the room, all painted glossy white.

Nell opened the door to the left. "Here's the bathroom. You'll love it. This was one of the first houses in Manhattan to have full indoor plumbing. Our grandmother got the idea from her friends in London."

Thalia praised the bathroom plumbing sincerely, but she was distracted by the door to the right. "Is that a closet?"

Nell opened the door to reveal a flight of steps running downward into darkness. "This goes to the Changing room."

"There's plenty of room to change clothes here," Thalia pointed out, then caught herself. "Wait. That's where you Trade?"

Nell regarded Thalia with approval. "We learn to Trade here in the nursery, so that's why there's nothing fancy or breakable in here. But sometimes it turns out a member of the family Trades to something wet. Or something large. That's what the Changing room is for. Anyway, it's fun."

Thalia took another look around. "Why aren't there any windows?"

"Manticores, of course." Nell sat on the narrow bed and gestured to the writing desk. "I expect you'll want to tell someone that you're moving your things here to stay. Write a letter. We'll send a messenger with it. It's not something you can explain in a telegram, is it?"

In the drawer of the writing desk, Thalia found writing paper with the Ryker address printed on it. *Riverside,* the house was called. What would it be like to live in a house so big it needed its own name?

Thalia wrote hastily to Nutall, explaining her situation in brief. She did not outright ask Nutall to come to her, but she hoped he would accompany her things. Putting it down on paper for Nutall made it all seem, if anything, less likely. As she sealed the envelope with wax, Thalia silently scolded herself for taking Professor Evans at his ill-informed word.

Nell showed Thalia the bell rope to ring for a servant to collect the letter and find a messenger to deliver it to Mrs. Morris's boardinghouse. "If you get hungry or need anything else, just ring. Any time, day or night. We have an excellent staff."

A maid answered the summons with a neat curtsy and took the letter Thalia offered her.

"Come to think of it, you never ate your sandwich." Nell told the maid, "Have Cook send a dinner tray." The maid curtsied again and left. To Thalia, Nell said, "I'm happy to help you with anything I can. Do you have any questions?"

Thalia regarded Nell blankly for a moment. She had a hundred questions. Sitting there in the quiet simplicity of the nursery, Thalia could think of only one. "How do I Trade?"

Nell stopped smiling. "I can't tell you that because I don't know. I've only just learned how I Trade myself. It's different for everyone."

Thalia hung on tight to her patience. "All right. Tell me how you Trade, then. You said something before. You find a common thread? What does that mean?"

"That's right." Nell paused to gather her thoughts. "Since I'm a Trader, I have two forms. To Trade, I figured out what the two forms have in common. I Trade to an otter. When I want to Trade, one form to the other, I think about how funny it is to be an otter. Then, when it's time to come back to this form, I think about how funny it is to have fingers and toes."

"That's it?" Thalia sat back in her chair, trying to hide her disappointment. There was nothing funny in her situation.

"It's different for everyone," Nell reminded her. "What do you Trade to?"

"I don't know." Thalia tried to find words for that night in Philadelphia. "My hand turned white." She did her best to describe the experience to Nell.

By the end of Thalia's story, Nell was wide-eyed. "That's wonderful. Whatever you Traded to was a form that let you slip that handcuff. That rules out lots of things."

Thalia didn't know exactly what her own facial expression was, but something about it made Nell say soothingly, "Don't be sad. You're safe from the manticore and you're in the best possible place to learn to Trade. Once you've Traded properly, you'll know exactly what your other form is. It often runs in families. What does your family Trade to?"

"I don't know. Nutall told me that my mother's parents Traded. That's all."

"What about your father?"

"I don't know. He was an orphan. I don't think he was a Trader at all."

"If you're a Trader—and you are—then both your parents

were Traders," Nell assured Thalia. "It takes two to make a Trader child."

"Oh." Thalia thought that over. "Even if I do Trade 'properly,' and find out what I am, I've just begun, haven't I? I'll need to control my Trades. I'll need to get the Board of Trade to give me an ordeal, won't I?"

"You will when you're ready."

"What about your ordeal?"

Nell gave a tiny shrug of her shoulders before she answered. "I don't know what it is going to be. That's up to the Board of Trade. But there are two other parts of the process of coming out in society. I need to Trade on command. I need to resist the urge to Trade."

"Right. Good. Three parts." Thalia thought it over. "What if I don't pass it?"

Nell waved Thalia's concern away. "Don't worry about that now. No one takes their ordeal until they're sure they'll succeed."

"Why is that?" asked Thalia. "Or don't I want to know?"

"You need to know," Nell assured her. "If you fail the ordeal, you can't Trade back. You stay in your other form."

"How long?" Thalia demanded.

"Until you die. No, Thalia, don't look like that! It's not that bad. We usually die in our other form anyway, because being a Trader means we are hard on ourselves. When our memory starts to go, it's easier to live in the other form."

"Easier to die, you mean." Thalia wiped her eyes. "Tell me about your parents. Your brother said he's running the family business now. Your mother and father. They're—gone. Right?"

Nell dropped her gaze to her hands, which she had folded in her lap. She nodded. When she spoke, her voice was full of tears. "Five years ago now. Papa was hurt in an accident. He didn't get better. Afterward, Mama didn't want to stay with us. So she Traded. She's never coming back."

Thalia made herself say the words. "Will you lose your memory too?" She did not add, *Will I?* She feared she already knew the answer to that question.

"Not for at least fifty years. But yes. I will. Nat says it's the other side of the coin." From somewhere Thalia didn't see, Nell produced another snow-white handkerchief and blew her nose delicately. "Being a Trader is full of wonderful things. But it doesn't last. If I welcome the wonderful things, don't I need to take this terrible thing too?"

Thalia didn't trust her voice, so she didn't answer. Nor did she ask Nell to tell her what so-called wonderful things were involved in being a Trader with no money, no job, and no idea how to Trade.

When a maid delivered the tray of food Nell had ordered, Nell left Thalia alone. Thalia had never been less hungry in her life, so she ignored the tray and explored her new lodging. Once she was finished with the quiet bedroom, her attention was drawn to the door that led to the Changing room stairs.

Thalia started down the narrow steps with caution. The air smelled moist and felt cool. There was no light, so Thalia moved by touch. As she descended, Thalia tried to estimate how deep the staircase went. Surely she would hit bedrock before long.

At the foot of the stair was a door Thalia judged identical to the one at the top. It was unlocked. Thalia entered a large, cold chamber that smelled of wet stone and river water. Like the nursery, it was windowless, but there was light. Gas fixtures in the ceiling, although set low, gave plenty of illumination. No furniture.

Limited floor space. The room was dominated by a pool of water. Despite the light, Thalia found herself unable to judge how deep the water was. It looked deep and felt cold.

Shallow stone steps led up from the far side of the pool to a pair of double doors. Thalia picked her way around the pool to try the latch. Locked.

Thalia judged this room was deep below the house foundations. She couldn't imagine where the double doors led. When her things came, when she had her set of lockpicks with her, she could find out. For now, she contented herself with pacing around the pool. She rubbed her cold hands and thought about Trading.

That night in Philadelphia, Thalia's hands had been cold enough for pins and needles, and then they had gone numb. Just now, in the Pierce-Arrow, her hands had been just as cold.

How close had she come to Trading right there in the backseat? How much closer could she come before she'd fall prey to the manticore?

Thalia shivered. Would her whole body go numb? Would she even know she'd Traded? What would she become once she'd Traded? Would it all fade away until she'd Traded back? What if she failed to Trade back?

When Thalia had recovered her composure, she climbed up the stairs again. If she moved far more slowly than usual, if her eyes were red, Thalia felt she had good reason.

Back in the nursery, Thalia ignored the covered tray. She sat on the bed with her head in her hands until the door opened and Nell came in. "Good news. Your luggage is here."

Nell stepped aside and the servants brought in everything Thalia owned in the world, doves, snake, props, and all. When the servants had gone, Nell handed Thalia an envelope. Inside was Thalia's letter to Nutall and a note from Mrs. Morris.

> *Dear Thalia,*
>
>   *The police have arrested Mr. Nutall for the murder of Von Faber the Magnificent. They want to talk to you. I haven't told them where you are because I didn't know. The police are sure to notice your luggage has been taken away, though. If you are hiding from them, go somewhere else. If you are helping Mr. Nutall, I'll help you all I can. Some strangers, not police, came asking for him. I think they were Sylvestri.*
>
>   *I will keep your money on account in case you are ever able to come back and lodge here again. You will always be welcome under any roof of mine.*
>
>   *With best regards,*
>   *Irene Morris (Mrs.)*

Thalia's knees trembled. She sat back down on the bed.

"What is it?" Nell sounded strangely far away.

Thalia handed her the letter.

After a moment, Thalia heard Nell say, "I'll get Nat."

Thalia was alone, but not for long enough. When Nell and Nat joined her in the whitewashed room, at first all she could make herself say was "He didn't."

Thalia realized she'd been pacing the room when Ryker put his hand on her shoulder to stop her. She had the urge to lash out at him, but somehow she rose above it. Instead she glared at him in silence.

Nell picked up the untouched tray of food. "I'll have Cook send you a fresher sandwich and a glass of milk."

"No." Thalia winced at the thought of food. "Thank you for thinking of it, but I can't eat anything."

"We'll have a big breakfast in the morning. If you've been trying to Trade this whole time, you'll be hungry by then. Very wise of you," Nell added. "I always think it's better to Trade on an empty stomach."

"Trade?" Thalia laughed bitterly. "I don't know how to begin."

"It doesn't matter how you begin. Stand up, sit down, lie on the floor—whatever you like."

"And then?"

"Then it depends. Nat Trades to a seal, which is what the Rykers have Traded to for generations. Mama was a Rothschild and Traded to an otter, same as I do. Once you know what you Trade to, it might be easier to start."

"Right. Good. What do you do exactly?"

"It depends." Nell looked thoughtful. "If I'm cold, I think about being warmer. If I'm hot, I think about being cooler. I think about how nice it is to Trade. Then I Trade."

"But how?"

"Go inside." Nell leaned close. "Listen for the rest of your soul."

Before Thalia could ask what on earth Nell meant, Nell had taken the tray and whisked out of the room. Once again, Thalia was alone. Nutall needed her help. Until she could protect herself from the manticore, Thalia was confined to the Ryker mansion. To protect herself from the manticore, Thalia had to Trade.

One of Nell's remarks came back to Thalia. Nell's determination to learn stage magic stemmed from the night she and her friends had gone to the Imperial Theater to see Von Faber the Magnificent. That birthday party of young Traders had been escorted there and back in safety. The fifteen-year-old boy that had been attacked had been saved by his bodyguard. There had to be a way to get an escort herself. Tycho Aristides was an expert on manticores. What would it take to hire him as her bodyguard? Thalia resolved to find out.

Meanwhile, Thalia meant to try listening for the rest of her soul, whatever that could possibly mean, if it took her the rest of the night.

The following morning, Thalia was at the breakfast table with Ryker and Nell when Rogers loomed in the doorway. "The police are here, sir. They wish to interview your houseguest."

Nell shook her head sadly. "You may refer to her by her name, Rogers."

Rogers showed no sign of having heard. "I have put them in the front parlor, sir."

Nell turned to her brother. "What about our lawyers?"

Ryker rose from the table. "I'll tell the police we can't speak to them until our lawyers are present."

"No." Thalia got up and smoothed her skirt. "I'll talk to them now."

Ryker frowned. "I don't advise it."

"I'll be careful." Thalia, with Nell and Ryker at her heels, followed Rogers to the front parlor, which was far more formal than the music room. Although a spacious room, it seemed somewhat cramped, full of heavy dark furniture grouped on a Persian rug of surpassing beauty. There were two policemen, only one in uniform, sitting stiffly in uncomfortable-looking chairs close to the center of the room. They rose when Ryker entered.

"Mr. Nathaniel Ryker." The white Solitaire man who spoke did not make it a question. He was wearing a navy pinstriped suit with a red paisley vest. "I'm Inspector Ottokar and this is Officer Kelly. We have some questions regarding the death of Mr. Johan Von Faber."

Ryker shook hands with both men. "Our family lawyers have been sent for, but until they arrive, Miss Cutler is only willing to speak with you briefly without legal representation." He introduced Nell and Thalia. The moment he did, Inspector Ottokar lost all interest in the Rykers. "Miss Cutler, you are the stage magician who calls herself the Lady of the Lake?"

Thalia drew herself up to her full height and gave Inspector Ottokar back look for unimpressed look. "I am."

Officer Kelly, a wiry young Solitaire with a roses-and-cream complexion, produced a notebook and pencil. He wrote something down, but Thalia couldn't tell what.

Inspector Ottokar continued. "David Nutall is your partner, correct?"

"Mr. David Nutall is my business associate, yes," Thalia replied.

"You have arranged legal representation and bail money for your partner."

Thalia stared at Inspector Ottokar until he snapped, "Answer the question."

"You didn't ask a question," Nell protested.

"On Miss Cutler's behalf," said Ryker, "our family lawyers have offered to post bail for her business partner, Mr. Nutall. They also offered to provide legal representation. I have been informed that Mr. Nutall declined both offers."

"Well, somebody bailed him out." Inspector Ottokar stared at Thalia. "If it wasn't you, who was it?"

Thalia stared at Ryker. "You got Nutall a lawyer?"

"I tried to." Ryker gave Thalia a flicker of a smile.

"Thank you."

"You're welcome."

Inspector Ottokar cleared his throat. "Whoever posted his bail, he can cool his heels with them until the trial. We're busy preparing the case against him. On the night Von Faber died, Nutall gave the police false names and addresses for the pair of you. As his—business associate—you need to give us a statement. Depending on the content of that statement, it is possible you too will be detained in police custody."

"No statement. Not without her lawyer present," Ryker declared. "Rogers, please send someone to the practice to urge them to join us immediately."

Rogers, who had been hovering outside the parlor door, withdrew.

"No statement?" Inspector Ottokar was incredulous. "Did I hear you right?"

Thalia, both heartened and astounded by Ryker's support, lifted her chin. "No statement until I have a lawyer to represent me."

Inspector Ottokar turned his glare on Thalia. "That's Trader talk, but you're no Trader. You're coming downtown with us."

Ryker stepped closer to Ottokar. "You may take Miss Cutler's statement here, but she does not leave the premises. She is a Trader, contrary to all appearances, but she cannot yet control her Trades. A manticore attacked her just yesterday. It isn't safe for her to go

out. Our family lawyers are well-versed in the limits of your juris-
diction on Trader property, on that you may depend."

"Let's all have a nice cup of tea," Nell suggested. "The lawyers
will be here soon, I'm sure."

"Keep your tea," Inspector Ottokar told Nell. To Ryker, he
added, "Keep your lawyers. Kelly, bring the girl."

Officer Kelly reached for Thalia. Thalia eluded his grasp. "I'm
not leaving with you." To Ryker, she said, "Get the Skinner, please.
If anyone can protect me from the manticore, it's the Skinner of
New York."

Nell's face lit up. "That will be exciting." She left the room,
calling for Rogers.

"Yes, it is." To Ottokar, Ryker said, "I forbid you to take Miss
Cutler from the sanctuary of this house."

"That right there should be good for a charge of obstructing
justice," Inspector Ottokar informed him. "Don't make us arrest
you too. For now, we'll just have the girl come with us, if you don't
mind."

"I mind very much." Ryker moved effortlessly out of Officer
Kelly's reach. "You are overstepping your authority, sir."

"I think you'll find that we officers of the law have greater
authority than you think, even over Traders," Inspector Ottokar
replied evenly.

"This is reckless endangerment," Ryker retorted. "Don't you
want her alive to make her statement?"

"I think the New York City Police Department is capable of
protecting a suspect," said Inspector Ottokar. "Kelly, bring her
along."

The walk from the front parlor to the courtyard of the Ryker
mansion was not long, but it took a while, as Thalia struggled with

Officer Kelly every step of the way. When they reached the front steps, Inspector Ottokar took Thalia's free arm and hustled her along to the horse-drawn police van waiting in the street beyond the Rykers' locked gate.

Thalia braced herself against her escorts' urging and stayed on the top step long enough to draw in a deep breath. No manticore smell that she could detect. After so long indoors, Thalia found the fresh air enlivening. There was a light breeze that smelled of the city. Daylight was welcome. Thalia felt light and strong, nerves strung tight by her situation. She didn't want to go with the police, but she could see no alternative. She thought she could trust Ryker to tell the truth about sending for a lawyer. She was sure Nell had sent for the Skinner. Unfortunately, unless they arrived immediately, neither one would do her any good.

Inspector Ottokar ordered that the gate be opened. The servants at hand looked at Ryker first. Only when he nodded, his reluctance evident, did they move to obey.

Wrought iron swung wide, almost noiselessly, and Ottokar urged Thalia forward. "No time to waste. They're waiting for us downtown."

If there was a manticore stalking her, Thalia knew it would be fatal to Trade shape now. Since she had become the Rykers' unexpected houseguest, she had been focusing her thoughts on how to make this mysterious transformation. Now, no matter what happened on her way to be questioned at the Tombs, Thalia was determined not to Trade. She would remain in her human form. If she could not Trade on purpose, she would not Trade by accident. She would control herself at all costs.

There were two more white Solitaire policemen with the van, one on the box holding the reins, the other standing by at the horses' heads. Thalia was pushed toward them. Ryker and Nell were still watching. Thalia was very conscious of every step she took away from the safety they represented. She was on her own again.

"Let's go, missy," called the van's driver from the box.

Thalia didn't like his face. She decided he was nobody. He was nothing. She stopped dragging her feet and put on her Lady of the Lake manner, impassive and graceful, as she moved through the open gate.

The team of horses drawing the police van startled uneasily. They tossed their heads, harness jingling, struggling against the traces as they tried to shy. Too late, Thalia caught the scent of something dead and rotten.

The manticore knocked over the policeman holding the horses as it ran past, headed straight for Thalia.

Thalia's hands and feet went cold. Pins and needles danced in her arms and legs. The abrupt sense of something new stirred deep within her. Another part of her mind—or perhaps another part of her soul—rose within her as fear held her still. *Do not,* she told herself. *Do not Trade.*

Both Ryker and Nell shouted a warning. Officer Kelly released Thalia and clawed at his holster, desperate to free his pistol. Inspector Ottokar pushed Thalia aside as he stood between her and the manticore. "Halt!"

The manticore shoved Ottokar away as Kelly took his shot.

With the gunshot so close, Thalia's ears rang. If anyone was shouting orders, she couldn't hear them. The world narrowed around her as she focused on the deathly face of the manticore.

It took no notice of the policemen, although Kelly's shot had been true enough to strike the manticore in its leg. It was intent on Thalia.

Thalia stood her ground, sure this was the last minute of her life. Ryker had been right to try to keep her safe from this. She held fast to her human shape while her familiar senses melted into utter numbness. Half of herself longed to Trade. She ignored that half. Even in extremis, Thalia noted the scent the manticore's proximity lured from her. She smelled menstrual blood and warm milk.

The smell steeled Thalia's resolve. If she had to die, if she had to die stinking, right. Good. She wasn't going to die screaming. This was her last exit—let it be a good one.

As the manticore closed in on Thalia, time moved with exquisite slowness. She couldn't hear anything, but Thalia saw its chest move in deep panting breaths, as if it was savoring the scent it drew from Thalia.

Stronger than it had been that night in Philadelphia when it had saved her life, the urge to Trade deepened. Thalia ignored it. Resisting the Trade, staying entirely human, would be her last act of defiance.

Looking into the manticore's bright but sunken eyes, she saw how unnatural it was, how filthy, how intent upon taking her life, upon taking her very self away. For the first time, she *knew* she was a Trader. Traders had magic. Manticores lived by feeding on that magic. The manticore's hunger burned in its eyes.

The manticore smiled at Thalia.

Something sliced past Thalia from behind.

The manticore was thrown back from Thalia. It fell writhing to the ground. Spittle flew from its mouth as its human disguise yielded to its true manticore form. The head remained human, but the trunk became a compound of lion and hyena, its tail hairless and scaly. When the manticore went limp, its smell became a visible stench, meaty and rotten, as vapors rose from the carcass.

Thalia's knees were like water. She took an involuntary step backward, then lost her balance and sat down hard on the flagstones of the courtyard.

Tycho Aristides, the Skinner of New York, stepped past Thalia and stood over the manticore, intent on the carcass, which was already beginning to decompose. Deftly, from an inner pocket in his coat, he produced a small glass jar filled with clear fluid. He took back the dagger he had lodged in the manticore's throat and used it to open the creature's abdomen. He plunged his leather-gloved hands into the cavity, sliced something within, and brought out a purplish bit of meat. He put the gobbet of flesh in the jar. Then he took off his soiled gloves and cleaned his big dagger and his little jar with a crumpled red bandanna.

Thalia turned aside until she was on hands and knees. She threw up. Ryker dropped to one knee beside her. He put an arm around her shoulders. Thalia felt his breath warm on her ear and heard him say, "You did splendidly."

Thalia shook him off and threw up again. His help was more welcome than she liked to admit, even to herself. Any more sympathy and she might burst into tears.

"Rogers," Ryker called, "brandy all around."

Thalia crouched on all fours and shivered while the dead manticore was loaded into the police van. Her hearing was back. She wished there were something she could do about her sense of smell.

"Don't think of going anywhere, miss." Inspector Ottokar, with help from Officer Kelly, had regained his feet. "Given how seldom manticores share a territory, you should be safe now. These manticore formalities take precedence, but that paperwork won't take very long. We'll be back for you shortly. You'll have a lot of questions to answer."

"I'll come with you, Inspector," Aristides declared. "There's a reward for every manticore I kill, and I don't see any point in waiting to collect." He offered Thalia his hand and she let him help her up.

Rogers distracted the policemen with his tray of glasses and the brandy decanter.

"Thank you, Mr. Aristides." Thalia brushed at her skirts. Her clothing was creased and dusty, but she'd managed to avoid both the manticore's blood and her own vomit. Good. She felt exhausted. Apparently resisting the urge to Trade took it out of one.

"You're welcome, Miss Cutler." Aristides gave her a formal bow. "I've been stalking the beast for days. It never went far from this doorstep. I thought it would pay to keep an eye on you, and when the Rykers' man came out to summon me, I knew I was right again."

"What's in the jar?" Thalia asked.

Aristides looked surprised by the question. "This? Just a bit of alcohol. Preservative. Manticores don't last long once they're dead."

"What did you take out of the manticore?" Thalia persisted. "It looked—"

"Disgusting, I know," said Aristides.

"Purple," Thalia finished.

"Gallbladder. You can't imagine how rare they are. Trader scientists will pay a lot of money for one." Aristides patted the pocket of his coat. "As much as the reward the Traders put up for killing one."

"Why? What is it good for?" Thalia couldn't imagine what a piece of a manticore could possibly do to be worth what it took to get one.

Aristides spread his open hands and shrugged. "Trader scientists are still Traders. They just say *research*. Who knows?"

Rogers offered them brandy. Thalia accepted a glass. Aristides declined with thanks. "I'm going with the policemen. Time to collect the reward."

The police van departed. The Rykers' servants closed and locked the gates, then set about cleaning up. Thalia stood in the middle of the courtyard trying to take it all in. There was manticore's blood on the flagstones. There was the embarrassing stain left when Thalia had vomited.

Little by little, Thalia's detachment faded away. Her hands began to shake. Her knees were less watery now, but she still felt as if they might buckle beneath her at any moment. This weakness, now that there was no danger whatsoever, made her feel ashamed. What was the matter with her?

Thalia reminded herself that this was her second manticore attack in as many days. Her friend Nutall had been accused of Von Faber's murder. Soon the police were going to come back to arrest her. It might be that only milk bottles were upset, but she had a right to feel shaken.

Thalia stood there until the servants had finished their work and left. Not a trace remained in the courtyard to show that a manticore had ever been there. Order was restored.

Overhead the sky was the usual mass of clouds, but otherwise it was a lovely day. Calm now, Thalia sipped her brandy and felt profoundly grateful that she was still alive to see it.

Chapter Ten

Spurred on by the manticore attack, Thalia returned to the damp chill of the Changing room. Now that the existence of another part of her soul had become evident, Thalia was determined to learn to Trade. The brandy she'd consumed might also have contributed to her zeal.

Nell had learned to Trade, Thalia recalled, when she had found a common thread between her two forms. Thalia knew she had to find out what her other form was and how she could cross the bridge between. Her very life depended on it.

The pool in the Changing room had a walkway all around it, broad on the side with the stairs to the nursery, narrow on the other three sides. Thalia found this an ideal spot to pace. Pacing helped her think. Pacing also kept her mind off how cold it felt down there.

Someone knocked at the double door at the far side of the pool. Thalia put her hand on the doorframe. "Who is it?"

"Who do you think?" Nathaniel Ryker unlocked the doors, joined Thalia, and locked them again. "Rogers will let us know when the police get here. Nell is sending for our family lawyers."

Thalia tried to rub warmth into her hands. "If the police take me in, I want Aristides as a bodyguard."

"I'll arrange it." Ryker was staring at her. Thalia tried to read his expression. His spectacles made it difficult to see his eyes. It was like trying to judge the depth of the pool by looking at the reflections of the gaslight, she thought.

Thalia spoke her thought aloud. "Why are you doing this?"

Ryker didn't waste time pretending he didn't know what she was talking about. "I'm helping you because you need it."

"You're helping me because I'm a Trader."

"And you need it." Ryker looked her over. He seemed to approve of what he saw. "You're very calm for someone who was recently attacked by a manticore."

"Am I?" Thalia shivered. "I haven't had time to think about it. A week ago, I had a career. Even just this morning, I thought I knew who I was. Now I don't know anything."

Ryker took off his jacket and put it around her shoulders. Thalia was annoyed with herself for noticing how good he smelled. "You'll learn."

"Any year now." Thalia didn't try to hide her bitterness. "I want my life back."

"Understandable." Ryker gave Thalia's shoulders a little pat, then stepped away. "You are in a devilish awkward situation."

"I am." Thalia frowned at him. "How long will you help me?"

"As long as it takes." Ryker was entirely calm. "It's all right."

"It's all right that I sit here like a cuckoo in the nest for weeks and months and years? It's all right that you feed me and house me indefinitely? It isn't all right."

Ryker's crooked smile held bitterness of its own. "That, I can assure you, is the least of your worries right now. You are welcome here as long as you need sanctuary."

"I can't stay here forever."

"Forever is impossible, I admit," said Ryker. "But I urge you to consider how long or short 'the rest of your life' might be. Don't forfeit your time out of impatience."

"How do you Trade?" Thalia demanded. "Tell me how to do it."

"I will gladly tell you how I Trade, but that won't help you. Each of us must find our own way." Ryker sounded embarrassed. "Listen carefully. This is my way. There are days when I find running the Ryker Trust and our family's businesses wholly engaging. Sometimes it is even exciting. Those days don't come very often. The rest of the time, things can get so boring. I feel how much more engaging it would be to Trade, how much more exciting. Then. I Trade."

"But how did you start? How did you begin to Trade?" Thalia took a step closer to him. "Before you had business to be bored with? How did you do it the first time?"

Behind his thick spectacles, Ryker had a sweet reminiscent look in his eyes. "We were staying at our house in Sag Harbor for the whole summer. It's not as big as this house, but it is very near the shore. The grounds there have a stone wall all around to keep it safe. I was in the garden. It has a shallow pond I like. Middle of the summer, middle of the night. There was a full moon. I could hear the tide coming in. . . . " He trailed off, smiling at the memory.

"Go on."

Ryker shook his head. "It was more interesting to Trade to my other form. That's all."

Thalia sighed. "I don't know what to do. I don't know how."

"Remember, your danger is not the only danger. Until you control your Trades, the manticores you attract will endanger Nell too." Ryker lifted his hand, as if to pat her shoulder again, but stopped himself. "Keep trying. I'll be upstairs, waiting for the lawyers." He let himself out the double doors and closed them firmly after.

Thalia was alone again. She told herself she was glad. She paced around the pool trying what others had tried. There was nothing amusing in her situation. Although Thalia suspected it would be possible to be bored with pacing eventually, she would never be bored into Trading.

From one end of the chamber to the other, around and around the pool, Thalia paced. As she paced, her temper rose. What kind of nonsense was this?

On what might have been her fiftieth circuit of the pool, Thalia decided to change direction. As she turned, Ryker's jacket fell from her shoulders. She stepped back to try to catch it but failed. Then she stumbled as her foot caught in the crumpled fabric.

Too close to the edge, Thalia thought. She twisted to regain her balance. For a moment she was sure she could. She was wrong.

Thalia fell into the pool.

The water was cold. It was far deeper than it looked from above. Thalia discovered that even as she flailed her arms she could not reach the side.

Thalia could not swim.

As she sank, Thalia saw the bubbles from the air her clothing held float up around her, at first so many they blocked her vision, then fewer, then none. As Thalia sank, the light above her seemed to dim.

Thalia fought the water but it was too deep. Once she bobbed to the surface, but her clothes pulled her back down and she sank before she could get a deep breath. Gasps and half breaths were all she could manage.

Thalia was possessed by anger at her own stupidity. Yet even as she redoubled her effort, she discovered she could not fight her way back up. The struggle lasted too long. Defeated, she exhaled. She knew it was only a matter of time. She could not keep from inhaling long. Then water was everything.

Thalia knew she was dying. She could feel her hands go numb. She tingled everywhere, but the strange sensation could not distract her from the underlying pain.

Thalia went cold to the bone. She flailed again, still enraged, still determined to go out fighting. She would not end like this.

Thalia's vision came back. The wicked cold had gone. The water had released her. She could breathe freely. All the pain was gone. She was on the surface of the pool, but in no danger of drowning. She rode the dwindling ripples with ease.

The water moved up and down beneath Thalia in a way she found pleasant until she remembered these were the ripples she'd made when she was drowning.

Behind her, the double doors opened.

Thalia looked around without moving her body. It was no trouble to turn her head farther than she ever had before.

Ryker was standing on the threshold. The gaslight reflected on his spectacles, which made it hard to see his eyes, but she could tell he was smiling.

Beside him stood the two policemen, Inspector Ottokar and

Officer Kelly. They were not smiling. Their eyes were wide. Their mouths were open.

Thalia turned to face them, spread her wings wide, and hissed at them with every iota of anger and aggression she could muster. It felt wonderful.

"As you see," Ryker told the policemen, "we were telling you the truth. Miss Cutler is a Trader."

"You Traders." Inspector Ottokar glared at Ryker. "Think you're funny, don't you? Where have you hidden the girl?"

Thalia hissed at them all again, and Ottokar in particular.

"I assure you, this is Miss Cutler." Ryker's sincerity was clear.

Inspector Ottokar choked, "She's turned into a goose!"

"Oh, no. Take a closer look." Ryker's smile was wide. "In fact, Miss Cutler is a swan."

Being a swan, even after Ryker had urged the policemen to stop gaping and leave with him, suited Thalia to perfection. She wasn't cold. She wasn't tired. The water was comfortable. It filled Thalia with wonder to spread her wings, then furl them again. Every sinew, every muscle held strength she had never known she had. Her neck was long and strong. It was not infinitely flexible, of course. Her wings were not infinitely powerful. But this strength was different from her strength as a human. She delighted in it.

Thalia used her time alone in the Changing room to experiment with her new grace and power.

When playing in the water lost its charm, it was a short hop to the edge of the pool, where she could settle down to the soothing and necessary work of preening her snow-white feathers to look their best.

Thalia was pleased with herself right up until the moment it occurred to her that she had no idea how to Trade back to her original shape. Experimenting with her wings and beak was no more successful than pacing around the pool had been.

Drowning had been terrifying. Waiting for the sword to fall that night in Philadelphia had been terrifying. Fear had driven Thalia to Trade. Thalia considered the knot of emotions she remembered. Not merely fear. Anger. Sadness. Terror of what came next. Sorrow at losing her life so soon.

If falling in the water had caused the Trade, Thalia was going to have a hard time duplicating the knot of emotions. Falling out of the water was impossible. If she Traded when she thought she was about to die, then the knowledge that the Trade would save her meant she would never believe she was about to die.

At last, thoroughly disgusted with herself and the entire world around her, Thalia tucked her head beside her wing and fell into an exhausted sleep.

When Thalia woke, she was huddled in an uncomfortable heap on the walkway. She was soaked. Her clothing was heavy with water, her hair a sodden tangle around her shoulders. She was shivering. She was human. She was a Trader.

Thalia leaped to her feet, narrowly missing another fall into the pool. "I am starving," she said aloud to nobody. She went up the staircase to the nursery. It made no sense to talk to empty space, but she was so glad to have regained the power of speech, she didn't care. "What time is it? Is there breakfast?"

It turned out to be ten in the morning. As Thalia changed out of her wet clothing, she saw that someone had tended to the doves and the snake for her. There really was no limit to the luxuries a Trader household supplied, she thought gratefully.

The marvelous plumbing beckoned. Once she was clean and dressed, Thalia was too hungry to wait for her hair to dry, so she braided it, pinned it up, and tied a scarf around her head to conceal the worst of her dishevelment.

By the time Thalia was ready to emerge, Nell was in the doorway. "Nat says you did it! Congratulations!"

Thalia smoothed her white lawn shirtwaist as she tucked it into her dark serge walking skirt. "Thank you for letting me use the Changing room. It worked."

"You are welcome, of course, but you did the changing. The room has no magical powers. That's all you."

"Is there any breakfast left?" Thalia winced at the whining, plaintive note in her voice. "I'm sorry I overslept."

"You must be quite hollow." Nell beckoned Thalia to accompany her. "I slept the clock around the first time I Traded deliberately. Tell me, how did you manage it?"

Thalia felt her face and ears get hot. "I tripped over your brother's jacket and fell in the pool. I thought I was going to drown. I Traded. That's how I felt in Philadelphia when I thought the sword would drop on me. Apparently that is what it takes for me to Trade, the imminent threat of death."

"How inconvenient." Nell looked intrigued. "But perhaps not insurmountable. How about Trading back?"

"I couldn't. It's lucky I got out of the pool before I fell asleep. I suppose if I'd stayed in the pool, I might have Traded back while I was floating in the water. Oh!" Thalia covered her mouth with her hand. "I'm afraid your brother's jacket is still down there. I forgot about it."

"That's all right. Nat can fetch it for himself next time he goes down." Nell ushered Thalia into the breakfast room. "What shall I ask Cook for? Coffee, of course. Eggs?"

Thalia gulped. "Not eggs. Not today."

Nell went to see about the meal while Thalia took a place at the table. The contrast with Mrs. Morris's boardinghouse dining table could not have been greater. No reach and grab from fellow diners here. Thalia was certain that no one in this house would mock her for the careful table manners Nutall had drilled into her.

When Nell returned, she was carrying a linen napkin and a china cup of coffee on a saucer, which she set before Thalia. "Start with this. The rest will be up soon."

Thalia took a sip of coffee and savored its warmth. "Thank you for having someone see to my doves. And the snake. I appreciate it."

Nell shook her head. "That was Nat, not me. He did it himself."

Thalia paused, cup in midair. "What do you mean, he did it?"

"I mean he tended to your doves and your snake," Nell said, "with his own fair hands."

Thalia searched for a solution to this mystery. "Does he like doves or something?"

"No. Nat isn't squeamish, but it was quite out of character for him to do someone else's dirty work. Also, take this into consideration. He positively dislikes snakes."

Thalia's breakfast arrived, borne by the cook herself. There was a small bowl of brandied cherries along with plates bearing toast, three sausages, and half a steak, accompanied by a bowl of oatmeal that must have been prepared for someone else's far earlier breakfast. Even the Rykers' cook could not prepare oatmeal in the time since Nell had been in the kitchens.

"That was helpful of him." Thalia applied herself to demolishing her breakfast.

"I think Nat expected you to take much longer to Trade. You might have been down there for days for all we knew. Nat has strong opinions about people who neglect animals."

Thalia touched her lips with the napkin and took another sip of coffee. "Does he have pets?"

Nell laughed. "Traders don't have pets. Solitaires need to keep animals around to help them remember that they're animals too. We're Traders. We don't need reminding."

"That's not why Solitaires have pets," Thalia began.

Nell waved her protest aside. "Don't tell me. I know. Your doves and the snake are part of your stage act. Nat won't let you neglect them, but he wouldn't order a servant to do something like that. I think it is quite possible that he likes you."

"Now that I'm a Trader," muttered Thalia. The oatmeal was still too hot, so she moved her attention from the toast to the sausages.

"He liked you before he knew you were a Trader," Nell confided. "Aren't you going to try those cherries?"

Thalia's mouth was full, so she simply pushed the bowl across to Nell, who ate one with her fingers.

It was a slow process, for there was a great deal of food, but by the time the clock struck eleven, the plates were as clear as Thalia intended them to get. Hunger dealt with for the moment, Thalia finished her coffee and settled back in her chair. "Thank you. That is so much better."

Nell gave Thalia a long, measuring look. "Are you ready for the newspapers? Von Faber's death is filling up the Solitaire papers but in the Trader press, all the headlines are about the manticore."

Thalia rose from the table. "Show me."

Nell took Thalia to the music room, where a dozen different newspapers were spread out. Nell had been correct. The manticore dominated the Trader newspapers. Photogravure images of the triumphant Skinner of New York adorned every front page.

"Oh, my." Nell regarded the likeness of Tycho Aristides with interest. "Don't you think he has lovely eyes?"

"Yes. Definitely. He also has a lovely knife. That's what I liked best about him." Thalia folded the *Transformer* and reached for the biggest Solitaire newspaper, *The Times*.

"A keen eye," Nell said appreciatively, "and a steady hand."

Von Faber's murder, *The Times* proclaimed, was all but solved. David Nutall, the prime suspect, was now under guard at the Sylvestri embassy, the Dakota. The Sylvestri ambassador himself had posted bail, a truly extraordinary sum, and informed the press that Mr. Nutall was a kinsman of his. Mr. Nutall was innocent. He could never have committed such a heinous act. The ambassador's family had already engaged the best legal representation available for Mr. Nutall. The Sylvestri ambassador would not rest until the truth had been revealed and the actual murderer, whoever that would prove to be, brought to justice.

When Thalia had finished reading that news story, she did not lower the newspaper. She wanted to hide her expression, even though she could not tell exactly what her expression was. She could feel that her face had twisted strangely. She knew she must be blushing. She didn't understand why she couldn't control herself better. Why couldn't she just deal calmly with the situation at hand?

Her thoughts would not stop circling. Nutall was Sylvestri.

Nutall—her father's companion, her mentor, her vade mecum of trustworthy advice on all matters of importance—was not a Solitaire after all. All her life, Thalia had been mistaken.

What a stupid person Thalia had turned out to be. She had been wrong about herself all her life. She wasn't a Solitaire. She was a Trader, of all ridiculous things.

Now Nutall wasn't a Solitaire either. Some small things fell together into a pattern. Nutall's extraordinary patience wasn't so extraordinary if he was Sylvestri.

The Sylvestri had an understanding of time and space that they claimed was not the same as the Solitaire worldview. Nutall's patience, always deep, was never more evident than when he stood in a line waiting for something.

The Sylvestri knew nature intimately, every flower, tree, and bird in the sky. There was little need to identify trees on the vaudeville circuit, so Thalia could not attest to any particular skill Nutall possessed in this area. He did understand the tides, she knew, and the phases of the moon. Once, when their train had stopped for hours in the Delaware Water Gap, he had demonstrated a surprising knowledge of rock formations.

Nutall's abstemious ways fit as well. Sylvestri, as a rule, never drank alcohol.

Sylvestri held themselves aloof from Solitaires and disliked and distrusted Traders. It was true that Nutall didn't fully trust Traders, but that was mere common sense. Even Traders, Thalia suspected, didn't trust other Traders.

Nutall had often said he considered an opportunity to haggle to be an experiment in Solitaire nature. Had that kill-fee conversation with Manfred been such an experiment?

Thalia was thrown out of her reverie when, from the doorway, Ryker announced the obvious. "Miss Cutler, you're back." He seated himself next to Thalia, who held the newspaper at an angle that concealed her face from him. With sudden concern, he added, "Are you all right?"

"Perfectly all right, thank you." Thalia knew her voice sounded strange, but she couldn't help it. To her absolute consternation, Ryker put his arm around her shoulders and gave her a gentle shake that was strangely comforting. "Mr. Ryker! What are you doing?"

"You aren't all right, are you?" Ryker let Thalia go on holding her newspaper, but he crumpled it enough to peer at her around the edge. "Thought not." From a pocket, he produced a handkerchief, took her hand, and put the handkerchief in it.

Thalia put the newspaper aside, took the handkerchief, and put it to good use. When she could speak clearly again, she asked Ryker, "Why are you being so good to me?"

"You Traded," Ryker said gently. "You even Traded back. Cause for celebration, I'd say."

"'Celebration,'" Thalia echoed bitterly. "Not the word I would have chosen."

"You're alive. You're a Trader. Soon you'll be in control of yourself."

"You can't be sure of that," Thalia said. "I may be forced to accept your hospitality forever."

"Doubtful."

"I ruined your jacket," Thalia confessed. "I'm sorry. I'll replace it when I can."

"Forget it." Ryker waved any concern for his clothing away with an airy gesture. "You have bigger problems. You're involved in a murder investigation. Yesterday you narrowly escaped death by manticore for the second day running. I suppose you're right to wait to celebrate until your affairs are less—complex."

Thalia blew her nose.

"Any word from our imaginary lawyers?" Nell inquired.

Ryker turned his attention to Nell. "I've received an apology and a promise that they will be here shortly."

"What good is having an entire law firm on retainer if they don't come when you call?" Nell sounded unimpressed.

"I'm sure they will answer that question for us," Ryker replied. "Start a list of your other questions while we're waiting."

"I think I will." Nell set aside her newspaper and left the room.

"Where were we?" Ryker asked Thalia.

Thalia tried to maintain a facade of calm but it kept shaking loose. Finally she let out a deep exasperated breath and told the truth. "I'm a Trader, a manticore tried to kill me, and my father's closest friend, who has been looking after me almost half my life, turns out to be Sylvestri." Thalia shook her head. "He never trusted me enough to tell me."

That gave Ryker pause. "Miss Cutler, I don't know what to say. That must be—confusing."

"It is." As an afterthought, Thalia added, "Yesterday I discovered that I can only Trade when I think I'm about to die."

"Good lord." Behind his spectacles, Ryker's eyes went wide. "Don't let Nell know. She has a fertile imagination and she likes to be helpful. If she decides you need to believe you are about to die, I'm not sure what she'll do about it."

Thalia gave that thought due consideration. "I will add that to my list of troubles. It's possible that one of the people helping me might decide I need to believe I'm going to die."

Ryker nodded. "Best to be prepared."

Rogers the butler appeared in the doorway. "The lawyers have arrived, sir."

"Show them in, Rogers." Ryker muttered to Thalia as he stood, "At last. This will take some time. We might as well be comfortable here."

Thalia followed his lead, heartily wishing she'd done something different with her hair.

"Mr. Aurelio Tewksbury and Mrs. Sylvia Hopkins of the law firm Tewksbury, Giorgione, Hopkins, and Associates." Rogers ushered in a cross-looking elderly white man without a hair on his head and a middle-aged black woman with kind eyes. Both were dressed for an afternoon call in the most elegant of clothing. Thalia assumed they were both Traders.

Ryker did the honors. "Mr. Tewksbury, Mrs. Hopkins, allow me to present Miss Thalia Cutler." He made sure his guests were seated comfortably. Nell slipped in quietly and sat on the nearby piano bench.

Thalia held Mrs. Hopkins' gaze as she made her most polite curtsy to the older woman.

Mr. Tewksbury spoke first. "I must observe, Miss Cutler, you don't look like a Trader."

"Don't be rude, Aurelio. Neither do you." To Thalia, Mrs. Hopkins continued, "When the police returned yesterday, they had a warrant for your arrest. Fortunately, you had Traded to a swan. Well done. Excellent timing."

"Even the dimmest policeman knows not to arrest a Trader in her alternate form," said Mr. Tewksbury. "They'll be back for you, of course."

"Of course they will," Mrs. Hopkins agreed. "But we'll be ready for them."

Ryker cleared his throat. "I'm sure we will, but it would have been helpful to hear from you yesterday. May I ask what was the delay?"

Mr. Tewksbury made a rumbling noise of disgust. "We were both with our respective spouses in Newport, I'm sorry to say, attending something the Mellons called a house party. It didn't deserve the name. Chaos, I tell you."

Mrs. Hopkins continued, "When we received your wire, which had been forwarded from our office, we immediately made our farewells, and returned to the city. Given the nature of your difficulty, some research was required."

"That's putting it mildly." Mr. Tewksbury leaned back in his chair. "Any chance of refreshments, my boy? Dry work, research."

"Nell?" Ryker turned to his sister, but she was already up and on her way out of the room. He turned back to the lawyers. "Trader law is clear on the subject of arrests while transformed. I am surprised your research took so long."

Mr. Tewksbury barely suppressed a guffaw. "That wasn't what we were researching."

"We wished to explore the finer points of the case." Mrs. Hopkins seemed not to notice Mr. Tewksbury's amusement. "The police are interested in you only because of the circumstances of Von Faber's death, Miss Cutler. Nothing more."

"She knows that," Ryker pointed out. "Did you need to investigate her background before you agreed to represent her?"

"Because Tewksbury, Giorgione, Hopkins, and Associates is competent and well thought of, Mr. Ryker, your family has had our law firm on retainer for many years," said Mrs. Hopkins gently. "We would not have the excellent reputation we do if we failed to do our homework. It was necessary to familiarize ourselves with the facts in the case."

Nell returned, followed by three servants, each bearing a tray laden with refreshments: coffee, sandwiches, and cake. Mr. Tewksbury rubbed his hands delightedly.

Ryker did not let the distribution of refreshments distract him. "You are here. At last. Therefore you and your firm are equal to the challenge. What happens next?"

"Three or four of these excellent little sandwiches," said Mr. Tewksbury through a mouthful of crumbs. "A sip of coffee, a morsel of cake, and we'll prepare Miss Cutler for her interview with the police."

"The Von Faber case is clear-cut." Mrs. Hopkins had ignored the sandwiches, but she was already on her second cup of coffee. "The police have hired an expert gunsmith to examine the weapon. That gunsmith is prepared to testify that someone tampered with the firing mechanism. Originally the chamber was designed to ignite only the charge in the lower cylinder. Some kind of tool, possibly a small metal file, was used to breach the barrier that prevented the upper cylinder from discharging."

"Sylvia means that somebody buggered up the gun so both the fake charge in the gun barrel and the tricky bit beneath it fired at the same time." Mr. Tewksbury helped himself to another cup of coffee. "That's what killed the poor devil."

"As you may imagine, the number of people who would know how to sabotage such a weapon is limited." Mrs. Hopkins nudged Mr. Tewksbury's cup with her own and he refilled hers as well. "Not only is Mr. David Nutall one of those people, not only was he at the theater on the night before Von Faber's last performance, but he actually threatened Von Faber. Several witnesses agree."

"Who are these witnesses, exactly?" Thalia demanded. "How do we know someone hasn't paid them to agree?"

"What excellent questions. I have obtained a list." Mrs. Hopkins handed Thalia a sheet of paper from the portfolio she carried. "See if you can recognize any names."

"It took special knowledge to rig that murder weapon," Mr. Tewksbury said. "Nutall had the knowledge. He had the means, the motive, and the opportunity. Nutall did it. Plain as the nose on your face."

Thalia dropped the list as she sprang to her feet. "That's not true."

Mrs. Hopkins was calm personified. "Every witness agrees that Nutall told Von Faber that he would regret it if he didn't drop the noncompete clause. Von Faber had interfered with Nutall's livelihood. That will make an impression on the jury it could be hard to counter."

"What the police are going to want to hear from you, Miss Cutler, is precisely how much you were mixed up in it all. It was your livelihood too," Mr. Tewksbury pointed out. "You had good reason to wish Von Faber dead."

"Nutall didn't do it and neither did I." Thalia took a deep breath and made herself resume her seat. If storming out would help, she would storm out gladly, but she knew it would only make things even harder. No matter what they said about Nutall, she had to control her anger. "If the police are only trying to frame Nutall, I don't want to talk to them at all."

"I cannot recommend that course of action," said both lawyers in unison.

"Very well." Ryker sounded soothing. "What course of action do you recommend? What should Miss Cutler do, since she knows that neither she nor her friend Mr. Nutall are connected in any way with Mr. Von Faber's death?"

"Same thing we would do if she were guilty," said Mr. Tewksbury.

"We petition the court for permission to submit all Miss Cutler's testimony in written form on the grounds it is unsafe for an immature Trader to risk a manticore attack by going out in public."

"But the Skinner killed the manticore," Nell protested.

"More than one recent report of a manticore means more than one manticore," Mr. Tewksbury stated.

"No, it doesn't," Nell said. "Manticores do not share territory."

"The Skinner is hunting the city on the assumption that the manticore he killed was not alone," said Mrs. Hopkins.

Mr. Tewksbury added, "For all we know, there could be a pack."

"That's ridiculous. Manticores don't run in packs. They hate each other," Nell pointed out.

"Hearsay," Mr. Tewksbury said crisply. "Inadmissible."

"I believe the court will grant our petition for Miss Cutler to submit her testimony in writing. There is precedent. She is not the only person imperiled by a manticore attack. Other immature Traders could be hurt as well. It is a matter of public safety that Miss Cutler not leave these premises." Mrs. Hopkins added, "Written testimony isn't subject to emotional outbursts in court."

Until now, Thalia had been doing her best to control any emotional outbursts, but now she protested. "I can't stay here. I have to talk to Nutall."

"You couldn't speak with Nutall directly, even if you were already in control of your Trades. Nutall is lucky to be out on bail at all," said Mr. Tewksbury. "He's not leaving the Sylvestri embassy, and you're certainly going nowhere."

"You can write to Nutall," Nell suggested. "Or is it possible he might write to you first?"

"Be advised that anything you write to Nutall will be read by everyone who touches it, including the entire embassy staff," said Mr. Tewksbury. "Don't get fancy."

"We need to use our time wisely. Rather than taking the time to confer directly with Mr. Nutall, which the police are bound to consider suspicious behavior, instead we will focus on offering the police a better suspect. Take a closer look at the list of witnesses," Mrs. Hopkins advised. "Everyone on that list was there the night before the incident. Do any of them have the kind of special knowledge of stage-magic props that Mr. Nutall does?"

Thalia looked at the list again. Each name had the person's occupation after it. She recognized only two of the names, Anton Ostrova, listed as shopkeeper, who had been visiting friends backstage, and Nora Uberti, who, as Von Faber's assistant, was obliged to be there. Before she said as much, Thalia considered. Both of them would know how the muzzle-loader worked in theory, but would either one know exactly how to rig it to misfire?

Anton Ostrova's name on the list was a surprise. Madame Ostrova would be livid with him. If Thalia gave the police reason to take a closer look at him as a suspect, Madame Ostrova would be livid with her.

Nutall had told her that Nora Uberti styled herself Mrs. Von Faber. If the photogravure of the Mrs. Von Faber who had offered a reward in the Solitaire newspapers could be trusted, she was even older than Von Faber himself. If not the original Mrs. Von Faber, she was certainly a far earlier edition.

Thalia picked her words with care. "Could you find out more about Nora Uberti? She called herself Mrs. Von Faber, but I think Von Faber must have lied to her. Certainly, he lied to everyone else he ever met."

"We can do some research on her, Miss Cutler." Mrs. Hopkins made a note.

"Now we come to the matter of exactly what you are to tell the police when they next come to speak to you." Mr. Tewksbury gave Thalia a very hard stare over his slice of cake. "You may tell them your name."

"They know her name, Aurelio," Mrs. Hopkins reminded him. "They also know she was foolish enough to let Mr. Nutall give their false names to the police at the Imperial that night."

"Why on earth did you do such a silly thing?" Mr. Tewksbury demanded. "Your rival was dead. Your career was assured."

"I was wearing my landlady's sister's hat," Thalia explained. "Even if I had been willing to admit that I'd gone to the theater to see a rival stage magician, which I was not and never would be, I couldn't let anyone recognize me while I was wearing that hat."

"I quite understand, Miss Cutler." Mrs. Hopkins made another note. "Now, Aurelio, precisely what should Miss Cutler say? More to the point, what mustn't she say under any circumstances?"

There followed a lengthy conversation between Mrs. Hopkins and Mr. Tewksbury in which they cited legal precedents at each other in both Trader and Solitaire common law. Thalia had some difficulty following it all. She did her best, for she had no intention of letting them place blame on Nutall to help her case. If she were driven to it, she would tell them about Anton's association with stage magic. Madame Ostrova's approval wasn't worth her life or Nutall's.

Thalia kept her attention focused on the threat to Nutall and to her all the while the legal jargon washed over her. In the end, the lawyers gave Thalia permission to confirm that her name was spelled correctly, but otherwise she was to say as little as possible and admit nothing.

Chapter Eleven

In the end, good legal representation won the day. When Inspector Ottokar returned, this time with Officer Kelly and several others in tow, their interview with Thalia took place in the front parlor with Ryker, Nell, Mr. Tewksbury, and Mrs. Hopkins in attendance. In the exceptional circumstances, Thalia was granted permission to remain in the custody of the Ryker family, given her delicate situation with regard to manticore attack.

In the statement Thalia gave the police, she admitted that she had allowed Nutall to give the police false names at the Imperial Theater the night Von Faber died. She asserted that she did so to protect her professional identity as a stage magician. Under questioning, she admitted that Von Faber's noncompete clause had caused her to lose work.

"If I were you," Thalia told Inspector Ottokar, "I'd question Mr. Cadwallader. He owns the syndicate. Von Faber must have had some information that Mr. Cadwallader didn't want to come out, or why would he consent to that stupid noncompete clause?"

"Strike that from the statement," Mrs. Hopkins told the police stenographer. "Miss Cutler, that is hearsay. You must limit your statement to facts, such as your name and birth date."

"It's a fact that Nutall is innocent and so am I," Thalia stated. "He couldn't kill anyone, not even Von Faber."

"This interview is at an end," Mr. Tewksbury announced. "Inspector, you have all you need to proceed with the investigation."

The police stenographer finished his notes and closed his notebook. The policemen made ready to leave.

"Miss Cutler," said Inspector Ottokar. "I have two pieces of advice for you. One. Remain here in the Ryker household, safe from theoretical manticores. If you do that, I won't need to arrest you. Two. Stay away from Mr. Nutall. Even if you're right about him, even if he's innocent, he's still Sylvestri. No one, Solitaire or Trader, can ever really know what a Sylvestri thinks."

Thalia scowled at Ottokar but held her tongue. She stayed in her chair while the policemen and the lawyers took their leave. The front parlor was far from her favorite room in the Ryker house, but she wanted a moment of peace to gather herself after the interrogation.

Before Thalia had a chance to do so, Ryker joined her. "I've seen our police visitors off the premises." He took the chair nearest hers. Thalia waited for him to speak, as she felt certain he was about to come out with an order or a lecture or a piece of advice. To her surprise, Ryker sat quietly and said nothing. The silence between them was easy, almost companionable. Thalia didn't want to break it. Fifteen minutes passed, and Thalia grew calm. She remembered something she'd meant to tell Ryker.

"You took care of my doves." Thalia added, "My snake, too. Thank you."

Ryker regarded Thalia with surprise. "You're welcome?"

"I thought you Traders don't like animals."

"*We* Traders do like animals. It's true we aren't as likely to keep a pet as Solitaires are. We have a different relationship to animals, that's all, since we know we are animals ourselves."

Thalia knew she must sound stiffly formal, but she spoke anyway. Owing Ryker even this additional small favor made her uncomfortable. "You didn't have to feed them and clean up after them yourself."

"Didn't I?" Ryker was smiling faintly. "I don't order my servants to do something just because I dislike doing it myself."

"No?" Thalia found herself smiling back. "Then you're the only one in the world who doesn't."

"You have a distorted idea of Trader behavior."

"Not just Traders, anybody." Thalia repeated herself, this time with genuine gratitude: "Thank you."

"You are welcome." Ryker's smile was wider and warmer. "I won't say 'any time,' since doves are messy and your snake is indifferent to me. But you are welcome, all the same."

"It was nice of you."

"I wish you weren't quite so surprised by that," Ryker said. "When have I not been nice to you?"

Thalia widened her eyes at him reproachfully. "When you as much as told me I was a fallen woman because I work in show business. Oh, how about when you criticized my piano playing?"

"Clearly, I was wrong about your character." Somehow Ryker's face went a darker shade of pink than usual. "I thought we'd put that misunderstanding behind us."

Thalia pressed on. "And my piano playing?"

Even the tips of Ryker's ears were blushing red now. "Do you think I waste my breath advising people who have no musical ability whatsoever? Your playing, surprisingly, isn't hopeless. I offer constructive criticism."

For the first time, Thalia noticed that when Ryker said things like that as he refused to meet her gaze, he was actually smiling. Was it possible he thought he was joking with her? Thalia considered the implications. Ryker liked her. Given the fact that she had been smiling at him while they discussed his abominable behavior, it was possible she might like Ryker.

This idea startled Thalia into silence. Dealing with Ryker as an adversary was a challenge. Liking Ryker had the potential to be a significant distraction. She was still trying to take in the possibilities when Rogers the butler entered to ask his employer a question.

Thalia excused herself and returned to the nursery. Before she could give this development her full consideration, she had more urgent work to do.

Thalia sat at the nursery writing desk, paper and pen before her. She couldn't leave the Ryker mansion, and Nutall couldn't leave the Sylvestri embassy. The embassy had no telephone, Nell had informed Thalia after some research. To send Nutall a telegram would be possible, but to put her thoughts into words that would fit on a telegraph form impossible. She had no real alternative. Thalia would have to write Nutall a letter.

David Nutall had been Thalia's mentor long before Thalia's father had died. Her father had shared a deep friendship with Nutall. On her father's death, Thalia might well have been left on the streets. Her best fate, as an underaged orphan with no family, would have been an orphanage. Nutall had never even mentioned such a choice.

As far as Nutall was concerned, Thalia had inherited her father's talent, her father's props, and Nutall as her stage manager. They had worked hard to create the Lady of the Lake act. Thalia had invented the trick in which she appeared to transform a large stick into a snake, but it was Nutall who had purchased the doves and painstakingly trained them, even as he trained Thalia in how to use them.

By rights, Thalia told herself, she should be onstage this very evening. Nutall should be there with her. It was all Von Faber's fault that Nutall was in trouble. It was all Von Faber's fault she was out of work. It was all Von Faber's fault that he had been so beastly to so many people that the police couldn't pick the person who had really killed him out of his crowd of enemies. Her anger and her loneliness pushed Thalia close to tears.

It took a little while for Thalia to recover her equilibrium. No telling how many people would read this letter before Nutall did. When she was calm, Thalia dipped the pen in the inkwell and wrote.

> *Dear Nutall,*
>
> *I know you are innocent. You would never kill anybody, not even Von Faber.*
>
> *It turns out that I am a Trader. This disagrees with what Professor Evans said, but as he is only a professor of literature, I suppose I should have known to question his opinion.*

*It turns out that you are Sylvestri, and you didn't
tell me. I would have liked to know that. But I guess you
couldn't trust me. Did my father know? I'll bet he did.*

*I can't come visit you yet, because I can't control my
Trades. I will learn how to do that as soon as I can. When
I see you, you had better be ready to tell me the truth. I
want to know why you think I can't be trusted to know
things. Are there any other questions I should ask you? I
will make a list.*

*I wrote to you when I first came to stay with the Rykers
but that letter got returned to me. There was a manticore.
That's why I had to move in with the Rykers. The doves
are fine. I think the snake is fine too. It is hard to tell.*

Sincerely,
Your friend,
Thalia Cutler

When the ink was dry, Thalia folded the sheet of writing paper
and put it in an envelope. There was wax to seal it with. Thalia was
mildly surprised there was a candle and matches to melt the wax
with. She had the impression that people who lived in a nursery
were not ordinarily given an easy way to make a fire. Apparently
the Rykers trusted her with a box of their matches. Thalia thought
it over and decided that when it came to such household items, she
must be at least as reliable as Nell.

Thalia simply addressed the envelope to Mr. David Nutall in
care of the Dakota, which was the Sylvestri embassy in New York
City.

The Dakota were only one of the many tribes in the Federation of First Nations, but they owned the stately building on the west side of Central Park. The Sylvestri among the First Nations had worked together with the Sylvestri of every other ancestry to implement the treaties signed with Solitaires and Traders. The Federation of First Nations controlled much of the western half of the continent, and no one traveled overland without letters of transit issued by the Sylvestri of the First Nations.

Thalia thought about ringing for a servant and trusting that the letter would be sent on her order. Better to find Nell, Thalia decided, and ask her to make sure the letter was sent.

Thalia stepped into the hall and found herself face-to-face with Rogers the butler, who not only held a shotgun but was aiming it at her. As she took in the betrayal, Thalia's hands went ice cold with pins and needles.

"Just following orders, Miss Cutler. Nothing personal," said Rogers.

In the fraction of a second that followed, Thalia Traded. As a swan, she threw herself hissing into Rogers' face, wings beating, doing all she could to kill him where he stood.

The shotgun went off, but Thalia's attack had spoiled Rogers' aim. The noise seemed thunderous to her, but Thalia felt no pain, no scatter of buckshot.

Rogers had fired a blank shotgun cartridge, a distant part of Thalia's mind realized. That bit of good news did nothing to abate her swan fury. Thalia let the instinct to attack run free. She was hissing and striking with her beak even as her wings punished Rogers. He dropped the shotgun and scrambled away from her, fleeing down the back hallway to vanish behind the door to the servants' quarters.

Thalia remained poised in the center of the hallway. There was no room to fly properly, but although her fear was ebbing, plenty of fight remained. Ready to meet another attack, she held her ground.

From a spot halfway up the staircase, Nell called down. "It's all right, Thalia. Don't blame him. It was all my idea. Rogers would never hurt you."

Thalia hissed to show what she thought of that and waddled back to stand over the abandoned shotgun.

Ryker and half the rest of the household came running. Rogers emerged cautiously and took shelter among them. Ryker adjusted his spectacles. "Nell, what have you done?"

"What needed to be done." Nell descended a few more stairs and addressed Thalia again. "You can Trade back any time. Just try."

Thalia's instincts told her to spread her wings and hiss at Nell again, so she did. Nell went back up the stairs two hasty steps. The swan in Thalia's nature felt fierce satisfaction.

As both her swan and her human halves calmed, Thalia was better able to distinguish the two. Thalia's swan was always there, she realized, waiting inside her for a chance to hiss and strike at the threats that filled the world around her. Thalia let her human understanding that she was safe and among friends soothe the swan within. The swan, little by little, calmed down.

When Thalia reached the point where the need to groom her feathers became irresistible, she let her guard drop completely and yielded to the urge.

Nell came the rest of the way down the stairs and stood beside her brother, who had sent the servants away. They watched in silence as Thalia worked. Finally, when the last feather was in place, Thalia let her other half shoulder the swan aside. Slowly, carefully, she Traded back and found herself human, huddled on the hallway carpet three feet away from her forgotten letter.

"Welcome back," said Nell.

Thalia, yielding to impulse, hissed at them.

"Not funny." Ryker pointed back the way Thalia had come. "Back to the nursery with you."

"I Traded." Thalia sprang to her feet. "I Traded back."

Ryker shook his head. "Only because you thought you were going to be killed. You need to be able to Trade when you want to, only because you want to do it."

"Don't you ever stop giving advice?" Thalia replied tartly.

"Never, so long as your life depends on it. We are all on the same side, remember? You also need to be able to keep from Trading when the circumstances warrant. If we let you go now, you would be easy meat for a manticore. The moment you met one, your fear would drive you to Trade. The manticore would consume your magic and leave you to die."

"First you won't let me leave because I can't Trade. Now that I can, you'll keep me here because I can't help Trading."

"Exactly." Ryker gestured at the nursery door again. "Believe me, the moment you pass your ordeal, I will let you go. I don't like giving lectures any more than you like listening to them."

Thalia found her letter to Nutall on the floor outside the nursery. She retrieved it and held it out to Nell. "Post this for me, please."

Nell accepted the letter. "I will, gladly."

Ryker regarded his sister sternly. "Yes, do that. But first, apologize to our guest for your bad behavior. I'm disappointed in you."

"But it worked," Nell protested.

Ryker glared at her. Nell put her chin up and glared back. When she had won that staring contest, she dropped her defiant air and turned to Thalia. "I am sorry, truly. I can't say I didn't mean to frighten you, because I did. But it was rude of me. I regret it."

Thalia said, "All right."

Nell went on. "It wasn't fair to make Rogers be my cat's-paw, either. I'll go apologize to him, too."

"You've left just one thing out of this apology," Ryker prompted.

For an instant, Nell looked puzzled, but her expression soon cleared. "I won't do it again, I promise." She held out her hand. "I apologize."

"Apology accepted." Won over by Nell's sincerity, Thalia shook hands. Then she returned to the nursery. She used her lockpicks to secure the door from the inside and went doggedly back to work trying to find a way to control the swan within her.

Two days passed. Thalia spent the time trying unsuccessfully to Trade at will. Without the fear of immediate death, the swan half of Thalia remained stubbornly quiet within her.

No reply of any kind had come from Nutall. Thalia wasn't entirely sure he'd received her letter. Nell had posted it, but there was no telling what had happened to it since.

At a sharp knock, Thalia opened the nursery door to accept the luncheon tray she'd rung for. To her surprise, it was Rogers there in the hallway, not a maid with her meal. Thalia gave him an inquiring look. "Rogers."

"Miss Cutler." Ever since the incident with the shotgun, Rogers' attitude toward Thalia had been respectful as well as apologetic. "Mr. Tycho Aristides is here. He wishes to speak with you."

"Of course."

"I have put him in the front parlor."

Thalia followed Rogers down the hall, abruptly aware that her muscles were stiff and sore. Was this from her attempts to Trade? How long had it been since she'd done more than walk a few flights of stairs? A longing to be outdoors filled her. Thalia was startled by the strength of that feeling. She had never been one for hearty exercise. Her life onstage and backstage had largely been spent indoors. Thalia decided to blame her sudden desire for the great outdoors on her swan nature. It was only natural a swan would resent being cooped up indoors.

Tycho Aristides, the Skinner of New York, was inspecting the windows of the front parlor when Rogers entered the room. He turned when Rogers intoned, "Mr. Aristides says he is here to see you on business, Miss Cutler."

Thalia stepped into the room and Rogers closed the door, leaving her alone with Aristides.

"Miss Cutler." Aristides shook her hand.

Thalia gestured Aristides to take a seat, then sat down in the same leather armchair she'd used when she met Tewksbury and Hopkins.

Aristides took the chair nearest Thalia's. "Hello again." As he'd been on the day he'd saved Thalia from the manticore, he was heavily armed and casually dressed. He fairly exuded competence.

Thalia regarded him with interest. "You wanted to see me on business?"

Aristides smiled at her charmingly. "How would you like to help me make New York City safer for everyone, including you?"

Thalia knew a rhetorical question when she heard one, so she didn't answer. Instead she gave Aristides a patient smile back and waited.

"You gave me the idea yourself. When the police were going to take you in for questioning, you and the Rykers sent for me." Aristides continued, "It took a while for the message to catch up to me. I was already here, of course. I'd been hunting that manticore for two days. By the time the summons from the Rykers reached me, I'd already killed the manticore and collected the reward."

"Thank you."

"Truly, my pleasure," said Aristides. "At the time, you offered to hire me as your bodyguard."

"I did," Thalia agreed warily. "I've heard that Traders too young to control their Trades hire escorts when they want to go to parties or the theater. Nell told me that's how she first saw stage magic performed."

"Traders hire escorts," Aristides agreed. "They don't hire *me*. That's like trying to hire an *on*-duty policeman to walk you home."

"If I've offended you, I'm sorry."

Aristides waved Thalia's apology away. "You gave me the idea, that's all."

"You want me to hire you to be my bodyguard?" Thalia guessed.

"No. Quite the opposite," said Aristides. "That manticore came right out to shake your hand the moment you set foot in the street. How would you feel about doing that again?"

"Setting foot in the street?" Thalia echoed.

Aristides looked pleased. "You attract them, I'll kill them. When we don't find any more manticores, then we will know New York City is safe for young Traders."

"You mean you want to use me for bait." Thalia kept her tone polite with some difficulty. For all her wild longing for the outdoors, she had not yet become completely irrational. "I'm against that."

"No, that's not it at all," Aristides assured her, in a tone that made Thalia certain that was exactly what he meant. "Let me explain."

"No, let me. You plan to risk my life to use me to attract a manticore, which you will kill. You are given a reward when you kill it. You also sell selected parts of the manticore and keep all that money too." Thalia gave him a very hard look indeed. "How could I possibly resist such a generous proposition?"

"There's no call to be sarcastic about it. I earn every penny of that reward," Aristides protested.

"If I took you up on this offer, I would be earning every penny of it too."

Thalia's vehemence seemed to surprise Aristides. "You're a Trader. Traders are rich. Why do you need a reward?"

"I'm a Trader," Thalia agreed. "But I am not rich. Quite the contrary."

"Oh." Aristides thought it over. "We'll split everything fifty-fifty. How's that?"

"Better, but my answer is still no."

"I'm good at my work. You're safe as houses while you're with me. I don't know how long you've been cooped up here, but you must have some errands to run, some personal business to conduct?"

More strongly even than the urge to be outdoors and away, free under an open sky, Thalia felt a new impulse. She wanted to see Nutall. She needed to make sure he was all right. She'd been told his Sylvestri family had bailed him out of the Tombs. Was that news to be trusted? Thalia sat on the impulse ruthlessly. To

Aristides, she said, "I have no personal business worth risking my life over."

Before Aristides could reply, an otter emerged from beneath his chair, moved to the middle of the parlor carpet, and Traded into Nell Ryker. "What do you mean by splitting the reward fifty-fifty?" Nell asked Aristides. "You aren't running half the risk, so I don't see why you should get half the money."

Thalia could only stare for a moment, during which Nell drew up a chair for herself and folded into it with a silken rustle of expensive petticoats. Aristides gazed across at Nell with wonder. This mollified Thalia. She wasn't the only one struck dumb by Nell's intervention.

"You Trade to an otter," Aristides breathed. After a moment, he cleared his throat. "Some folks call them river weasels, but I've always thought otters to be wonderful cunning beasts."

"Some people think otters are 'cute,' I'm told. Do you think otters are charming fuzzy creatures, Mr. Aristides?" Nell asked.

"No, ma'am. I've seen their teeth."

"That's a good answer," said Nell.

"Mr. Aristides was telling me about his business proposition," Thalia told Nell.

"I heard him." Nell smiled at Aristides so that a dimple appeared by the corner of her mouth, and then she actually batted her eyelashes. "Why make this business proposition to Miss Cutler and not to me?"

Aristides looked confused. "Because you've made your debut in society, Miss Ryker."

Nell shook her head. "I haven't, although I'm ready to at any moment. So, by the book, I'm as likely a subject to play bait for you as Thalia, but don't think for a moment either of us would be so foolish."

"I want to see Nutall, but I'm not about to risk my life for the chance." Thalia turned from Nell to Aristides. "You're full of confidence, but how many Skinners do the manticores kill?"

"Lots," said Nell, just as Aristides replied, "Don't be morbid. I'm fit for the task."

Thalia raised an eyebrow at him.

Undaunted, Aristides continued, "Skinners don't often live long enough to resign, I'll grant you that. But manticores are rare. They hate each other. It's common for the city to go for years without a single sighting. We haven't had two manticores at the same time for thirty years. You can help me put a stop to it."

"I'll stay in until they go back to being rare, thanks."

"You're the very reason they're here, Miss Cutler," Aristides reminded her. "You draw them. Until you master your Trades, you're endangering every young Trader in the city."

"Yes, thanks. I know that." Thalia's voice came out much more quietly than she'd meant it to.

The door opened and Ryker was standing there. "Enough."

All three turned to face Ryker. Aristides' smile went crooked. Nell looked indignant. Thalia felt numb.

"Mr. Aristides, leave this house. Immediately." Ryker gave Aristides a glare that brought the Skinner to his feet, hands up.

"Your sister is in danger because of Miss Cutler," Aristides told Ryker. "You know it as well as I do."

"Out. Don't come back unless you're sent for."

Aristides left, still with a crooked smile on his face, with Rogers close at his heels.

"He looks like such a lovely man," Nell told her brother, "but he's actually dreadful. Thalia, you mustn't pay attention to a word he says."

"It's true, though. You are in danger because of me." Thalia felt cold and distant. She couldn't meet Nell's eyes, let alone Ryker's. It was time she did what everyone needed her to do. Why had she wasted time chatting with the Skinner in the first place? Once and for all, she needed to master her Trades.

"I have work to do." Thalia rose from her chair and headed for the door. "I'll be in the Changing room."

Ryker stopped her as she passed. "Leave us for the moment, won't you?" Ryker asked his sister. "I'd like to have a word with Miss Cutler alone."

Nell rose. "As long as you remind her again that she's welcome to be our guest indefinitely, and that Mr. Aristides is rude, and that you disagree with him entirely, then yes. I will leave you two alone."

"Thank you." Ryker closed the door after her, then took Aristides' chair and leaned forward to look into Thalia's face. "You have had a shock."

Thalia shook her head. "Not really. I knew I was luring a manticore. I just hadn't thought it through. Until now, I hadn't realized just how much danger I'm putting other people in."

"Manticores are what put other people at risk. Not you."

"But I can't control myself—Trader children control themselves better than I do."

With much hesitation, Ryker gently touched the back of her hand. "You will learn control. It is inevitable."

Thalia turned her hand to take his before he could withdraw

that gentle touch. "Why are you so nice to me? You think I'm go-ing to corrupt your sister. You think I am debased."

"I never thought you were debased."

"Yes, you did. Admit it."

"All right. When I thought that, I didn't know you were a Trader. Now that I know what you truly are, I know it is our fam-ily duty to help you."

Thalia meant to be sarcastic, but somehow her words came out sincerely. "Do you know what I truly am? Tell me. What am I?"

Ryker was just as sincere, meeting her eyes fully, his expres-sion open and warm. "You're a Trader in trouble. If my sister were somehow in your position, what would have happened to her? It doesn't bear thinking of. It is my duty as a Trader to help you find your way through this. Not only my duty. My pleasure."

Thalia stared at him. "Mr. Ryker—"

Ryker released her hand and sat back, embarrassed and apolo-getic. "I'm sorry. Forgive me. That was honestly meant, but poorly timed. Please forget I said that."

"Yes." Ryker was a Trader, so Thalia could not help distrusting him, but where had her dislike of the man gone? "Of course. I am grateful for your help."

"You are welcome to be our guest indefinitely." Somehow, Ryker made his sister's words his own.

"I'm not going to spend the rest of my life as your houseguest," Thalia insisted. "I can't. I have responsibilities. I have friends who need my help."

"Of course. Your Mr. Nutall." Ryker sat up straight, not easy to do in the big armchair. "You are very certain of his innocence in Von Faber's murder."

"I am." Thalia thought of saying more, but decided there was no point. To Ryker, her certainty in Nutall's innocence would probably sound like nothing but a child's blind faith. "Thank you for helping me. I can never repay you." Thalia didn't try to conceal her relief and gratitude. "Please understand—I don't want the debt to grow any larger. No matter how generous you are, I am not going to stay here for the rest of my life."

"If a manticore attacks you the moment you leave the premises, you might find that the rest of your life is shorter than you think," Ryker pointed out. "The neighbors have already complained about the manticore's visitation here. I am in no hurry to repeat any part of that unpleasantness."

"I know that Nell won't be safe from manticores until she's passed her ordeal. She is sure she can control her Trades now. Is there any way she can prove that?" Thalia ventured to add, "If there is, could I—"

Ryker cut her off. "Could you have your ordeal at the same time she does? You want that so badly you'd risk it before you're ready?"

"I just want to prove I can control my Trades."

Ryker shook his head. "Listen, Thalia. It's not that simple. There are three parts to it. You must Trade when you are told to Trade. You must return to your human form when you are told to, and you must refrain from Trading no matter what."

"I refrained when I met the manticore by the police van," Thalia pointed out.

"Three parts, I said." Ryker's troubled expression cleared. "That's the ordeal. Nell's will be chosen specifically for her. Yours, when the time comes, will be chosen for you. It's called an ordeal for a reason. It's something like the coming-of-age ritual in a primitive society."

Thalia regarded Ryker with narrowed eyes. "You mean it *is* a coming-of-age ritual, because Traders *are* a primitive society."

"Nonsense." Ryker tried again. "For Traders, the ordeal isn't mere superstition; it is essential to life."

"You're making my point for me," Thalia informed him.

"Traders are not primitive, and this is no mere ritual. The ordeal must be undertaken to become an adult in our society."

Thalia decided to leave enlightening Ryker for another day. "Traders sometimes do fail the ordeal, though. Nell told me what happens to them."

"Yes." Ryker looked as if he'd eaten something bad. "They take their animal form permanently."

"I suppose you passed your ordeal at an uncommonly early age," Thalia ventured.

"In fact, I did." A becoming blush suffused Ryker's face. "I'd been well prepared for my ordeal."

Thalia persisted. "Did all your friends succeed as well? Aren't there stories about the Traders who didn't succeed? Tales told late at night? In whispers?"

"In fact, there are." Ryker's voice went soft. "Although one risks the mockery of one's peers, one can attempt the first two steps as many times as one wishes. The third step, the real ordeal, may be undertaken only once. Those who do not manage their ordeal do not try again. They are not able to. They take their alternate form and stay that way. This is why it is essential that Nell and you both wait until you are thoroughly prepared." Ryker's shuttered expression told Thalia that despite his own success, Ryker had firsthand knowledge of what such a failure meant.

Thalia did not permit herself to wonder whom he had lost. She suspected she was in one of those rare situations when ignorance was as close to bliss as one ever came. "If I fail, if I am doomed to be a swan for the rest of my life, will I know it?" Thalia suspected the swan inside her, that fleeting awareness she was slowly coming to know, might have a very different view of such a fate.

"For a while." Ryker looked tired and sad. "In time, you are filled by the form you Trade to. There is no more room for the human half of your soul."

"So I would know and I would not know." Thalia considered the situation. "The worst of both worlds."

"The greatest waste," Ryker agreed. "There are never so many of us Traders in this world that we can afford to let anyone go needlessly." To Thalia's profound astonishment, Ryker kissed the back of her hand. "Take care with yourself, Miss Cutler."

Ryker left her there, alone in the parlor. Thalia stood there thinking, gradually becoming aware of the physical residue of her encounter with the manticore days ago. Her muscles twinged. Her bones felt heavy. Her heart ached. She found herself rubbing the back of her hand, just at the spot where Ryker had kissed it.

Nutall was in trouble, but Thalia couldn't help him.

Thalia was in trouble herself, but she couldn't help it.

Meanwhile Professor Evans sailed blithely on, Thalia reflected bitterly, telling Traders they were really Solitaires. In all fairness, Thalia had to admit it wouldn't have helped to learn she was a Trader back in Philadelphia. She'd been extremely fortunate to meet the Ryker siblings. Did the Ryker standard of ethics hold for other Traders? Had circumstances been different, would Thalia have found herself a permanent houseguest anywhere else? She doubted it.

Had circumstances not been precisely what they were, Thalia might well have been dead days ago, her belated magic consumed by the first manticore.

Until that night in Philadelphia, all Thalia had ever wanted out of life was to be a famous stage magician. Now that lost ambition seemed more remote to her than the possibility of finishing her life as a hissing, angry swan.

This time when Thalia returned to the Changing room, it felt like she was returning to a sanctuary. She locked all the doors and sat on the walkway beside the pool with a blanket from her bed in the nursery wrapped tightly around her shoulders. She was safe, Thalia told herself. It was all right to hide for a while. She could put the interactions she'd had, first with Aristides, then with Ryker, out of her mind. She made herself put it all out of her mind, even the burning necessity of learning to Trade. For a long time, she let herself sit there in the chill of the Changing room and think of nothing.

Thinking of nothing did not help Thalia learn to Trade. Thinking of nothing, safe in the silence, did, by slow degrees, restore Thalia's calmness. When she was ready, she let herself think about the fact that her undisciplined state was endangering young Traders because she could be drawing another manticore to her. To Thalia, being responsible for endangering others felt much more terrible than endangering herself. After long analysis, Thalia decided that what she was feeling was shame. She let that emotion drive her back to the business of learning how to Trade.

Trial and error, Thalia reminded herself. That was the only way she'd ever learned anything. There had once been a time, though she couldn't quite remember it, when she didn't even know how to shuffle a deck of cards. Trial and error was the only way.

Chapter Twelve

Thalia's ongoing effort to master her Trades was broken only by occasional evening meals with the Ryker siblings, the ongoing chores involved in looking after her doves and the snake, and one domestic upheaval, caused by Nell arguing with her brother over a substantial wooden crate, delivered early one morning.

After yet another morning spent fruitlessly trying to Trade, Thalia was introduced to Nell's delivery. After lunch, Nell took her through a passage Thalia hadn't seen before, which led them out a pair of French windows into an enclosed garden with carefully trimmed shrubs and a gravel path underfoot. It was a quiet space tucked behind high stone walls. This pocket garden lay on the south side of the house, and even so early in the afternoon, it was warm in the April sunlight.

In one corner of the garden rested a metal tripod topped by an expensive-looking device bristling with knobs and dials, with a lens like a snout pointing toward the center of the garden.

"Isn't it wonderful?" Nell caressed the top of the device as if she were petting a sleeping cat. "It's a kinetoscope. I ordered it through the mail. It's from New Jersey."

"What's it for?"

"We've talked about this before. It makes moving pictures." Nell steered Thalia into the center of the garden and stood behind her device, by turns consulting a small meter in her hand and then peering through the lens. "Yes. There should be plenty of light if we start right now."

"Plenty of light for what?" Thalia let Nell adjust her position.

"I'm going to make a moving picture of you doing your card tricks so that I can watch and learn even when you're busy learning how to Trade."

Nell's evident satisfaction with her own ingenuity silenced Thalia. She handed Thalia a deck of cards. Thalia shuffled them in patient silence while Nell fussed with knobs and dials.

"Now!" Nell began to turn the crank that operated the device. "Action!"

Performing for an audience was one thing. Performing for a machine was something else. Mindful of the stage magicians' oath she had sworn, meant to keep her professional secrets from laymen, Thalia confined herself to the simplest card pass she knew. Despite Thalia's restraint, Nell exclaimed with delight as her device clicked away.

Feeling embarrassed, Thalia went through the pass again and again until Nell's supply of film finally ran out. Afterward, Nell thanked Thalia so profusely for her help that Thalia actually blushed. Could it be this simple to repay her debt for the Ryker family's hospitality?

"When will you watch the moving pictures? Today?" asked Thalia. *Not now, I hope,* she did not say aloud.

"Oh, no. I need to have the film sent out to be processed first," said Nell. "I need to send it back to New Jersey to have it done."

"That will take quite a time, I expect." Thalia tried to phrase her concern as delicately as she could. "You won't show it to just anyone, will you? You are my pupil. I have no problem showing you, but I don't feel right about letting just anyone see the trick, in case they learn it themselves."

Nell paused in the process of taking her contraption down for storage inside the house. She frowned thoughtfully. "Oh. I hadn't thought of that. No, I promise I will limit the viewings as much as I can. But I do think other people would like to see the moving pictures. You look quite pretty."

In another two days, Nell's supply of film had been replenished. The first attempt at making her own moving pictures had come back with the fresh film stock and was ready to be viewed. Nell set up the kinetoscope's special experimental projector to point at a sheet hung in a darkened room and ran the short film over and over again.

Thalia watched the flickering images through once and then refused to look at it again. Was that how she really looked to the audience, devoid of grace and charm, shuffling cards mechanically?

Nell went delightedly through it again and again. Her enthusiasm for the project would have resulted in another trip to the garden if it hadn't been raining. The next sunny afternoon, Nell wheedled another session. Thalia tried to put a bit more life into her performance.

Shuffle, cut, shuffle, fan, Thalia worked through the tricks without taking her eyes off the gleaming black disc of the kinetoscope lens. She made the machine her audience. She made each flick of her wrist a scientific exhibition. If Nell was going to learn from her moving pictures, this time Thalia wanted her to learn the right technique.

While Thalia watched the lens of the kinetoscope and made sure her wrists and hands and fingers were all moving perfectly, Thalia's mind wandered back to that night in the Imperial Theater, when Von Faber and his assistant had prepared the rifle for the Bullet Catch.

Thalia had to admit the assistant had been good. She had the kind of grace found in ballet dancers. Her focus on each stage of loading the weapon had made it easy for the audience to think they knew what was going on. *Shuffle cut, shuffle fan.*

Thalia and Nutall had been in good seats. Thalia had seen the effortless pass in which the silver musket ball with the initials had been switched for the dummy lead one that would have stayed in the rifle had the trick gone properly. The one with the initials had gone with Von Faber, ready for him to produce it when he mimed the catch.

Shuffle cut, shuffle fan.

Thalia had seen that pass, but there was something else, something that she had noticed at the time. Something had been pushed out of her thoughts by the events that followed.

Nell had stopped cranking and begun talking. Was she

addressing Thalia? Absorbed in thought, Thalia went on working the cards. Her entire focus was on her recollection of that night.

There was something that had troubled Thalia. If there had been a kinetoscope that night, if she could watch it all again, it might come to her. But there was no film to watch. There was only Thalia's recollection of the night.

Shuffle cut. Shuffle fan.

Frowning to herself, Thalia kept the cards going. She went back in her thoughts, slowly working through her memory of the evening from the moment they had taken their seats to the moment Von Faber had announced he would perform the Bullet Catch.

The volunteer (a plant, no question) was chosen from the audience. The weapon was inspected.

The initials were scratched into the silver ball.

Von Faber took his place while his pretty stage assistant loaded the rifle under the volunteer's eagle eye. The gunpowder, the cartridge paper, the leaden ball—not the one with the initials—and the rod that plunged it all into position in the rifle barrel.

Shuffle cut, shuffle fan.

The gunpowder, the cartridge paper, the leaden ball, the rod.

Thalia stopped shuffling the cards. *The gunpowder.*

Nell was standing right in front of Thalia. "Are you all right?"

The world leaked in a little at a time.

"Yes," Thalia answered absently. "I am quite all right. I've just remembered something, that's all."

That graceful stage assistant had used a generous amount of gunpowder, much more than either Nutall or her father would have permitted. Since what the audience actually heard was the charge from the smaller cylinder, it was unwise to use more in the pantomime of loading, lest some observant audience member shout out that the crack of the weapon firing had been too small for the amount of powder used in loading. To prevent such misfortune, Nutall had insisted that the powder horn her act used must contain only the precise amount of gunpowder he measured out for each Bullet Catch.

Von Faber's powder horn had held far more gunpowder than even the lavish amount the stage assistant had poured.

No wonder there had been a louder report that night than Thalia was used to hearing. At the time, she had put the disparity down to her place in the audience compared with her usual position onstage, holding the chalice in which she would pretend to catch the bullet. Now Thalia was sure that the increased amount of gunpowder had been the cause.

Thalia remembered that sharp report. She remembered what a performance the pretty, graceful stage assistant had given. Every gesture, every tear had been convincing.

"Nutall didn't kill Von Faber." Thalia handed Nell the deck of cards. "I always knew it, but now I know how to clear his name. Von Faber's stage assistant killed him." Thalia explained her theory to Nell. "All I need to do is prove it."

Nell was intrigued, her kinetoscope forgotten for the moment. "How will you do that?"

Thalia took stock of her situation. No one involved with Von Faber's murder had any reason to listen to Thalia or to answer her questions. Her friend David Nutall was out on bail, taking shelter with his Sylvestri family. He couldn't provide any help whatsoever. The police already viewed Thalia with suspicion. Nothing would suit them better than to arrest her as an accessory to the murder. Thalia had little money, no influence, few friends, and a pressing need to learn how to Trade to a swan. "I don't know yet."

Nell frowned. "When do you think you will know?"

First things first. Nutall was with his family, the lawyers had said, safe with the relatives who had bailed him out. Nutall was at the Sylvestri embassy. Thalia would tell Nutall what she had remembered. A telegram would be far too short for a proper explanation. "I need to write another letter."

Nell led the way to the nursery, where the writing desk held paper, ink, and a pen with a working nib. She gazed at Thalia expectantly.

Thalia frowned back. "I can't write a letter if you're watching me."

"Can't you?" Nell dropped into a nearby chair and picked up the instructions that had come with her kinetoscope. "Go ahead. Try. I promise I won't read over your shoulder."

Dear Nutall,

If you have already answered my letter, your reply has gone astray. I haven't heard anything from you. I'm worried about that, but my chief reason for this letter is to tell you that Von Faber's stage assistant was responsible for his death. I am sure of it. For all I know, you've come to the same conclusion. If we can somehow find evidence to prove she did it, your name will be cleared.

I will do all I can, but I'm afraid I can't be of much help until I can safely leave this house, which won't happen until I pass my ordeal. The Rykers have been wonderfully generous. They claim it is their duty to keep me safe from the manticores. I am very grateful to them, but I hate incurring debts I can't repay. Still, it means I can give you a return address where a message from you will reliably reach me. In case my first letter never reached you, I am still at Riverside House.

I know you are out on bail, which your family posted. I hear you are staying at the Sylvestri embassy. May this letter find you there in excellent health and spirits. It's wonderful that your relatives are helping you. I find it curiously difficult to picture what your family must be like. I always thought Dad and I were all the family you had. Of course, I always thought you were a Solitaire like me. Now it turns out neither of us is a Solitaire. That is curious too. I still can't quite believe it.

Professor Evans was wrong about me. I am a Trader. More than once, I have Traded to the form of a swan. It is pleasant in a way, but strange. That was what happened that night in Philadelphia, although I didn't understand it at the time. I Trade when I'm frightened. I was frightened that night.

How do you find being Sylvestri? I suppose it isn't as strange for you, given that you've always known what you were. Why have you kept it secret from me? You've never behaved in the least as if you were anything but Solitaire. I'm sure your family missed you and are glad to have you back.

I miss you. I miss working. Miss Ryker is still practicing the tricks I've taught her, but she has used a kinetoscope to record me so she can watch that instead. That way she can keep learning card and coin magic even while I'm busy learning to Trade.

Write to me if you can.

Your friend,
Thalia

Three hours later a messenger brought a thick envelope containing her unopened letter and a sheet of stationery from the Sylvestri embassy. Thalia opened it in the music room.

Dear Miss Cutler, said the missive. *The man you know as Mr. Nutall has no wish to communicate with you. Desist.*

It was signed by Peter Viridian, the Sylvestri ambassador to the entire eastern seaboard.

"How annoying," said Thalia. "For all the ambassador knows, that could have been my suicide note."

Nell looked up from the Shakespeare play she was reading. "Bit of a crushing disappointment, Mr. Nutall not even opening it."

"I don't think Nutall ever knew of its existence." Thalia resisted the urge to crumple the ambassador's letter and throw it in the fire. Instead, she set it carefully aside. It was time to think again.

Thalia could ask for help from a third party. Madame Ostrova had always been fond of Nutall. She would be a good place to start.

Thalia cursed softly to herself. If she were a true Trader, as almost any other Trader her age would be, she would not need to beg for help from Madame Ostrova or anyone else. If she were a true Trader, she wouldn't be endangering every young Trader in the city.

That bitter thought reminded her of Aristides and his business proposal. If Thalia let the Skinner accompany her to Nutall's sanctuary, he could deal with any manticore that she attracted. If she did not attract a manticore, Thalia would know one of two things. Either she was in control of her Trades enough that she wasn't drawing manticores to her anymore, or Aristides had killed the last local manticore.

How far did manticores travel, Thalia wondered. How long would it take for a different manticore to come hunt an empty territory? Thalia began to draft a telegram. She had a counteroffer to make.

The next morning brought Tycho Aristides to the Ryker house in time for breakfast. With some reserve, the Rykers welcomed him and invited him to join them at the table.

"You summoned me, Miss Cutler?" The Skinner was looking particularly spruce. His hair was clean and looked freshly trimmed. His buckskin trousers were spotless, and he smelled of boot polish and good tobacco.

"Very much against my advice," said Nathaniel Ryker. "We should give our legal representatives time to sort this out."

"Nat, we've talked this to death." Nell gave Aristides a warm smile as she served him breakfast. "Let Thalia speak."

"What do you know about the Sylvestri?" Thalia asked Aristides. "You're well acquainted with Traders, and you are an absolute authority on manticores. How far does your Sylvestri expertise extend?"

Aristides swallowed a large bite of the Ryker household's excellent smoked fish and cleared his throat. "Let's start with what you know about the Sylvestri. In the beginning, the world made itself. The first humans who came were the Sylvestri, who helped keep things in balance."

"Fairy tales?" Ryker asked dryly. "Isn't it a bit early in the day for bedtime stories?"

Aristides continued, "The Sylvestri moved the mountains, they cared for the forests, and they kept the water clean. After a while, the Solitaires came, and the Sylvestri felt sorry for them, so they shared some of the world with them. Last of all came the Traders, and they bought things and sold things until they ran the parts of the world the Sylvestri had shared with the Solitaires."

"That's not the way the story goes," Nell protested.

"That's the way the Sylvestri tell it," said Aristides. "What exactly do you want to know, Miss Cutler?"

"My friend is at the Dakota." Thalia explained Nutall's situation. "The ambassador won't let him receive my letters."

"Sounds about right. There are a few Sylvestri who tolerate Traders, and more who believe in mixing freely with Solitaires. Such Sylvestri are never chosen as ambassadors." Aristides paused as Nell refilled his coffee cup. "Thank you, Miss Ryker. Ambassador Viridian is a Sylvestri separatist. He mistrusts most Solitaires and absolutely all Traders."

Ryker raised an eyebrow and Nell made a small noise of disagreement, but neither actually said anything aloud.

Aristides said, "Solitaires, he considers treaty breakers and weaklings, but he'll take their money when they come to the embassy for letters of transit to cross Federation territory on the way westward."

"What does Ambassador Viridian think of you?" Thalia asked.

"He knows my worth," said Aristides. "He knows my word is good. He knows I'm no weakling."

Thalia leaned closer. "Can you get me to the embassy?"

"And safely back again," said Ryker firmly.

"Let's see if I have this straight." Aristides produced a detailed map of Manhattan and its boroughs. He spread it out and tapped the Upper West Side in the approximate location of Riverside House. "You want to go from here—" He ran his index finger south and tapped the street running up the west edge of Central Park at Seventy-Second Street. "—to here. The Dakota. To see your Sylvestri friend, who is a guest there."

"And safely back again," Nell prompted.

"And safely back again," Thalia echoed. "How far is it? Two miles? Two and a half? Think you can manage it?"

"I can get you there. They probably won't let you in." Aristides smiled grimly. "Provided the Sylvestri haven't sheltered a manticore without telling anyone, which even they wouldn't do, and provided you keep yourself from Trading if we do flush out a manticore, I believe I can get you back here alive and in your current form."

"Right." Thalia sat back in her chair and pushed her plate away. Food was out of the question if she was going to risk luring a manticore. Her stomach was already twisting at the mere thought. "We are in agreement."

"Slow down." Aristides held up a hand. "I am the Skinner of New York, remember. My time is valuable."

"I'll pay you ten dollars for the round trip," Thalia assured him. "You offered to split the reward money if I would work with you to lure out a manticore. Consider this a rehearsal of the idea, only you won't have to share the reward."

"Twenty dollars," said Aristides. "I'm not in this for my health."

"Done." Thalia shook hands with Aristides.

Ryker said, "I know I can't stop this, but take a moment to think. You're not stupid, Thalia. I know you aren't. Think it through. Explain to me why it seems reasonable to you to risk your life because the ambassador won't deliver your note to Mr. Nutall."

"I have no intention of risking my life," Thalia assured him. "If I lure a manticore out, Aristides will kill it. If I don't, it may mean that I've mastered the ability to Trade, so I don't attract them anymore."

"It won't mean that at all. You have to pass your ordeal to be certain you're safe," Ryker retorted. "I know you are a stranger to our ways, but this should be a simple enough concept to master."

"I have to do this," said Thalia.

"I thought she was brighter than this," Ryker told Nell.

"Well, I'm not." Thalia opened her reticule, the largest she owned, showed Ryker the pearl-handled pistol nestled within, and closed it again. "I inherited it from my mother."

"Do you know how to handle that?" Ryker was dubious.

"I had more than just piano lessons," Thalia said. "If a manticore gets past Aristides, I know what to do."

"Don't worry about it," Aristides told Ryker. "Miss Cutler won't need her weapon, but it won't hurt to let her carry it."

"Thanks." Thalia turned from Aristides to the Rykers. "Given that the ambassador told me Nutall didn't want to hear from me ever again, I think I should make my visit a surprise."

Chapter Thirteen

Tycho Aristides used his map of the city to show Thalia and the Rykers the route he intended them to take and what he expected to happen on the way to the Sylvestri embassy. There were places a manticore was more likely to hide than others. There were places that would probably be safe, given the number of people likely to be there in the middle of a weekday afternoon. There were places that weren't safe under any circumstances.

"We need to take your motorcar," Aristides said to Ryker. "Speed is safety."

Ryker's jaw tightened. "Fine. I'll drive."

"Oh, by all means," said Nell. "I have to stay home all alone while you will be off having fun without me."

"Yes, poor you." Ryker turned his attention from his sister to Aristides. "When will you be ready to start?"

"Now. I don't go out until I'm equipped to do my job." Tycho Aristides spread his arms. His black coat, unbuttoned, fell open. Thalia could see the butt of a gun protruding from a shoulder holster on either side. Throwing knives were ready in two leather bandoliers that made an X on Aristides' chest. At either hip, another set of pistols rode in low-slung holsters. A sling over one shoulder held a sawed-off shotgun. "Any more questions?"

Thalia counted five guns and twelve throwing knives. "How many manticores are you expecting?"

"This outfit"—Aristides gave a little shrug of his shoulders so all the weaponry shivered menacingly—"is just for daytime."

Thalia said, "You have a lot of experience in this line of work."

"I have, yes." Aristides stood a little taller. "I killed my first manticore when I was fifteen. That made me a Skinner, but I became the Skinner for Manhattan and its boroughs two years ago. I went up for it the time before that, but they chose the mayor's nephew instead. He got killed in the Bronx in 1903. After that, they picked me for the job."

Thalia asked, "What's the difference between *a* Skinner and *the* Skinner?"

Aristides smiled. "The manticore that attacked you outside looked like a man at first because that's the shape they Trade to. A Skinner makes the manticore Trade. Anyone can call himself—" With a glance toward Thalia and then Nell, Aristides added, "— or herself, as the case may be—a Skinner the first time they kill a manticore on purpose. *The* Skinner, on the other hand, has to take responsibility for any manticores in his range. He—or she—has to manage any freelance Skinners on the job, lest they muck things up. He has to talk politely to the mayor and the chief of police upon any manticore topic they'd like to discuss. He has to be brisk with the newspaper reporters—lie to them sometimes, even."

Nell looked intrigued. "Can women truly be Skinners?"

Aristides nodded. "There have always been women who were Skinners, yes. Not so much these days, not here in the East. It's civilized here, in the nicer neighborhoods anyhow. But last I heard, the Skinner of San Francisco is a woman."

"Don't even think about it," Ryker cautioned his sister. "You may train to be a stage magician. You may operate your kinetoscope. Under no circumstances may you undertake a career killing manticores."

Nell frowned. "You never let me do anything fun."

Ryker frowned back. "No, and I will never let you get yourself killed either."

To forestall Nell's next objection, Thalia clapped her hands briskly. "Time we set off."

Aristides made short work of loading up Ryker's Pierce-Arrow. Ryker was behind the wheel, Aristides in the front passenger seat, and Thalia in the rear seat immediately behind him.

Aristides brought out one of his pistols, as Ryker signaled his servants to open the gate. To Thalia, Aristides added, "Keep your bag closed. I'll be the one shooting when the time comes. That's enough lead to be flying around. I don't need you blazing away too."

The car pulled out of the Ryker courtyard, of necessity going slowly at first, but gathering speed while Ryker worked his way up the gears as they headed for Amsterdam Avenue. Disorderly traffic, horse-drawn and motorized, meant the potential for speed inherent in the Pierce-Arrow was never realized. They crept southward.

Pedestrians were more than mere distractions as Ryker
threaded their way among the carriages and horse-drawn buses.
Any one of them could be a manticore in its human disguise. Despite Aristides' instructions, Thalia kept one hand on the weapon
in her reticule as she watched out the windows. Aristides was vig-
ilant as they made their way downtown, but there was no sign of
a manticore.

Ryker drew up before the stately assembly of towers and tur-
rets that housed the Sylvestri embassy. Aristides let himself out
and stalked around the car, ready for any threat, until it became
obvious that no one, not even the doorman, took any notice of
their presence.

Although the architecture was French château, the magnificent pile was named for the people who had funded it, the Dakota.
Although some Dakota were Solitaires, and a few were Traders,
many of their people were Sylvestri.

Aristides came back to the driver's window. "Stay in the car,"
he told Ryker. He opened the rear passenger door and offered
Thalia his hand. "I'll escort you inside, Miss Cutler."

They were met on the doorstep by a white Solitaire doorman
of great stateliness. Thalia presented her card and introduced
herself and then Aristides. "I am here to see Mr. David Nutall."

"Come in, Miss Cutler, Mr. Skinner." The doorman held the
door for them, but from the dubious expression on his face, it was
clear he didn't think they'd be staying long. "I will see if he is at
home."

Thalia raised an eyebrow. It wasn't Nutall's home, this place.

"Do you want me to come in with you?" Aristides asked.

"No. Keep an eye on things out here." Thalia closed her reticule and let the doorman escort her indoors.

"Sit here." The doorman indicated a simple wooden bench. He left the room without waiting for Thalia to obey.

Thalia did not sit. She took her time looking around the foyer as she waited. Every inch of the anteroom was decorated, an assembly of plasterwork, frescoes, and mosaic tiles, and all the decoration had the same theme—greenery. Vines, trees, flowers, or shrubbery—it was all portrayed with such realism that Thalia could pick out individual drops of dew on the foliage.

At last, the haughty doorman returned, accompanied by a middle-aged Dakota Sylvestri woman, haughtier still.

"I am Mrs. Peter Viridian, His Excellency's wife. The ambassador is busy at the moment. You are Miss Cutler?" Everything about Mrs. Viridian, from her expression to her inflection, made it clear she'd expected someone far better than Thalia. She wore a morning gown that seemed made of autumn leaves and velvet. She looked disapprovingly at Thalia through a gold-rimmed pince-nez strung from a black grosgrain ribbon, which made her eyes seem piercing.

"I am." Thalia stared right back. "As I told the doorman, I've come to see Mr. David Nutall."

Mrs. Viridan sniffed. "I believe the ambassador has written to tell you that the man who told you his name was Nutall does not wish to communicate with you."

"I know no such thing." Thalia glared at Mrs. Viridian. "I won't believe that unless he tells me so himself." *Maybe not even then,* Thalia thought. "Let me see him. If he tells me to leave him alone, I'll go."

Mrs. Viridian examined Thalia as if she were a new kind of bug. "Rudeness like yours would undoubtedly camp on the doorstep until it gets its way. I have the ambassador's permission to admit you to Mr. Nutall's presence for half an hour, no longer. Don't abuse our courtesy."

Thalia said, "Show me some first, then we'll see."

"Follow me."

For a lady of her years, Mrs. Viridian moved fast. Thalia had all she could do to keep up. Their way led through a maze of corridors and stairs, all decorated as lavishly with artful greenery as the foyer.

Thalia knew perfectly well it was still morning. Yet as they climbed and descended steps, as they moved through the corridors of the palatial building, Thalia's sense of time and place wavered as the light shifted. Surely it was late afternoon on a hot summer's day? Unless it was very early morning? Or dusk come early on a winter day?

Thalia kept her mouth shut but her eyes open, taking careful notice of their route. She did not trust Mrs. Viridian to bring her to Nutall without trickery. She might need to find her own way back on short notice.

At last Mrs. Viridian ushered Thalia into a small but sunlit room, and shut the door upon her before Thalia could protest. She heard the key turn. Thalia tried the door—locked—before she registered a presence behind her. She turned quickly. The sunlight angling in through the slats of the narrow wooden window blinds made it hard to see all the way into the dim corners beyond.

"There you are. How spruce you look." Nutall, entirely composed, entirely calm, regarded her from a rattan chair that he seemed to find very comfortable. His feet, in carpet slippers, rested on a matching ottoman.

To judge from the tidy blizzard of newsprint and teacups in his immediate vicinity, Nutall had been peaceably drinking tea as he read the newspapers, but he looked delighted at the interruption. "Forgive me if I don't get up. Do sit down and join me. You'll find the green chair most comfortable, I think."

"Thank you." Thalia took the cup of tea he poured for her and sank into the chair he'd recommended.

Her friend looked very different. His hair had been cropped so short the parts he'd dyed were gone. What little hair remained was pure gray. It made him look surprisingly old. His carefully tended mustache was gone. It made his upper lip seem longer than she remembered. He appeared to be tired but not in any kind of distress.

Now she'd finally rejoined Nutall, Thalia could hardly choose where to start with her questions. "Who is that harpy? Does she actually keep you locked in here? Did she intercept my letter?"

"Sandwich?" Nutall offered her a half-demolished plate of assorted tea sandwiches and bonbons that would have done credit to Mrs. Morris on a lavish afternoon. "Pay no attention to Dorcas. She has an overdeveloped sense of my importance."

"I came equipped. I can open the door." Thalia read Nutall's expression at last and found herself adding, falteringly, "—if you want."

Nutall still held the plate out to her, so Thalia took a sandwich—watercress, she noted—and subsided into her chair to wait for him to speak.

Nutall helped himself to another sandwich. For a few moments, there was the silence of utter contentment as they shared the meal. At last, Nutall sighed and put his cup and saucer down on the newspaper. "You've changed, my dear."

"*I've* changed?" Puzzled, Thalia glanced down at herself. She was wearing the tan walking dress that Nutall must have seen at least fifty times before. "Well, yes. It's been days, I know. I'm sorry

I didn't come sooner, but I have an excellent excuse. Turns out, I'm a Trader after all. I turn into a swan. Well, I'm not good at Trading yet. As I'm what they call an immature Trader, I attract manticores."

"Dear me." Nutall regarded her with alarm. "Don't manticores eat young Traders? What on earth are you doing here if a manticore could eat you?"

"It wouldn't literally eat me, only my magic," Thalia assured him. "I would die soon, true, but I wouldn't be eaten."

"I repeat. What are you doing here?"

"I have questions."

"Write me a letter, then. Don't go jaunting about town luring out manticores. It isn't safe."

"I did write to you, only my letters were returned unopened. Did you know that?"

Nutall shook his head. "It doesn't surprise me."

"Why not?" Thalia demanded. "Why would they do that?"

Nutall left her questions unanswered. "So. Professor Evans was wrong."

"Couldn't have been any wronger."

"I blame myself. I should never have settled for help from a professor of the humanities."

"Never mind that now. They didn't let you have my letters. Why not? Are they keeping you here as a prisoner?"

"By no means. I am treated as an honored guest. A member of the family, if you will." Nutall poured them both more tea. "They are my family, in a far more literal way than you and I are family."

Thalia was warmed by Nutall's acknowledgment of their connection. Thalia's father was always going to be her father, of course, but Nutall's deep friendship with him had made him a different kind of father to Thalia.

"You never said you were Sylvestri." Thalia hadn't meant to put that much accusation into her voice. She tried again. "You don't seem very Sylvestri to me."

"I'm afraid I can't help that. I've spent most of my adult life teaching myself to pass as Solitaire, so I've done my best to winnow out all my most Sylvestri habits." Nutall waved his teacup, as if he were dismissing the entire topic of the Sylvestri, and set it down on its saucer. "I'm very sorry I didn't get the chance to read your letters. You're a Trader after all. I am surprised."

"That's not all I wrote to you. Von Faber's stage assistant sabotaged the rifle." At the blank expression on Nutall's face, Thalia prompted him. "Don't you remember the way she poured the gunpowder when she loaded it? She must have known the trick would go wrong. She killed Von Faber. I only have to prove she did, and you'll be safe. Your name will be cleared. You'll be free."

"I'm sorry." Nutall regarded Thalia with an apologetic air. "I don't think that your professional opinion will be sufficient evidence to prove the unfortunate young woman's guilt."

"I'll convince the police," Thalia said. "Don't worry about that."

Nutall went on. "I don't think, even if you do succeed in finding the true culprit and proving their guilt to the satisfaction of absolutely everyone, that I will be free. My family is intent upon helping me." He pronounced the word "help" with a twist that made it somehow mean the opposite. "They want me to stay with them."

That was awkward. Thalia knew that even if the murder charge could be dismissed at once, it would be a few days before they could find a new theater booking for their act. If Nutall's family detained him, the delay would be even longer. "How long, do you think?" Thalia asked.

"For good, my dear." Nutall pushed the sandwich plate an inch farther away. "I am not to waste my time among the Solitaires any longer." He sounded like he was quoting someone, someone who strongly disapproved of Solitaires.

"Lucky I'm not a Solitaire, then," Thalia countered.

Nutall shook his head. "Listen. From now on, you have to find your way without me."

Thalia watched him closely, holding his dark gaze, hoping he would relent. Finally she broke the silence. "Do you want to stay here?"

Nutall shook his head but murmured, "Yes."

Thalia sat back, her thoughts racing. Was someone listening? She looked around the room. There was no telling what lay behind those serene walls. Could there be someone who could hear but not see them? Thalia did her utmost to conceal her instinctive response to take action. Calm. She must play the game for Nutall's sake. "You mean I should work the act alone? For how long?"

Nutall looked sad. "When the murder trial is over, when the syndicate takes you on again, you may find someone else to be the host in your act. Or else you can create a new act working alone."

Thalia dismissed the idea of permanently working as a solo act with a wave of her hand. "I don't care about that right now. I care about what really happened during Von Faber's act. I'm told you were at the theater the night before, or you wouldn't be in this predicament. Just think. Is there anything else you can tell me? Anything you saw that night or the night before that might help clear you?"

Nutall sat in silence.

Thalia hoped he was searching his memory and not just staring at her blankly.

"I intended to ask Von Faber to waive the noncompete clause," Nutall said at last. "That was why I was there the night before he died. I couldn't see how we would ever find you another gig at a decent theater so long as he insisted on that stupid clause."

"He refused to listen," Thalia guessed.

Nutall shook his head. "I never had the chance to speak with him. He was quarreling with his wife. She's spent all these years in Baltimore raising their children on her own. When she brought them to New York for a visit, she was far from pleased with what she found here."

"Which was what?"

"The rumors are true. Three months ago, Von Faber bigamously married his assistant, young Nora. He had kept the affair from his first wife, which didn't seem to surprise her in the least, but he hadn't bothered to divorce her first. She took issue with that. Most distressing."

"Distressing for Nora," said Thalia.

"True. His assistant was understandably furious to find herself his bigamous partner, and not legally married, as she had believed."

"She didn't know he was married with children?"

"Von Faber kept their existence a secret. He told his first wife that he'd done it for their protection. She laughed at that."

Thalia asked, "Who else was there to hear the fight? Stagehands, for sure."

"Oh, yes. Plenty of witnesses to the argument." Nutall frowned. "I did not mention it to the police, but as I was leaving, young Anton Ostrova arrived."

Thalia frowned. "The lawyers the Rykers hired for us showed me the list of names the police have made of people who were at the theater that night. They know Anton was there. Do you know why he came?"

"It is barely conceivable that he had been sent there by Madame Ostrova to ask Von Faber about the rifle missing from our inventory. But given Von Faber's wide range of unpleasant behaviors, it could have been something entirely unrelated to our problem. There were people there that night not directly involved in Von Faber's show. I'd be surprised if the police know about every single one." Nutall turned his attention to the final sandwich on the plate. "Won't you have another? To help me finish these off?"

Thalia shook her head. "I'm not hungry. I just want to help you."

"You can't. My family have made their wishes plain."

"I thought I was your family." Thalia didn't know why that made Nutall smile.

"You were, for a very long and very happy time," Nutall said. "In a way, you always will be. But I'm subject to my blood kin now."

"You don't have to be. I'll get you out of here," said Thalia.

Nutall went on as if she hadn't spoken at all. "In a way, it's a relief to talk about it with you at last. I find Solitaires quite fascinating. It was an interesting exercise, living as one. Ironic, that you were pretending to be a Solitaire too."

"I was not pretending," Thalia reminded him.

"The longer I spend in sanctuary here, the more my life in disguise seems like a dream." Nutall took the last sandwich himself.

"What's it like, being Sylvestri?" Thalia asked.

"Tell me what it is like to be a Trader. An immature Trader," he corrected himself.

Thalia closed her eyes while she tried to think of an answer for him. "I have Traded, only I can't Trade on purpose yet. It happens when I'm afraid. So it's hard for me to tell what it is really like under all that fear."

"Despite the danger from manticores, you set forth from your sanctuary without yet being in control of your Trades—dear me. Aren't you taking unnecessary risks?"

Thalia admitted, "There's a chance I'll attract another manticore, yes. They tell me they are rare, but you couldn't prove it by me. But I've made arrangements. I needed to see you, but I'm not crazy."

"Arrangements. Very well." Nutall did not look convinced. "So you've not quite come into your powers."

Thalia could feel her eyebrows rise until they were all but knotted in puzzlement, but she couldn't seem to do anything to stop it. "Oh, do I have powers?"

"You will." Nutall's smile this time was all crinkles and warmth, exactly the way it always ought to be in Thalia's opinion. "You resemble your mother in more than mere looks, it seems."

"Do I?" Thalia couldn't help the chime her cup made when she put it back on its saucer, the trembling of her hands betrayed by the rattle of porcelain on porcelain. "How do you know about my mother? Why wait until now to tell me about her?"

"I know what your father told me, nothing more. I've seen only what he showed me. The wedding portrait you found among his personal effects—I've seen that. Your father was afraid—knowing you, with good reason—that if you knew anything more about your mother, you would be determined to know everything. The memory of that loss caused him nothing but pain."

"Still." Thalia swallowed hard. "Don't I have a right to know?"

"Absolutely. But your father feared you would insist on looking for your mother's family. Once they knew of your existence, he thought they would take you from him. When your mother married your father, her parents were furious. He was determined to protect you. I have tried to honor his wishes in every detail." Nutall's expression clouded. "You and your well-being were all Jack cared about in the world."

"He cared about you too," Thalia pointed out.

Nutall continued as if she hadn't spoken. "Your parents met in Vienna, at the World's Fair held there, as you know. That was a great undertaking, the 1873 Exposition. They changed the channel of the Danube to accommodate it. Foolish of them, as it turned out. The river disliked the disturbance. There was an outbreak of fever."

Thalia said, "You make the river sound like a grumpy neighbor."

"Do I?" Nutall went on, "Your mother was a swan maiden, one of the Danube river folk."

"A swan maiden?" Thalia cleared her throat. "Like me?"

"Apparently so. After they married, your mother became your father's stage assistant." As an afterthought, Nutall added, "She had the original idea for the pigeon squeezer, Jack told me."

"Did she?" The knowledge that her mother had helped invent magic tricks cheered Thalia.

Nutall nodded. "For a long time, they were happy on the vaudeville circuit. Their only sadness was the bad times your mother had when she was pregnant. They lost two stillborn children before you came along."

"I never knew that."

"Your father told me that the loss of your mother and brother only six months after your brother's birth nearly killed him too. You were the only thing that kept him going." Nutall's eyes were full of pride. "You have grown into a fine young lady. Yet when you Trade, you turn into a swan. How does that work?"

Despite the terror of her Trades, despite the threat of manticores looming over her, Thalia could not hold back a wild smile. She found herself blazingly happy to be sitting there with Nutall, able to share her new truth. "I can't explain it. I think it doesn't matter whether I Trade or not. I am a swan all the time."

"Dear me."

Thalia went on, "The swan gets scared. The swan gets angry. It hisses and tries to break things."

"You always did have a temper," Nutall said. "From what Jack told me, so did your mother."

"I always thought the only things I'd inherited from her were her clothes, her pistol, and her pearls."

"She would have been very proud of you." Nutall smiled sadly. "As proud as your father was."

"Did he know you're Sylvestri?"

Nutall nodded. "Jack knew all about me. He helped me elude my family. The day I met your father was the first day of my life I felt free, not just of my family's expectations, but completely free. Now I learn that Jack was a Trader. He must have been, or you would not be able to Trade at all, no matter how strong your mother's heritage."

Thalia demanded, "Father knew he was a Trader and never said?"

"Oh, no. I'm sure he never knew. He had no family. He never, ever Traded."

"You're sure about that?"

"I am. I knew him as he knew me. We broke every rule to be together. I can't regret it, but I am sorry that our secret is something that hurts you now."

Thalia knew it was childish to feel resentment, yet she did. She did her best to conceal it. Nutall had never been in such a forthcoming mood before. She ought to take advantage of it. She knew she should ask for more details about his life with her father. Yet Thalia, most profoundly, did not want more details about that. She wanted not to know more about their life together behind her back. "Mrs. Viridian said Nutall is only an alias you use. What's your real name?"

"Muir." Nutall looked sad. "I was named David Muir."

Thalia asked, "What happens next? The trial?"

"This may be the last time I see you outside a courtroom. That is why I burden you with truth you may not be ready to hear. Thalia, you still have your whole life before you. It is a different life than the one you expected, that's all. Embrace your heritage. Trade bravely, deal honestly, and plan a solo act."

"If I must. But I'm going to prove you innocent."

The light in the room dimmed, as if the sun had gone under a bank of clouds. The door opened. Mrs. Viridian stood waiting.

"Goodbye, Thalia," said Nutall gently.

Thalia sprang to her feet. "No! Now that we don't have the noncompete clause to worry about, I just want to get back onstage as soon as possible. I'll work out a solo act, but I'll still need you. You are my manager."

"Not anymore."

"You can stay behind the scenes. You can prompt me from the wings."

"Forget about me. You have problems of your own and you can't solve mine. No one can."

"That's enough." Mrs. Viridian peered coldly at Thalia through her pince-nez. "You must leave now." To Nutall, she said, "You've had your time."

Nutall rose to his feet slowly, as if it hurt him to move. Thalia embraced him carefully. How old *was* Nutall, anyway? He seemed much older than she remembered.

"I'll be back tomorrow," Thalia told Nutall. "I'll send a message if I find out anything useful before then." She turned to Mrs. Viridian. "You let him read his letters from now on."

"Let it be," Nutall murmured in her ear. "Leave it."

"Never." Thalia refused to let her emotions go free with the likes of Mrs. Viridian watching. "Until tomorrow."

"If you think you must," sighed Nutall.

Thalia left him there, in the once-sunny room. Mrs. Viridian marched her out through the cleverly decorated corridors. Despite the beauty of the place, despite the fact that she was leaving her oldest, closest, and most trusted friend behind, Thalia found herself restless and eager to leave. This was not the place for her. Perhaps nowhere built by Sylvestri would ever feel natural or comfortable to a Trader.

Chapter Fourteen

The doorman, looking peeved for some reason, accepted Thalia from Mrs. Viridian's custody, and so she found herself back on the doorstep, put out like a cat.

Ryker and his motorcar were exactly where Thalia had left them. Had it been an hour before? Thalia was usually good at estimating time, but something about the Dakota had thrown her off. The doorman's displeasure, it became clear, stemmed from Mr. Ryker's refusal to move the car from beneath the sheltering canopy of the porte cochere.

There was another motorcar waiting behind Ryker's, a gleaming black Mercer with its distinctive cylindrical hood, reminiscent of a steam locomotive. Unlike Ryker's Pierce-Arrow, the heavier Mercer looked solid and secretive. Even as Thalia watched, the driver opened the rear passenger door. The well-dressed white Solitaire who emerged, radiating impatience, was Cornelius Cadwallader, head of the Cadwallader theatrical syndicate, himself. He brushed past Thalia, and the doorman admitted him to the quiet elegance of the Dakota without a word of challenge.

"Does Mr. Cadwallader come here often?" Thalia asked the doorman.

"Go away," said the doorman. "Take that car with you."

"Is he here to get his letters of transit to take the train to the West? Or is he here on some other business?"

The doorman said nothing, and merely glared at Thalia. She felt his disapproving stare between her shoulder blades as she walked away from him toward Ryker's Pierce-Arrow. When that doorman looked at a person, she reflected, a person stayed looked at. She felt as if she were being watched by a small crowd, not just one tall man in a uniform. She wondered if he might secretly be Sylvestri too.

To Thalia's surprise, Aristides was missing from the front passenger seat. "Where is Aristides?" As Thalia put her hand on the door, the overwhelming sense of something wrong descended upon her. The hand that was touching the door had gone pins and needles. Thalia felt herself watched. This was no disapproving doorman. This was far stronger. She felt as if someone were gloating over her discomfort.

"He said he smelled something." Ryker opened the door and beckoned her inside. "Shall we leave without him?"

Something moved behind her. Thalia ducked her head, preparing to throw herself into the relative shelter of the car, just as Aristides' voice called out sharply, "Get down."

A shotgun fired, both barrels. Thalia distinctly felt something brush at her skirts. She wasn't sure if it was shotgun pellets or something even worse. Through the ringing in Thalia's ears there came a sound like someone dropping an extremely large sack of potatoes.

In the struggle to join Ryker in the car, Thalia's hat had come askew, blocking her vision entirely. She clawed it aside and looked.

On the pavement beside the car lay the manticore. This one had been in a different stage of transformation. Its body was shaped like a lion, if lions had claws like razors front and back. It had the head and shoulders of a man, so hairy it was almost furred. It smelled bad in exactly the same way her first dead manticore had.

Tycho Aristides, the Skinner of Manhattan and its surrounding boroughs, stood over the dead manticore and put fresh cartridges in his shotgun with finicking care.

Thalia felt dizzy with relief. This time there had been no accompanying compulsion to Trade. Maybe she was actually making progress in controlling her Trades. "Where were you?"

"Right where I was meant to be, watching for you to come out." Aristides slung the shotgun over his shoulder and rolled the carcass on its side to go after the gallbladder.

"Thank you." Thalia took her place in the backseat, glad to sit quietly while her knees felt so watery. Belatedly, she remembered the pistol in her reticule. On the whole, she was glad she'd left it there. They'd caused enough stir without her shooting holes in something. Or someone. As things stood, Aristides had all the fuss well in hand. "Thanks for the help."

"You have to admit." Aristides looked up from his gory work with a crooked smile. "I get results."

Once Aristides had consigned the manticore to the authorities and returned to his seat in the motorcar, Ryker finally started the engine and turned for home. Thalia leaned forward to speak in his ear. "I have another errand. This one is downtown."

After emitting a wordless hoot of exasperation, Ryker set their course southward. "Of course you have. Where to, madame?"

Thalia gave him the Sixth Avenue address of the Ostrova Magic Company, and as she'd expected, Ryker recognized it without her adding the name of the business. "What are you planning to do?"

"Take me there and find out," Thalia countered.

"Where are we going?" Aristides demanded. "I still need to go collect my reward, you know."

"Nutall gave me an idea. I have some questions to ask at the Ostrova Magic Company."

"That makes sense." Aristides settled down in the front passenger seat. He looked entirely relaxed, but Thalia noticed he kept a sharp eye on their surroundings as Ryker exploited every gap in the traffic.

"You aren't going to order anything for your stage act, are you?" Ryker inquired.

"If I have to, I will."

"Try to restrain yourself. Nell is already sorry to miss this little promenade. If she misses a chance to meet and do business with Madame Ostrova as well, she will certainly feel hurt that we left her out."

"You never took her there?" Thalia answered her own question. "Of course you didn't." Given that Ryker had done his level best to discourage his sister's interest in the stage, he would never risk letting her make Madame Ostrova's acquaintance.

Thalia could understand his reasoning. Nell would adore Madame Ostrova. It was likely that Madame Ostrova would take to

Nell in return. Ryker was probably wise to postpone introducing them as long as possible.

The trip downtown took hardly any time. Ryker threaded his motorcar through the traffic skillfully. He ignored the shouted remarks his driving style provoked. For the first time, Thalia could see similarities between Ryker's behavior and his sister's. She supposed family resemblances took many forms.

When they drew up outside the Ostrova Magic Company, Ryker asked Aristides, "Are you coming in?"

"I'll stay here and keep an eye on your car." Aristides regarded Thalia with caution. "Unless you think there's a chance of a manticore hiding inside?"

"If there is," said Thalia, "Madame Ostrova will be designing a trick around it."

Ryker followed Thalia through the door.

Within, the bell chimed merrily, but no one came to greet them at the counter. Thalia stood waiting, and Ryker made himself comfortable in one of the wing chairs. The place smelled the same as always, but Thalia couldn't remember it ever being so quiet. She lifted her voice. "Hello? Anyone there?"

The silence stretched out long enough that Thalia called again. "Hello?"

Without a rustle or a footfall, Madame Ostrova came through the bead curtain, eyes narrowed. "You."

"Yes, me," Thalia agreed. "May I have a moment of your time?"

As Madame Ostrova scowled at her, Thalia added smoothly, "Or, if you are busy, may I make an appointment to speak with you at your convenience? Only I've just talked with Nutall. I'm helping to prove his innocence."

"Oh, really?" Madame Ostrova looked far from convinced. "How do you mean to do that? How can you do anything for anyone when you are a Trader now?"

Thalia was taken aback. "That doesn't change anything, me being a Trader."

"Ha," said Madame Ostrova, but she wasn't laughing. She wasn't even smiling.

"Well, it does make it difficult to leave the house," Thalia admitted. "I'm working on it."

"You are not a Solitaire but a Trader, Nutall is not a Solitaire but Sylvestri, and your boyfriend there is another Trader, so who knows what is true?" Madame Ostrova shook her head in disgust. "What do you want with performing stage magic, either you or Nutall, when all the time you *are* magic? Stage magicians should be plain Solitaire and nothing else."

"Nutall never let on that he was Sylvestri, on stage or off," Thalia said. "Even I didn't know."

"Very likely." Madame Ostrova gave a disapproving sniff.

"I didn't know I was a Trader. I've certainly never used Trading in the act." Although without Trading, that night in Philadelphia would have ended her career abruptly, Thalia realized. That might count as cheating, only she hadn't done it on purpose. She stated firmly, "I promise I never will."

"You swear?" Madame Ostrova looked down her nose at Thalia, a feat considering that Thalia was taller than she was.

"I swear." Thalia meant it and she let all her honesty show. "Nutall is innocent. Please help me prove it."

Madame Ostrova's severity relaxed, but only slightly. "I liked

Nutall. Whether he is Sylvestri or Solitaire, he's no murderer. I don't know what I can do to help you, but I won't hinder you."

"May we speak privately?"

After a moment of consideration, Madame Ostrova inclined her head in silent consent.

Thalia turned to Ryker. "Wait here. Madame Ostrova and I have something to discuss."

Ryker, clearly amused, waved her off. "Don't leave without me, that's all I ask."

Thalia, relieved, smiled back at him. "Don't you leave without me, either."

"No chance of that."

Madame Ostrova let Thalia go through the bead curtain first. Once in the little office, Thalia looked around carefully before closing the door. "No one can overhear us, can they?"

Madame Ostrova took her chair. "Not unless I tell them. What's going on in your head, Trader girl?"

Thalia said, "Nutall hasn't told anyone but me, nor will he, but when he was leaving the theater the night before Von Faber died, he saw Anton arriving."

"My boy Anton?" Madame Ostrova's eyebrows shot up. "He is mistaken."

"You know he isn't. And even though Nutall didn't tell the police Anton was there, someone else must have. I saw the list the police have. Anton's name is on it."

"So why haven't the police arrested Anton?" Madame Ostrova asked. "Why do they wait to blacken our name?"

"You and I both know Anton would never knowingly be involved in anything like what happened to Von Faber. But if you didn't send him there on business, why was he there?"

Her expression thunderous with disapproval, Madame Ostrova shook her head. "Anton thinks he's a grown man. He's wrong, but still I let him do as he likes. I thought it less trouble. I was wrong. But maybe the police will leave Anton alone because they know—or think—Nutall killed Von Faber."

Thalia said, "Maybe. But even if the police haven't yet questioned him, that doesn't mean they won't do it soon. I do think Anton may know something no one else does. May I talk to him?"

Madame Ostrova eyed Thalia warily. "If I say no, what will you do then?"

"Nothing." Thalia answered hurriedly, hoping somehow to win back Madame Ostrova's former approval. "I won't tell anyone anything. Only I'll have to poke around while I'm clearing Nutall's name, and who knows what I might stumble into that way?"

Madame Ostrova shook her head. "I will talk to him, not you. To me alone, he will tell the truth. Our name must not be dishonored by lies. If Anton is involved in this wickedness, he is not an Ostrova anymore."

Thalia covered her mouth with her hand. "Don't say that. Anton is always an Ostrova."

"You don't know anything about our family, Trader girl."

"Don't I? When we were children, I played with Anton and the others. I think I know everything that matters about the Ostrova family."

Madame Ostrova drew a deep breath and let it out in a sigh. "Very well. What do you want me to ask him? I have questions of my own, mind. But I will share what I can with you."

"If he wasn't there on your behalf, why did Anton go to the theater? Nutall said he was on the point of leaving as Anton arrived. Who did Anton talk to? Did Anton see anything that seems suspicious now?"

Madame Ostrova held up her hand to stop Thalia. "Enough. Go home. I will send for you when I'm ready to tell you what Anton has done."

"Can't I just sit here and listen, quiet as a mouse, unless there's something I need to ask him?"

Madame Ostrova shook her head. "A mouse you never were. I talk to him alone."

"I'll wait."

"Not here."

"I can't just come and go as I please now. I'll wait at the professional entrance, then. With Mr. Ryker," Thalia conceded. "But I'm not leaving until I know what you find out from Anton."

"Oh, very well." Madame Ostrova rose and escorted Thalia back to the front room. "Sit. I'll tell you when I'm finished."

Thalia took the chair beside Ryker and listened so hard her ears rang, but she heard nothing once Madame Ostrova had retreated through the bead curtain. Not the slightest footfall told which way she had gone.

Ryker looked hopeful. "Are we done here?"

"Not yet. Now we wait."

No one else came to the professional entrance while Thalia sat there with Ryker. There was nothing to read. Thalia had no desire to make small talk with Ryker. None of the things Thalia wondered about Ryker, she suspected, would fit into anything but the largest possible talk. She wasn't yet ready to put that to the test.

Ryker, luckily, had no apparent wish to chat either. They sat in silence for half an hour. Thalia found it restful.

At last, the bead curtain rattled. "Come," commanded Madame Ostrova. Behind her, Anton Ostrova stood chastened, eyes reddened. "Not you," she told Ryker, who sank back obediently in his chair.

Thalia joined Madame and Anton Ostrova in the office. Before she could say anything, Anton Ostrova had seized both her hands in his. Even through the leather of her gloves, Thalia could feel how cold his hands were.

"I am so sorry, Miss Cutler, so ashamed of what I've done. Please don't let my crime damage my family's honor. If you can't forgive me, try to forgive my family."

"What crime?" Taken aback, Thalia glanced quickly from Anton to Madame Ostrova and back again. "What have you done?" If Madame Ostrova had discovered her son was the true culprit in Von Faber's murder, surely this was not how she would deal with it?

"I stole a rifle from the tricks you and your family put in storage here. Your father trusted us and I have betrayed that trust."

Thalia stared at Anton. "That's where it went? You took it? Not Von Faber?"

Anton looked distraught.

"Go on," Madame Ostrova prompted.

"I gave it to a girl." Anton suppressed a sob. "I've known the rifles were there ever since Mother had me help with inventory. She asked me to help her get one, and I did."

"Who asked you?" Thalia demanded, although she had a very good idea indeed whom Anton meant. "Which of your girls exactly did you give it to?"

"She's not my girl. I'm not that lucky." Anton squared his shoulders and straightened as if ready for the firing squad. "Nora Uberti. She's a Solitaire girl from downtown. Her parents are back in Italy. She has to support herself. I love her. So I stole your rifle."

"When?" Thalia dearly wanted to shake Anton, but she didn't permit herself to move. "Why? What did she tell you she wanted it for?"

"Miss Nora is a stage magician too," Anton said. "She wants her own act. Von Faber promised her he would help but he lied, of course. Nora needed her own rifle to do the Bullet Catch for her audition."

Thalia frowned. If the syndicate enforced a noncompete clause against Thalia, or any other stage magician in the five boroughs, there was no chance they would let Nora Uberti perform. Clearly Anton hadn't cared about a noncompete clause. He might not even know it existed. "When did she get the rifle?"

"I gave it to her a month ago," Anton said. "It was for her birthday."

"We will make this right," Madame Ostrova stated. "No matter what it takes. You tell me, Trader girl. How do we make this right?"

"Do the police know about this?" Thalia asked. Anton shook his head. "Have you told anyone any of this?"

"The police haven't asked me anything." Anton's eyes filled with tears. "I don't want to talk to them."

Thalia suspected that the only reason the police hadn't come after Anton was because they had fixed on Nutall as the murderer. "You went backstage at the Imperial the night before Von Faber's last performance. Tell me about it."

"Yes." Anton glanced at Madame Ostrova, who nodded encouragement. "I was there. It was after the performance. Nora was cleaning the gear and putting it in order for the next show. I helped her. No one else ever did."

Thalia kept her voice casual. "Who else was there?"

"Von Faber, of course. He was in his dressing room with fat old Mrs. Von Faber. I heard them arguing. Mr. Nutall was there when I arrived, but he was on his way out the door."

"What were the Von Fabers arguing about?"

Anton shrugged. "Mrs. Von Faber had finally found out about Miss Nora being married to Von Faber. She was mad. Then Mr.

Cadwallader arrived, so Von Faber told his wife to go back to their hotel. He said he had to talk to Mr. Cadwallader. To remind him who was the boss, he said."

"What did Von Faber know about Mr. Cadwallader?"

Anton shrugged again. "If I knew, maybe I could persuade Mr. Cadwallader to offer Miss Nora a contract of her own."

"So do you think Von Faber was blackmailing Mr. Cadwallader?" Thalia asked.

Anton said, "Miss Nora believed he was. I don't know anything firsthand. But from what I heard, it sounded that way."

"What made Nora think Von Faber would let her use the Bullet Catch if no one else was allowed to?"

Anton said, "Nora told me Von Faber had promised her she could have her own act."

Had Von Faber really told her such a thing? It was possible the girl was making it up, but the possibility that Von Faber had lied to her was well in character. Thalia wondered how much more provocation he had given Nora Uberti to kill him. "Go on. What happened then?"

"Von Faber kissed Mrs. Von Faber until she calmed down and did what he said. He was good at the love talk. Then his wife did as she was told. Mr. Cadwallader came into Von Faber's dressing room and shut the door. I couldn't hear them after that."

"What then?" Thalia prompted.

"Then Nora was angry."

"Why? What happened to set her off?" asked Thalia.

"I don't know. Maybe it was the love talk. It wasn't very nice to hear. I have never seen Nora so upset. We argued, because I wanted to walk her home, and she didn't want me with her. Finally she made me leave."

"What did she do then?"

"I don't know." Anton wouldn't meet Thalia's eyes.

"Come on."

"She called me names and made me leave. I don't know what she did after that. I don't care. She made me so angry. I walked all the way home from the theater."

Thalia glanced in surprise at Madame Ostrova, who was giving Anton another of her sternest looks. "That was not safe at such an hour."

"I didn't care." Anton's eyes were red. "I almost hoped for trouble. I wanted to punch somebody."

"What then?" asked Thalia.

"Then nothing." Anton shook his head as if to clear it. "Then, the very next performance, Von Faber dies. I try to talk to Nora, to see if there's anything I can do for her, but she won't talk to me. She won't talk to anybody. She never said it, but I heard Von Faber told her she would get the props if anything happened to him."

Madame Ostrova laughed bitterly. "The props won't go to Miss Uberti. I'll take them in lieu of the money he owed us for his props and storage. He never paid us all he owed for the trick he commissioned, either."

Anton shook his head. "Turns out that all the tricks, everything goes to old Mrs. Von Faber. She's going to sell them. I asked her if she'd let us handle the auction. She says she will think it over."

"And what else?" Thalia prompted. "Does anything else you saw strike you as important or odd in light of Von Faber's death?"

"I told you what else I saw. Nothing." Anton turned to Madame Ostrova. "Can I go now?"

"That was smart to ask Mrs. Von Faber about auctioning the props here." Madame Ostrova patted his shoulder. "You're a good boy, Anton. You can go."

When Thalia asked Madame Ostrova to show her the trick Von Faber had commissioned, she led Thalia to the workroom, where the trick, all but complete, rested comfortably upon a bed of newspapers.

The trick was a mirror-lined cabinet with doors front and back. Thalia looked at herself in the mirrors and imagined using the trick in her act. The grand finale began to take form in her mind, something out of *Through the Looking Glass*. She could send a stage assistant through the looking glass and bring them back again. She could rename herself the looking glass magician. No. Too long. The glass magician? Thalia put her wild ideas aside and thought hard about what it would take to get Nora Uberti to clear Nutall's name. "I'd like to buy this trick from you."

"For now, it is part of the Von Faber estate. You have to talk to the executor. If Anton is right, it will be Mrs. Von Faber. I think she will ask top dollar for it." Madame Ostrova smiled serenely. "We will certainly make her pay us top dollar first."

"Then may I rent it?" Thalia held Madame Ostrova's gaze. "It would help me prove Nutall's innocence—and Anton's."

Madame Ostrova's eyes narrowed. "Under such circumstances, I think yes. A short-term rental could be arranged."

"I would like one modification made to the trick. There needs to be a concealed trapdoor in the base."

Madame Ostrova gave a little shrug. "It could be arranged. Given time. And money."

"May I also rent your theater?" Thalia asked. "Only for a few hours once everything is ready. I have in mind a command performance."

"Rent the Ostrova Palace of Mystery?" Madame Ostrova gave

Thalia an approving look, the first since she had received Thalia as a known Trader. It was a pleasant change. "When do you want it?"

"The sooner the better. As soon as the box has been modified. I also need to work out a guest list. Would a matinee work? The day after tomorrow."

"I will reserve it for you." Madame Ostrova asked, "Tell me, what else do you have in mind?"

Thalia said, "Anton is familiar with the rifle Von Faber used. I want one of mine made to look as much like the murder weapon as possible. I plan to tell the audience it is the very weapon that killed Von Faber. I will use it to seek his murderer out."

"Very well. What else will you need?"

"Your help, and Anton's, and maybe Freddie's as well. I'll let you know the details as soon as I figure them out."

Madame Ostrova produced a small brown notebook and a tiny pencil. "What else?"

"I want two leaden musket balls, each engraved with the word 'Murderer.'"

Madame Ostrova didn't even glance up from the list she was making in her little notebook. "What else?"

"A gong, something suitable for the Bullet Catch," said Thalia.

Anton knocked at the workroom door politely. "Your Trader wants to know how much longer you are going to be here," he told Thalia. "He says—"

From behind Anton, Ryker himself called, "I said, it's not that I'm impatient, but the Skinner is."

"I'm coming," Thalia told Ryker. To Madame Ostrova, she added, "Make that two gongs."

Chapter Fifteen

What set the Ostrova Magic Company's building apart from the buildings beside it along Sixth Avenue was not to be seen from the outside. It had the same kind of red brick facade as the buildings on either side, stood at much the same height, and had windows like any other building of its kind, only cleaner.

If one crossed the neatly swept threshold of the main entrance, one entered the shop that sold Ostrova-made magic tricks and other gaudy items intended to appeal to the novice magician. The privileged could enter through the professional entrance, as Thalia had done, and admire the reception area or do serious business in Madame Ostrova's office.

The top floor of the Ostrova Magic Company's building held living quarters for Madame Ostrova and her extended family.

These were entirely off-limits to outsiders. Visitors who came on business were generally kept to the storage area in the cellar, the construction workshop on the ground level, or its adjacent space, the Ostrova Magic Company's Palace of Mystery.

This grand name belonged to a scaled-down version of a true theatrical stage, complete with a stage curtain of heavy red plush velvet trimmed in gold braid, twenty-four seats for the audience, proper flies above the stage for simple backdrops, and a small but effective set of ultramodern electrical stage lights.

As a show business venue, the Palace of Mystery was tiny. As a space in which to perform stage magic, it was perfection. Its chief drawback was a lack of room for an orchestra, but the acoustics of the place were so good, the gramophone provided by the management could fill the tiny theater with music.

The little theater allowed select clients to try out the tricks and stage props they had commissioned from the Ostrova Magic Company. Testing the new equipment before a discerning audience led to satisfied customers.

The centerpiece that dominated the stage the day Thalia had booked the Palace of Mystery for her matinee performance was the mirror box originally commissioned by Von Faber. Mrs. Von Faber had refused to pay the outstanding balance due for the mirror box out of the money left in her husband's estate, so Thalia had paid Madame Ostrova for it with the money she'd earned tutoring Nell. It was her trick now.

Like the building that held the Palace of Mystery, the exterior of the mirror box was deceptively simple in appearance. It was lacquered shiny black, with a set of bright brass hinges on the front double doors as its only ornament. Its interior was a compartment completely lined with mirrors, dazzling in the focused brilliance of the stage lighting. The mirrors distracted the eye from the precise dimensions of the box interior. Behind the mirrors an inner compartment could conceal a stage assistant.

Thalia had made one modification to Von Faber's original commission. She had insisted that a trapdoor be added to the base, and the whole box be positioned so it could rest over the stage trapdoor. Ordinarily a mirror box would be entirely self-contained— but Thalia had plans for that trapdoor.

Once every seat in the audience was occupied, Thalia took her place onstage. The general lights in the theater went out, leaving only the glow of the footlights and the glare of the spotlights that blazed down on Thalia and the mirror box. The audience stopped talking and stared at her.

Under the circumstances, Nutall couldn't introduce her, so Thalia did her best to capture his mixture of perfect diction and friendly impudence as she introduced herself. "Ladies and gentlemen, Sylvestri and Solitaires, Traders and Manticores, welcome to the Ostrova Magic Company's Palace of Mystery. I am Miss Thalia Cutler."

She paused for applause, but there wasn't any. In ordinary circumstances, standing in front of a stoically silent crowd would be an uncomfortable sensation, but Thalia welcomed a pause in the proceedings, no matter how awkward. It had been much too long since she had performed on a stage. The blaze of stage lighting in her eyes and the rising warmth of it on her skin felt wonderful. It felt like coming home.

Thalia went on. "This afternoon you are privileged to witness a command performance. Today you will see how all roads lead to the truth. Today the truth will be revealed. I refer, of course, to the true identity of the murderer of Johan Von Faber."

There. The audience had responded to that, a wordless rustle of anticipation. Time seemed to slow down as Thalia stared out at them. The audience stared back at her, although Thalia was careful not to meet anyone's eyes for more than an instant. Ryker was in the best seat, with Madame Ostrova impassive at his left hand and Tycho Aristides, as heavily armed as ever, on his right. In the back two rows Inspector Ottokar, Officer Kelly, and five policemen, all of whom glared suspiciously at Thalia, sat with half a dozen journalists Madame Ostrova had invited at Thalia's insistence. The seats closest to the stage were filled with the Ryker family's legal representatives, Mr. Tewksbury and Mrs. Hopkins; slender Miss Nora Uberti, dressed in black; and the original Mrs. Von Faber, who looked like a plump grandmother wearing her granddaughter's Dresden shepherdess costume. Right where she'd expected to find them, in the seats closest to the exit door, David Nutall sat with Mrs. Dorcas Viridian on one side and Ambassador Peter Viridian on the other. In the next row back, Mrs. Morris was sitting right behind Nutall, her cheeks bright pink with excitement.

As Nutall had taught her long ago, Thalia pitched her voice for the benefit of the last row of seats. "There is more in this world, my friends, than we can understand. Hamlet said, 'There are more things in heaven and earth, Horatio, than are dreamt of in your philosophy.' There are more things afoot at this moment than any poet ever told. If you value the truth, help me. Lend me your thoughts, lend me your vibrations. Together we will solve this mystery."

Thalia put her hands on the shiny black mirror box, turning it this way and that for the benefit of the audience. When her ritual concluded, she opened the double doors on the front of the box and let the stage lights show the mirrored lining. Brightness drew every eye. Once she had displayed the open box, she ceremoniously withdrew the props she'd placed inside: a mop, a broom, a bucket, a muzzle-loading rifle, and the sword she called Excalibur. All the while, Thalia reeled off a yard or two of standard stage patter about revealing the hidden truth. She hadn't used any of her recent wild ideas in this routine. Sending someone through the looking glass wouldn't suit Thalia's purpose today.

As she worked, Anton, Thalia's onstage assistant for the performance, accepted these trophies as she handed them out. He carefully arranged them in a semicircle around the mirror box.

"If we put away the distractions of the world, the truth becomes more clear." Thalia slowly spun the box, noiseless on the ball bearings set into the base, opened the less conspicuous double doors on the back panel, and gestured for Anton to enter the box and walk through it. Obediently, Anton demonstrated the mirror box's utter lack of mystery.

Once it was empty, Thalia slowly spun the box again, this time with both sets of double doors open. Now it appeared to be nothing but an unusually shiny armoire, mirrored within. Anton closed the back doors as Thalia closed the doors at the front.

Thalia waved Anton away for the moment and turned her attention to the audience. "Ladies and gentlemen, I require a volunteer from the audience." Thalia dropped her words into the silence as she locked her gaze to Nutall's and let it burn there.

Nutall was dressed with his usual attention to detail, dapper in a dark suit with a diamond stickpin in his dark blue silk cravat. Thalia thought he looked tired.

Mrs. Viridian put her hand on Nutall's arm and tried to keep him from rising from his seat. Thalia could have told her that was futile, but Mrs. Viridian found it out for herself.

Nutall was prompt to respond to his cue. Thalia felt her eyes fill with tears as she watched him approach. She blinked her vision clear.

It seemed to take a great effort for Nutall to clamber across the Ostrovas' miniature footlights, and take his place beside Thalia on the stage. "I volunteer," he said softly, but the acoustics of the tiny theater took his murmur to every corner of the room.

"You can't. You can't volunteer." Mrs. Viridian's voice did not carry as well from the audience as Nutall's had from the stage, but she wasn't murmuring. "You shouldn't even be here."

"You must," Thalia announced. "We cannot find the truth without you, David Nutall." To Mrs. Viridian, Thalia said, "I will return him unscathed."

That was an outright thumping lie, but Thalia did not hesitate to tell it. She used every advantage her position onstage gave her to influence Mrs. Viridian, who subsided with obvious reluctance. Her husband patted her hand consolingly.

"Thank you," Thalia whispered to Nutall, and the back row probably heard that too, so she said nothing more. Instead, she gestured to the mirror box and offered Nutall her arm to help him inside. As she did, she gazed at the floor of the mirrored compartment, willing Nutall to take her hint. Long before Thalia had opened the doors and spun the mirror box to demonstrate its emptiness, she and Anton had taken pains to position the box exactly over an unobtrusive trapdoor built into the stage itself.

"Thank you, my dear." Nutall was as well versed in concealed trapdoors as he was in the need for discretion. The warmth in his voice and the emphasis he put on the word "thank" told Thalia he'd caught her meaning. "I can manage."

With Nutall in the mirror box, Thalia shut all the doors.

The gramophone was ready. At Thalia's signal, Freddie Ostrova dropped the needle, and a Viennese waltz began to play.

Thalia used her movements, the tilt of her head, the sweep of her arms, to tell the audience what was happening. There was the mirror box; there was Nutall. Now Nutall had gone into the mirror box. Now the double doors were shut.

There really should have been a drumroll, but without an orchestra, all Thalia could do was time her move for the moment the scratchy music stopped. "Hey, presto!"

Thalia spread her arms wide to signal her reveal. As Anton opened the doors at the back, she opened those on the front of the box. Together they spun the box slowly for the benefit of every pair of eyes in the audience. The mirrored compartment was empty.

Mrs. Viridian leaned forward, glaring. "Where is he? Where did he go?"

Thalia read her intention in the stiff lines of her body. She held up her hand to gesture *stop*. "Please remain in your seat, or this performance ends now."

"What an excellent suggestion," Mrs. Viridian snarled. "Police! I demand you arrest this woman."

From the row behind, Mrs. Morris stretched forward to put her hand on Mrs. Viridian's shoulder, keeping her in her seat. "Oh, do hush up. I've never seen one of Miss Cutler's stage performances before, and she was just beginning. Go on, dear."

Bristling but silent, Mrs. Viridian settled down.

Thalia couldn't help smiling gratefully at her landlady as she resumed her patter. "You have lent me your thoughts. You have lent me your vibrations. We work together here to reveal the truth."

Thalia rapped twice on the rear door, spun the box back into its original position, and opened the front door. "Behold. I give you Innocence itself."

There stood Nell Ryker, elegant in a rose-pink silk ball gown made in the latest narrow French fashion. Thalia handed her down from the box, and Nell, jubilant, curtsied in response to a scattered round of applause from the audience. Thalia hadn't arranged for any paid enthusiasm, so the response delighted her. Scattered the applause might be, but it was genuine.

Squarely in the spotlight, Nell waved to her brother. "Hello, it's me!"

"Where is David Muir?" Mrs. Viridian shook off Mrs. Morris and sprang to her feet. "Where has he gone?"

At the same time, Nathaniel Ryker vaulted onto the stage. He caught his sister by one slender opera-gloved wrist. "What do you think you are doing here?"

Thalia picked up the gleaming sword she had used in the Siege Perilous trick, struck a noble pose, and watched the distraction play out from her position just outside the range of the brightest spotlight. She was still well lit, but, for the moment, not at the center of the audience's attention.

"Don't worry." Nell pulled away from her brother's grip. "Everything is fine."

"It is not fine," Ryker snarled. "What if a manticore decides to pay a call? What do you do then, you silly girl?"

"Haven't you noticed?" Nell glared at him and pointed at Aristides. "The Skinner of New York is right there in the seat next to yours. If a manticore somehow blunders in here, it will soon regret it. Go sit down. We're not finished."

"*You*," Mrs. Viridian said to the police officers in the audience. "Do your jobs. Get David—I mean Nutall—back."

Inspector Ottokar, Officer Kelly, and the other police officers, who had been about to take the stage, stopped where they were. If they continued, they would seem to be taking orders from a Sylvestri—and a Sylvestri woman at that. They didn't want to do that.

Thalia said imperiously, "Quiet, all of you. We are in the presence of the mystical. I cannot reveal the truth until you stop your squabbling."

Somehow, despite the racket of indignant denials that followed, Thalia distinctly heard Mrs. Morris say, "That's right. You tell them."

"Poppycock!" Clearly Mrs. Viridian was not impressed with Thalia's stage patter.

Thalia spoke to the audience at large but she focused her gaze entirely on Mrs. Viridian. "Kindly return to your seats, ladies and gentlemen, and the demonstration will continue." In truth, she didn't blame Mrs. Viridian for her reaction. She was spouting poppycock. But the longer her stage act lasted, the more time Nutall had to make good his getaway.

Mrs. Viridian approached the stage and halted only when Thalia raised the sword. "You're a fraud."

"You're mistaken. What I am, madame, is a stage magician. Once you cease your interference, I will prove it." Thalia made a sweeping gesture with the sword and held her Lady of the Lake pose until everyone, even the visibly fuming Mrs. Viridian, had returned to their seats.

Thalia caught Nell's eye and nodded toward the now-silent gramophone. As Freddie wound it up, Nell sprang to drop the needle on the wax cylinder. The music resumed in the wrong spot, but Thalia didn't let that worry her.

First Thalia swung her sword high, sweeping the air above the mirror box. "No wires, as you see."

Then Thalia set her sword down next to the muzzle-loading rifle, and moved around the mirror box, closing the doors front and back. Mrs. Viridian was still making disagreement noises, but they were small sounds and Thalia drowned them out without a qualm.

This time when Thalia spoke, she used her voice to command, letting the perfect acoustics of the place aid her as she spun out the patter.

"You all know who I am. I have the power to reveal the truth about Von Faber's death."

Thalia couldn't resist a pause to let those words sink in, but went on before she gave her audience a chance to think. "I can call Justice herself to witness. The police have accused David Nutall of this crime. Mr. Nutall is innocent. Now I shall prove it."

Thalia picked up the muzzle-loading rifle. The audience didn't move. They didn't make a sound. Yet Thalia felt their interest and anticipation rising. She reveled in it. "Some of you were there the night Von Faber died. I was. I can tell you exactly what happened."

Thalia showed them the rifle. "Here we have the very rifle that took Von Faber's life." This was a lie. The true murder weapon had been safely filed away in some police evidence locker since the murder investigation had begun. "It has two firing chambers, not one."

Thalia knew that the rifle she held, the one she'd used in her own Bullet Catch, was now so similar in appearance to the murder weapon that even an expert would be hard-pressed to tell them apart. "Someone meddled with this firearm so that a spark from the flint ignited the gunpowder in the wrong firing chamber."

Thalia could sense her power over the audience faltering.

Too much mechanical talk about things like firing chambers. She pressed on. "Gunpowder does not know who is using it or why. Gunpowder does one thing, and one thing only. Gunpowder explodes." Thalia held the rifle to her shoulder, taking care to aim it up into the shadows above the miniature stage. The audience's attention sharpened again, braced for a gunshot.

Thalia went on. "The trick went wrong that night. Someone tampered with this weapon. Someone used a jeweler's file to widen the passage between the trick firing chamber and the true one. The finest stage magician in the world couldn't catch that bullet. Mr. Von Faber had no chance."

Thalia lowered the rifle, aiming it down toward the stage. "I'll tell you the truth. I'll tell you who tampered with this weapon. I'll tell you who planned it all."

In the rapt silence that followed her words, Thalia surveyed the audience staring back at her. Mrs. Viridian's face was pinched, eyes narrow, waiting for her next chance to interrupt. Immediately behind her, Mrs. Morris was wide-eyed and smiling. Her evident confidence in Thalia's ability to save the day made Thalia's throat feel tight.

Nell stood next to Freddie at the gramophone, her brother beside her. Nell was radiant. Ryker was scowling. Both were focused on Thalia. Freddie was intent on winding up the gramophone next time the music faded.

Aristides, although still in his seat and looking ostentatiously relaxed, was sharp-eyed, his attention on the room at large, not just on the stage. Madame Ostrova, on the other side of Ryker's empty seat, watched with one eyebrow raised. The newspaper reporters appeared completely unimpressed. Only one had a notebook out. Thalia noticed another who was peeling a hard-boiled egg.

Nora Uberti, who had once thought herself to be the first and only Mrs. Von Faber, sat quietly in the front row, her expression pleasant. Her hands were folded in her lap. Her head was tilted to show she was giving Thalia all her polite attention. Thalia met her mild eyes and held them, counting the silent seconds until Nora dropped her gaze. Six. That, under the circumstances, impressed Thalia. A cool customer, Nora.

Thalia spun the moment out as long as her audience returned her scrutiny with interest, then resumed her patter. "May I have a volunteer from the audience?"

Mrs. Viridian climbed on the stage before anyone else could move. "I insist you choose me."

The Bullet Catch proceeded. Thalia showed Mrs. Viridian the special leaden ball. Then, holding it in the hollow of her hand, Thalia pretended to whisper to the bit of lead. Thalia palmed that musket ball and only pretended to put it into the rifle. "I have asked the powers of mystery for their aid. They will show us the truth."

Using every trick of timing she knew to keep her audience focused on her, Thalia aimed her rifle at a bronze gong hung at the far side of the tiny stage. A second gong, hung at the back of the theater, was struck as soon as the gun fired. Anton Ostrova timed the strike perfectly. The reverberation filled the room and even drew a note from the untouched gong onstage.

"Where is the bullet?" Thalia went through her pantomime with relish. "Where has it gone?"

Once it had been thoroughly established that no musket ball had struck the gong she had aimed at, Thalia intoned, "Oh, mystic powers, show us the truth. Murder will out. Speak the truth!"

In pantomime as elaborate as she dared, Thalia pretended to

hear the musket ball whispering to her. The spotlights followed her as she followed the inaudible voice of the bullet, letting it call her down from the stage and into the audience. She followed it to Nora's spot in the theater audience. "I hear it. Don't you hear it? Powers of mystery, show us a sign!"

"This is ridiculous," Nora said, arms folded tight, every line of her body full of scorn.

"Mystic powers don't lie," Thalia countered. "Turn out your reticule."

"Certainly not!" Nora glared at Thalia.

"Anything to stop this nonsense." Mrs. Viridian seized Nora's reticule and upended it into Nora's lap. Among the items that fell out were Nora's comb and pocket mirror, a packet of pastilles, and a leaden musket ball engraved with the word "Murderer."

"What is this?" Mrs. Viridian took the musket ball between thumb and forefinger. "What on earth? Now it says 'Murderer.'"

The audience shifted and murmured, more stirred by Mrs. Viridian's prosaic tone than they would have been by any dramatic announcement from Thalia, who considered the twenty-dollar gold piece she had given Madame Ostrova to slip that second musket ball into Nora Uberti's reticule money very well spent indeed.

"She's tricked you." Nora sprang up. "It's a child's trick. She palmed that musket ball when she pretended to load the gun. She planted it on me."

"She was nowhere near you," Aristides pointed out dispassionately.

"It was you." Thalia pointed to Nora Uberti with all the dramatic flourish at her disposal, which was considerable. "You are the murderer." This was a vital moment in the performance she had planned. Thalia relished the effect her accusation had on the audience. Whatever Nora Uberti said or did, the audience—for the moment—was in the palm of Thalia's hand. Time to make the most important point clear. "I told you. I was there. I saw you load the rifle that killed Von Faber. You used far too much gunpowder. There was no reason to be safe, to measure it, was there? You knew what was going to happen."

"You're a liar." Nora's manner was a perfect mix of pity and scorn. "Your friend is the real murderer, but you're trying to put the blame on me. That's why you're playing these stupid tricks."

Thalia let her tone soften. "Von Faber was a second-class magician and a first-class creep. Why did you stay with him? Why didn't you just find another line of work?"

"Oh, now you're my mother, giving me advice," Nora sneered. "You know how hard it is to find this kind of work. That's why you're pestering me. You don't want my competition."

Thalia kept right on asking questions. "Why did you use his stage magic act to plan his murder?"

"I didn't plan anything. You're out of your senses." Nora turned in her seat to call to the policemen. "You, you're officers of the law. Protect me from this lunatic."

"You made someone steal the gun for you." Thalia carefully omitted Anton's name. She was grateful for his help in particular and the Ostrova family in general. Anything she could do to protect him from the interest of the police, she would. "You knew how the rifle worked because Von Faber made you take care of his, along with all his other props. You cleaned it. You kept it in working order."

"That's true," said Officer Kelly. "The stagehands told us that."

"Was it hard to sabotage?" Thalia persisted.

"I don't know what you're talking about. Leave me alone," Nora snarled.

Thalia pressed on. "Was it hard to squeeze that trigger?"

"I don't have to listen to this." Nora sprang to her feet. "I'm leaving."

"You aren't going anywhere. You're guilty of murder."

"You're guilty of slander," Nora retorted. "You'd say anything to clear that creepy Sylvestri friend of yours."

Thalia took a position that focused the spotlights and the attention of the audience on her face as she revealed the jeweler's file she'd stowed in her sleeve for just this moment. "This is the tool you used, isn't it? I found it in your makeup box." Thalia did her best to let the light catch the drab object. "Small. Easy to hide. I knew it would be. I knew just what to look for. That made it easy for me to find."

As Thalia had sent Freddie Ostrova out to purchase a new file for this performance, it didn't surprise her when Nora sneered. "No! That's not the—"

What did surprise her was that Nora Uberti blushed as she bit off her retort, a blush so powerful that she looked as if she'd been scalded.

"That's not the one you used?" Thalia inquired mildly, still pretending to admire the little file. "Perhaps you'd better sit down again. I think the policemen want to talk to you."

Indeed, there were policemen on either side of the young woman now. While the unspoken end of her sentence could have been anything at all, even the dullest pair of ears in the audience had caught something false in Nora's tone. Even the least interested pair of eyes in the audience had seen that blush. A response that strong could not fail to suggest shame or guilt.

"She's lying. This is slander." Nora Uberti kept her head. "It's a trick! Let me go. I want a lawyer." Nothing in her words admitted guilt. Everything in her manner did.

Thalia watched the police officers take Nora Uberti into formal custody. She wondered if the young woman would ever confess to her crime. That was up to the policemen and the lawyers now. Thalia was no dime-novel detective. She hadn't accumulated circumstantial evidence proving Nora's guilt. She'd only assembled props and told a lot of lies. It was just a performance.

Every performance requires a grand finale. Thalia took her position in front of the mirror box and clapped her hands. "Ladies and gentlemen, if I may have your attention, please? As the mystic powers have revealed the truth about Von Faber's death, David Nutall has been cleared of all suspicion. Thus I shall restore him to you," lied Thalia.

The policemen began the process of removing their new suspect. As they moved her toward the exit, Nora Uberti raged at them, but tears of anger shook her words into sobs.

Thalia carried on with her act. By now, Nutall would be well away. Thalia had done what she could to clear him of the murder charge. The authorities wouldn't pursue him, although his Sylvestri kin would demand she bring him back. Aiding and abetting Nutall's escape would put Thalia on the spot, no question. But she owed it to Nutall to do all she could to help him, no matter the cost to her.

With a flourish, Thalia opened the front panel of the mirror box: empty. She spun the box on its axis to bring the back panel around and release it. The view through the empty mirror box impressed no one. Thalia stood tall just the same. Time to face the Sylvestri music. "Alas, even I cannot always command the mystic powers. I regret—" Thalia faltered, distracted by a familiar figure ensconced in the last seat on the left in the back row.

Nutall sat there smiling at her as if nothing at all were amiss.

Thalia knew that smile. It combined his pride in her with his satisfaction with himself.

Thalia made a regrettable choking sound, then caught herself. "I regret the powers have not returned him to the box itself, but if you will direct your attention to the back row . . ." Thalia made a grand gesture. The little crowd turned and gasped.

Nutall rose and acknowledged the audience with his most elegant bow, even though no one was applauding. "It was a lovely gesture, my dear. Thank you." Nutall joined her onstage. "But a gentleman never jumps his bail."

They faced the audience shoulder to shoulder as Nutall spoke in his most authoritative tone. "Miss Cutler and I thank you for your kind attention. This brings my final performance to a close."

His announcement brought only puzzled silence. The gramophone had long since run down. Nell, her wrist again held firmly by her brother, was in no position to reach it. Freddie was watching from the wings, ready to close the curtain.

Thalia looked out at their little audience and felt a sense of anticlimax. Was this all her grand gesture had amounted to?

"That's enough of this nonsense," Mrs. Viridian informed the entire room. "David, we're leaving."

Nutall ignored her.

Madame Ostrova clapped her hands sharply, the first of a scattered drift of applause. Thalia winced. That kind of polite clapping was almost worse than none at all. Nevertheless, Thalia made a deep curtsy in reply. Beside her, Nutall made his most formal bow.

The rest of the lights came on, illuminating the audience.

When Nutall came up from his bow, he leaned close and

murmured to Thalia, "I know the Skinner of New York when I see him, but who are those three behind him?"

Thalia followed his glance. The next five seconds passed in what seemed like five minutes. Immediately, she recognized Mr. Tewksbury and Mrs. Hopkins, but the man sitting between the lawyers and the journalists, apparently fascinated by his own shoes, was a complete stranger.

Still, there was something oddly familiar about the heavy line of his jaw and the slump of his shoulders. When the stranger raised his head to stare at her, Thalia knew what it was. Making herself speak took effort. When she managed it, her voice came out half strangled. *"Manticore!"*

Aristides was already on his feet and hauling out his guns, but the manticore, shaking off its human form, knocked him down as it charged the stage.

Nutall stepped in front of Thalia. Inwardly, she cursed herself for leaving her little revolver with her street clothes in her dressing room backstage. Even its small-caliber bullets would be better than nothing, faced with this. Or maybe not. She might shoot one of her friends by accident.

Ryker shouted, "Aristides!" He pushed Nell behind him, ready to protect his sister.

Neither of those actions were of any practical use, Thalia noted, in the distant, calm, and rapidly dwindling part of her mind that wasn't busy insisting that she Trade to her swan form and flee. Thalia noted with gladness that the manticore was ignoring Nell completely. Her friend had been right all along about her ability to control her Trades. The manticore paid no attention to anyone but Thalia.

In one bound, the manticore reached the space between the

front row and the stage, a seat that had been vacated by Inspector Ottokar. Thalia bumped into Nutall, took an involuntary step backward into her props, and trod on the Bullet Catch rifle. She fell, taking Nutall down with her.

Aristides produced a pair of Sibley-McKay pistols and fired at the manticore from close range. Now fully transformed into its monstrous shape, the manticore only paused for a moment to utter a pained roar, then leaped over the footlights, up on the stage.

The swan within her spoke to Thalia. It demanded to rise. The manticore called it forth. As she sprawled on the stage, Thalia caught her own scent, at once sweeter and more rank than her usual self. Thalia pushed the voice within down with all her might. *Shut up. Not now. Shut up.*

"Stay down." Nutall tried to pull Thalia beneath him to shelter her from the chance of a stray bullet.

Thalia shook him off and turned back to her discarded props. She could already tell she was going to have bruises from rolling among them. The muzzle-loader, now discharged, was useless, but beneath it lay her sword, the Lady of the Lake's Excalibur. Thalia seized it and scrambled to her feet.

The blade sang through the air as she swung it up to the ready position. Each moment stretched; she could not help grimacing in despair at how long it took her to come on guard. As Thalia started her attack, the manticore was already there, trampling Nutall underfoot.

Thalia kept her arms moving, letting the energy of her turn augment her swing. She missed her target completely, but the manticore sat back on its haunches in its haste to back out of range. Nutall rolled away stage left, apparently unhurt.

The swan inside Thalia, drawn near the surface by the

manticore, fought for dominance over her. Thalia put every bit of her will into ignoring the swan and every ounce of her strength into recovering her balance. She readied a better swing even as the manticore gathered itself to attack. Thalia's whole focus was the monster before her. Yet within, she welcomed the sense of the swan melding its fury with her fear, lending its strength to her arm.

Distantly, Thalia knew that the Skinner must be lining up his shot, even as her audience and assistants were scrambling for shelter from the fight. Only she and the manticore remained on-stage. Out of all the people in the theater, Thalia alone had what the manticore wanted. If she could resist the urge to Trade, her audience could flee. They were safe while the manticore attacked her. She was safe only as long as her strength lasted.

Thalia was no stranger to anger. Always, she had been best served by using her anger on someone else's behalf. Now, in defense of her audience, Thalia set her anger—and the swan's fury—free. She snarled at the manticore. "No Trading today."

The manticore snarled back at her, coming so near that its breath made Thalia gag.

Thalia and the manticore were joined by a third presence at center stage.

Tycho Aristides, the Skinner of Manhattan, Brooklyn, Queens, Staten Island, and the Bronx, shoved his way into position just behind the manticore's left foreleg. He leaned against the beast. It had to shift its weight to keep its balance. The manticore, still focused completely on Thalia, shouldered Aristides back.

Aristides aimed both his Sibley-McKay pistols at the base of the manticore's skull. He fired. The manticore went down and stayed down. The smell of gunpowder was sharp for a moment, then completely overwhelmed by the stench of the dying monster.

The overpowering urge to Trade left Thalia, snapped like a thread. That, as much as Aristides' professional air of limitless calm, convinced her she was truly safe.

Aristides used his knife to remove the creature's gall bladder and stow it tidily away in one of his collection of jam jars. While he worked, Thalia stayed on guard. Where one man could transform into a manticore, there could be another. It was unlikely, but Thalia earned her living on the border between likely and unlikely.

Time picked up its natural speed again as Thalia caught her breath. The audience regained its composure. Nutall came back to Thalia's side. "Are you quite all right?"

Thalia nodded. For the moment, words were beyond her.

"You could put the sword down now. If you like." Nutall put his hand on Thalia's wrist and guided her as she let the sword point come safely down. "Put it down, there's a good girl."

"It would have worked," Thalia said, meaning the sword. Even now, with the manticore dead at her feet, she felt she would never willingly put that sword away again.

"Probably." Nutall handed her the scabbard.

Thalia heard the doubt implicit in Nutall's dry tone. "No, it would. I can defend myself."

"Without a doubt." This time Nutall's voice held only honest encouragement. "Thank you for your willingness to defend me too."

Thalia frowned at Nutall. "You're really just going to do what they want?"

"I ran away from them for years." Nutall, still warily scanning everyone left in the theater, somehow managed to ignore Mrs. Viridian and her husband completely. "I've had a good innings, but now it is time to make my peace with them."

"All right." Thalia couldn't look at Nutall calmly for a moment longer, so she pretended that it took her entire attention to fit her sword back in its scabbard. She had risked a great deal to set Nutall free in the world. That he did not wish to be free had never crossed her mind. She had given him an expensive gift only to discover that he didn't want it.

"Are you? For someone who has just been attacked by a manticore, you're distressingly quiet," Nutall said. "This is a reversal of policy. I expected you to shout at me a bit."

Thalia regarded him in silence. Nutall knew Thalia better than anyone living. But Thalia had never really known Nutall at all, had she?

"You'll do very well as a solo act," Nutall assured her. "I was holding you back, really."

Thalia knew teasing when she heard it, but she was in no mood to tease back. "You weren't. Who will introduce my act while you're with your charming family?"

Mrs. Viridian approached, frowning. Nutall waved her away, but she ignored him.

"You will speak for yourself," Nutall told Thalia, "just as you did today."

"Enough talking." Mrs. Viridian put her hand on Nutall's shoulder and pulled him away. Together they left the theater, with His Excellency Mr. Viridian trailing behind.

Thalia didn't protest. She watched them go.

At her elbow, Nell spoke softly. "Your friend didn't look at all happy, did he?"

Thalia startled slightly. "No."

"Nor do you," said Nell. "But I have good news for us both. The patrons of the Board of Trade have come. They must have made up their minds about our ordeals at last. Come. Meet them."

To Thalia's surprise, there were now three women in the theater who had not attended her performance. They stood just inside the Palace of Mystery's main door, surveying the scene before them with eyebrows raised. The remaining members of the audience kept a respectful distance from them.

All three women were elegantly dressed. All three were in late middle age, rather old for Traders. None of them seemed impressed by Thalia or the little theater. The tallest of the three looked as if she smelled something bad. The other two were perfectly impassive.

Since a dead manticore was sprawled across the stage, the theater actually did smell terrible, but Thalia suspected that had nothing to do with the tall woman's expression.

"I'll introduce you, shall I?" Nell was ablaze with excitement.

"Right. Good. Perfect," lied Thalia. She put down her sword and followed her friend.

Chapter Sixteen

Nell curtsied as she greeted the newcomers. "Allow me to present Miss Thalia Cutler, stage magician. Miss Cutler, please make the acquaintance of the current patrons of the Board of Trade."

Thalia kept her curtsy as close to Nell's plain style as she could. She had a distinct sense that it was no time for the Lady of the Lake's elaborate version. "I'm pleased to meet you." Somehow her voice came out slightly askew, higher than usual, like a frightened little girl's. Thalia winced.

"This is Mrs. Isabella Kipling," Nell murmured respectfully.

Mrs. Kipling was a black woman with piercing eyes, high cheekbones, and a wide mouth bracketed by lines that hinted at frequent sarcasm. She wore flowing black and carried a walking stick. Beneath her Parisian hat, her cloud of graying hair was confined in a beaded snood. "Miss Cutler."

Thalia stood straight. "I am pleased to meet you."

"This is Miss Emma Carey-Thomas." Nell sounded reverent as she added, "And this is Madame Speranza Gillyflower."

Miss Carey-Thomas, a white woman somewhere in her sixties, had close-set eyes, a narrow mouth, and a long, pointed nose. Her silhouette was fifteen years out of fashion, a pinch-waisted corset and a voluminous bustle beneath layers of dark serge ornamented with black braid. Her straight hair was iron gray, parted in the center, coiled in a tight knot at the nape of her neck, and topped off with a cap of filmy gray tulle suitable for a woman half her age.

Madame Gillyflower, the oldest of the three, was also the broadest and the tallest. She was black and wore her hair in braids. She had a round face and a mole—or a beauty mark—on her cheekbone. Unlike her drab companions, she wore bright colors, a bottle-green velvet bodice over a white shift and full skirts of brown and orange. Her hat was a twist of the same green velvet piped with gold braid. Unlike Miss Carey-Thomas's unfortunate cap, Madame Gillyflower's hat suited her so well it made her seem younger than her advanced years.

Thalia had to clear her throat twice before she could trust herself to get out even a few polite words to greet Miss Carey-Thomas and Madame Gillyflower in their turn.

Mrs. Kipling and Miss Carey-Thomas were unimpressed but courteous. Madame Gillyflower regarded Thalia with disfavor. "Miss Cutler. You are theatrical, I see."

Beside her, Nell bristled, but Thalia felt calmness descend. How many times in her life had she been snubbed for being in show business? She'd lost count long ago. "I am, Madame Gillyflower. I have taken over the family business."

"No shame in that." Mrs. Kipling spoke up. "The point is, neither of them Traded."

"With a manticore so close at hand," added Miss Carey-Thomas. "Commendable."

"They aren't green girls," said Madame Gillyflower. "Restraint is to be expected at this age."

Nell drew herself up, possibly to dispute this point, possibly to explain Thalia's curious circumstances, but when Thalia nudged her, Nell subsided.

Miss Carey-Thomas said, "The presence of one dead manticore doesn't preclude another live one. For the sake of other young Traders, Miss Cutler needs to be assigned her ordeal. If she succeeds, she won't attract manticores any longer."

"If she fails, she won't attract manticores either," Mrs. Kipling pointed out. "Problem solved."

"Then we are unanimous." Madame Gillyflower turned her full attention to Thalia and Nell. "Are you prepared for your ordeal?"

"Yes, ma'am," said Nell.

"I am," said Thalia.

Madame Gillyflower gazed at Nell for a long moment, then at Thalia. Whatever softness had been in her expression when she looked at Nell, Madame Gillyflower lost as she regarded Thalia. "Very well. Here is your ordeal. From this spot, find your way home."

"Whose home?" Nell asked. "I am lucky enough to have one. Not everyone has."

Thalia was grateful to Nell for pointing this out. If Thalia had to choose her true home, where would it be? Onstage, she supposed, working. If the Palace of Mystery counted as onstage, that would be a brief journey indeed.

The three older women exchanged a long wordless look. Then

Madame Gillyflower stated, "Your home, Miss Ryker, will be the finish line for both of you. Once you are safely inside, we will ask you to Trade back to the form you now display." She put extra emphasis on the words "Trade back" and gave Thalia a searching look. "Only do that, when we ask, and you will have succeeded."

Miss Carey-Thomas added, "You will be adult Traders, one or both of you, and as such, accepted in Trader society."

"Or you won't have to worry about Trading anymore," said Mrs. Kipling dryly.

"Go forth," said Madame Gillyflower, "and Trade."

Thalia scanned the space around her. The Sylvestri had gone. The police had taken Nora Uberti away, and the journalists had followed them. There were only five other people left in the little theater. Ryker stood closest. Tycho Aristides was still dealing with the manticore he'd killed. Madame Ostrova, Anton, and Freddie were watching from the door. "Right now? Right here?"

"Come on, it will be fun." Nell added, "I'll race you." She Traded to her otter self and streaked for the door. Her brother walked briskly after her and opened the door to let her through.

Thalia watched them go, overwhelmingly aware of her own bulk, her intractable human shape.

"Go on," said Madame Gillyflower kindly. "You can do it." How many timid young Traders had she urged on with those very words?

I can't. Thalia refused to say the words aloud, but the truth of it held her motionless.

Each manticore had called to her and brought forth that powerful urge to Trade. Thalia had told that swan voice within to shut up. She had banished it. Now Thalia searched herself for her swan, but could detect no trace.

For the moment, there were no overt threats to Thalia's life.

Tycho Aristides was cleaning up after dealing with the most recent manticore. The Ostrova Magic Company and its Palace of Mystery were her sanctuary. Here, she was completely safe.

Thalia knew herself. So far her only Trades had come when she had been convinced she was in grave danger. How galling, to be in a situation where none of her difficulties were dangerous, when only imminent danger was any use to her.

Madame Gillyflower and her companions were still watching Thalia with interest. Thalia kept attempting to Trade, but her concentration was flawed. Only her disadvantages came to mind.

With Nutall gone, Thalia's stage career was on hiatus until she could invent a solo act. This bad luck had been balanced by good luck. The Rykers had given her hospitality in full measure, even lent her their home as she had none of her own. All she had to do was Trade and return to their mansion on Riverside Drive.

Thalia failed to Trade. The Board of Trade remained, but she could no longer meet Madame Gillyflower's eyes.

What was Thalia, if not a permanent houseguest of the Rykers? She had accepted favors, many more than she felt comfortable with. She had promised herself that one day, when she was rich and famous, she would repay those favors and redeem her pride. But how could she become rich and famous under what amounted to house arrest? She was a guest of the Rykers the way Nutall was a guest of his Sylvestri family. Was she going to do what he had done? Was she going to find a corner and hide there?

Thalia failed to Trade. Miss Carey-Thomas withdrew discreetly. Mrs. Kipling and Madame Gillyflower remained, but by now, Thalia was so close to frustrated tears, she didn't dare to look at them.

Even Nutall's unsatisfactory solution was beyond Thalia. How could she be a Trader without the ability to Trade? How could she live on charity? How could she continue as a figure of fun, a sport of nature, a danger to others as a Trader stuck in her first shape?

Thalia became aware at last that these hard hot thoughts had a voice of their own, a thread of anger wrapped in disgust. *What kind of life is that?*

Thalia felt her face burning. Shame and guilt and anger built within her. How far away was fear?

The thread of anger and disgust asked, *What do you care?* It answered, *You're worthless.*

Thalia's inmost voice countered, *Shut up, you.* To her surprise, it was the voice she'd thought of as the swan within. Now it had gained such strength it was like another person inside her. It said, *I am here.* It said, *You know who I am.*

Finally fear rose up in Thalia. She did know. This voice within was as strong as she was, stronger than her sense of herself as human. *Human? No. I'm no Solitaire. No simple swan. I am a Trader. I am you.* The voice fell silent, yet Thalia could feel it ringing within her still. She was angry, so angry, but now fear locked her every muscle. Her hands and feet were pins and needles. Her whole body had gone cold.

"High time," said Mrs. Kipling.

Thalia turned on her, head down, hissing. Thalia had to raise her arms to keep her balance and only then saw she was spreading her wings. She had Traded.

Mrs. Kipling took a hasty step back, well out of range. From the doorway, a safe distance away, Miss Carey-Thomas said, "Passable."

Thalia paused, poised to strike. She guessed that her exact state of mind was evident in every line of her swan body.

Madame Gillyflower only smiled. "Talking to yourself, are you?"

If Thalia had possessed the power of speech, she would have

said, "How did you know?" But even as the words sank in, she knew the answer. How many times had Madame Gillyflower witnessed the moment when both sides of a Trader's nature worked in unison?

That voice hadn't been some unreliable figment of her imagination. That voice had been herself. Madame Gillyflower might have been joking, but her words were true.

Thalia spread her wings and hissed. Madame Gillyflower wasn't afraid of her, but Mrs. Kipling and Miss Carey-Thomas were. At least for a moment, Thalia could intimidate the Board of Trade. Well, two-thirds of the Board of Trade. She suspected there was very little on earth that could intimidate Madame Gillyflower.

Miss Carey-Thomas held open the door to the Palace of Mystery. "Stand clear. Hold that outside door open. Miss Cutler needs to leave."

It was a muddle, getting out of the room, out of the building, and leaving the Ostrova Magic Company behind. Hissing and waddling had almost lost their charm by the time Thalia made it to the pavement outside. There, she had better ways to move. She sprang up and did not come down.

The world was intoxicating. Thalia's wings were strong. Her vision was even better than her human sight. Her swan self had skills she put to work while her human self simply marveled.

Thalia cleared the rooftops of Sixth Avenue and kept rising, moving westward until she found the river waiting for her, the dear Hudson River, half salt at the top of the tide.

The wind told Thalia things she'd never known before. She could see it moving as it rippled the surface of the water and smoothed it again. Beneath the brown and green gloss of the water's surface, she could see the currents twisting by the way the air met the water. She could read the water as easily as she rode the eddying currents of the air.

As Thalia flew north, following the Hudson upstream, she watched the sky. It was going to rain. She could feel it in the wind. The bluffs across the Hudson on the New Jersey side were already blurred slightly by the moisture in the air. The sense of the sky above her, the sense of the river beneath her, the ocean so near, the sense of the rain to come, all deepened as Thalia explored what it meant to be free in the swan half of her nature.

Thalia flew without a thought. Moving up or down, right or left, all was effortless as she climbed and dove and angled her way upriver. If she failed her ordeal, if she were to remain in this form for the rest of her life, what hardship would that be? Thalia reveled in her new nature.

Pigeons and sparrows were plentiful in the city, but on the water, seabirds were most dominant. Thalia saw how silly the ducks looked feeding, heads down and tails tipped up as they dabbled. Her human vanity warned her she would look exactly that silly when she fed as a swan. The swan side of her nature shrugged this off without concern. She didn't care if she looked silly feeding. She was elegance itself the rest of the time. Sometimes inelegance was necessary.

Thalia flew steadily on, as gulls wheeled and turned around her. Any one of them could be Madame Gillyflower or one of the other ladies of the Board of Trade. The last corner of Thalia's mind still fixed on words wondered if they ever kept a young Trader under observation by Trading themselves. It could certainly happen, Thalia decided, but not to her, not today. If they monitored any young Trader's ordeal today, it would be Nell's, not hers. They had as much as said that if Thalia attracted yet another manticore, she was on her own.

By the time Thalia had left the railway lines and the West Shore ferry station behind and below, her human side had gone silent. She'd given up trying to put her observations into words. Words were no use in midair.

All the other birds she encountered gave Thalia a wide berth, as if they sensed she was nothing like them. Any time she thought she saw a bird that could be a Trader, Thalia steered clear. Even in her angriest mood, she wasn't eager to encounter a Canada goose, whether fellow Trader or true bird.

Thalia's next clear thought was sharp awareness of how hungry she was. It had been a long time since her last meal. Every remotely edible morsel drew her attention: water weeds in the shallows at the river's edge, tender roots among the grass, and even the grass itself.

Was there a downward limit to Trader size? If Thalia accidentally ate a bug, was there a chance it might be another Trader? As Thalia flew resolutely along, hunger edged her every thought, but she resisted the impulse to indulge it. She had put miles behind her before she recalled what she was supposed to be doing and where she was supposed to go. This was her ordeal. For once, she had Traded on cue. Now she would need to Trade back. But the cue would be given by the Board of Trade, and first she had to satisfy their requirement: go to the Ryker mansion.

Thalia reminded herself she only had to get there and Trade back. It had been Nell's idea to have a race. The stakes were high enough, completing the most important Trade of her life. Thalia decided she really had no need of any additional excitement.

What were the odds an otter could swim upstream faster than Thalia could fly? She liked her chances. But as the rocks at the edge of the river gave way to the gentle slopes of Riverside Park,

Thalia remembered she would still need to find her way inside the house. Nell might win her race yet.

Even with the human side of her nature taking back Thalia's focus of attention, it was hard for her to turn away from the river and back to the city roofs and treetops. It was hard to fly low while the sky was still beckoning her to ride the wind. Thalia promised herself she would come back soon, whether she passed her ordeal or failed it. The prospect of failure held no terror for her now. There were good things about being a swan.

Ryker, Thalia remembered, Traded almost every day for his swim in the Hudson River. What would it be like to be able to do this daily? What would it be like to be able to depend on having the freedom of the air, the river, even the open sea?

The more Thalia thought about what could be, the less she was her swan self, fixed so firmly in the present moment. Her human side was overshadowing the swan. Thalia felt the moment to Trade back drawing near. She still had to follow the instructions given her by the Board of Trade. For the first time, she was confident she could.

With plenty of wing-space in the Ryker courtyard, Thalia wheeled as she descended and came to earth precisely where she'd decided to land, less than a foot from the front doorstep. She folded her wings neatly and waddled forward. There was no way for her to ring the bell or manage the latch in her swan form, so she gave the door an impatient peck. It opened at once.

"Good afternoon, Miss Cutler." Rogers the butler sounded both respectful and apologetic. Perhaps the incident with the shotgun was still on his conscience. More likely, Thalia decided, he simply had enough common sense to be wary of her swan form.

Rogers stepped back to let Thalia in. "Mr. Ryker, Miss Ryker, and, er, the others are waiting for you in the music room."

Chapter Seventeen

Thalia followed Rogers to the music room as quickly as her short swan legs allowed. There the members of the Board of Trade were ensconced in the best chairs, sipping tea and nibbling cakes. Ryker was seated on the piano bench. Nell, still in her otter shape, was curled comfortably beside him, her chin on his knee. She gave a single welcoming chirp when Ryker dislodged her and rose to his feet as Thalia entered the room. Nell sprang from her resting position on the piano bench to perch atop the piano.

Mrs. Kipling and Madame Gillyflower set their teacups down.

"Excellent." Miss Carey-Thomas helped herself to another little cake. "All present and accounted for."

Madame Gillyflower said, "You may Trade back now, both of you."

Taking them in turn, Thalia curved her long neck to eye the Board of Trade crossly. After her flight up the river, the music room was too hot, too stuffy, too small, and too full of things it would be easy to bump into and break. She wished she could be alone. The scrutiny of the Board of Trade was unavoidable, but it was embarrassing to have Ryker there watching too.

"Unless the ordeal was too much for you," Madame Gilly-flower added.

Thalia hissed scornfully at the very suggestion. She ignored the discomfort of being observed and let herself dwell on how hungry she was, and how good those little iced cakes looked. She thought about how thirsty she was. A cup of tea would be very welcome. She thought about what might be instead of what was.

Thalia Traded back. She found herself seated in a huddle on the floor. Her stage costume was undamaged. Her shoulders felt as if she'd strained something important. "Ow."

"You did it!" Nell, now fully human again, but still as graceful as an otter, did a brief hopping dance of triumph. "So did I! I passed my ordeal too!"

Beaming, Ryker came to help Thalia up. Such was Thalia's relief, she let herself lean on him for an entire second and a half. "I Traded." Thalia tried the words on for size. They fit. She had done it on purpose at last. "I really truly Traded."

"You did." Ryker gave her a formal handshake. "You're a Trader now."

"Congratulations." Madame Gillyflower addressed both Thalia and Nell. "You have both passed your ordeal. Once you have finished celebrating your success, demonstrate some restraint. I'm not certain polite society is ready for either of you yet."

"Thank you." Thalia followed Nell's lead and curtsied to the Board of Trade. "Thank you all."

"Thank goodness that's over with." Nell turned to Rogers, who was watching from the door. "Is there any smoked fish left, do you think? Perhaps a few sandwiches?"

"Very good, Miss Ryker." Rogers turned to go.

"Champagne, too!" Nell called after him. "This is a celebration." She twirled on the spot and returned to the piano bench. "I was sure you'd beat me here, but you took your time, didn't you?" Without giving Thalia a chance to reply, she explained. "Nat gave the Board of Trade a lift in the Pierce-Arrow, so I slipped in the back and hid beneath the rumble seat."

"Very clever." Thalia accepted the cup of tea and the little cake Ryker handed her. She ate the cake as slowly as she could, but it was still gone in a moment. She was grateful that sandwiches were in her near future.

"Very bumpy." Nell turned her attention to the Board of Trade. "It was so kind of you to grant us our ordeals today. I'm sorry we haven't planned a more formal celebration. A bigger cake, for one thing. Champagne and sandwiches will be here soon, though. Rogers is very good."

"We won't stay." Madame Gillyflower rose. Mrs. Kipling and Miss Carey-Thomas followed suit. "You have done well today. We shall leave you to celebrate *en famille*."

"It's best we don't become too familiar with you," said Miss Carey-Thomas.

"Nor you with us," added Mrs. Kipling crisply.

Ryker and Nell accompanied the Board of Trade out. Thalia let them go without her. Once she was alone in the music room, she took the chair Miss Carey-Thomas had occupied. Her knees had gone weak. She was now a true Trader, an adult, and quite literally a fully fledged one. She was safe from manticore attack, prey no longer, and since she would no longer attract them, she would endanger no one else. She would be of no interest to Aristides now. Thalia was surprised by how much that thought hurt.

Thalia could not only Trade and fly as a swan whenever she wished, she could come and go freely in her human form. The city was hers again. But where should she go? What should she do next?

Wherever Nutall had gone with the other Sylvestri, it was where he had chosen to go. Thalia had done her best to help him. Now she was on her own. Where would she choose to go? Her home was the theater, but she would need a new act, a solo, before she went back on the circuit. In the meantime, what to do?

It was tempting to plan an immediate visit to Philadelphia. Professor Philander Evans had been so wrong. There ought to be consequences for such ignorance. With regret, Thalia let that thought go. The responsibility for the error was all her own. Her mistake had been trusting in his knowledge without corroborating it.

What true knowledge about Traders existed? Where could Thalia find answers to her questions about Trader ways? She was certain Ryker and Nell would do their best to help her, but who were the authorities on the subject? Now that she knew how to Trade, how best could Thalia learn how to be the kind of person who Traded?

With a sinking feeling, Thalia admitted to herself her growing suspicion that the most reliable source of answers to her questions had walked out of the room with Madame Gillyflower and the other members of the Board of Trade.

The morning after the impromptu celebration of Nell's and Thalia's successful ordeals began far later than usual. Thalia, alone in the breakfast room with the morning editions of the newspapers, was cheered yet not surprised to read that all charges against David Nutall had been dropped. Miss Nora Uberti had confessed fully to her crime, which she had planned and carried out entirely alone. No charges were brought against any accomplice. Thalia, reading between the lines, thought she saw the words "especially not any member of the Ostrova family" implicit in every version of the story. The Ostrova Magic Company, although the site of the murderer's arrest, was not connected with the crime in any way.

The only reporters Thalia had asked Madame Ostrova to invite to her special performance were those she trusted to keep their promise to report the events accurately. Madame Ostrova, she suspected, had elicited a promise of her own, to keep the reputation of the family business unsullied. Thalia wished she'd thought of that.

The gossip columns in the Solitaire newspapers noted that the first Mrs. Von Faber, clad in deepest mourning, had been seen at the opera two nights running. Rumor had it that Caruso had arranged for her to attend as a distraction from her mourning, although the Great Caruso himself had denied it. Wherever the tickets had come from, Mrs. Von Faber seemed to be enjoying herself.

It was a surprise to Thalia when Rogers appeared in the doorway bearing a card with that very name upon it. "Mrs. Von Faber wishes to see you, miss. She says it will take only a few moments of your time." As Thalia rose, brushing out her skirts, he added, "She is in the parlor, miss."

Thalia followed Rogers out of the room and went to the parlor. There she found Mrs. Von Faber examining the porcelain figurines ornamenting the mantel. Seeing her close to, Thalia was surprised how well the white Solitaire woman had retained traces of her youthful air. Perhaps it was an illusion caused by the plumpness. Mrs. Von Faber's cheeks still retained an almost childlike fullness, and her careful application of rouge made her seem almost doll-like despite her age.

Thalia cleared her throat.

"Good morning, Miss Cutler. Thank you for seeing me." Mrs. Von Faber held up the figurine. "Meissen. Interesting. I would have bet good money it was Limoges." She put it back on the mantelpiece. From her jet-beaded reticule, she drew out a thin brown envelope. "I am grateful to you for finding out who killed my dear Johan. I offered a reward. You've earned it. So I will pay. But that's not why I'm here right now. I'm here because I've gone all through my husband's papers. He had a special box. I knew it was important, but no matter what I tried, I couldn't open it, so I had to pay a locksmith. He got it open last night. There were some envelopes inside. Since this one has your name on it, I thought you'd better have it."

Thalia eyed the envelope suspiciously. "What is it?"

Mrs. Von Faber chuckled. "It's not some kind of summons, if that's what you're worried about. Nothing legal."

"Is it illegal, then?" To Thalia's surprise, Mrs. Von Faber looked embarrassed. Any reply she might have made was broken off when a maid, bearing a tray with Rogers' idea of appropriate refreshments, joined Thalia in the doorway. Thalia let her past to arrange the tray, then invited Mrs. Von Faber to be seated.

"Oh, how nice." Mrs. Von Faber jostled the maid in her eagerness to take a chair. "Very kind of you, I'm sure."

"Very kind of my hosts." Thalia took the best chair and poured out coffee. "Cream? Sugar?"

"Both, please. Lots of both." Mrs. Von Faber put the envelope down when she accepted her cup from Thalia. There was a single word written on it in bold black letters: CUTLER. "If you don't want it, just put it in the fire. I won't take it back."

"What is it?" Thalia repeated.

"Read it and see." Mrs. Von Faber took a wafer-thin cookie from the plate Thalia offered. "There were half a dozen envelopes like that inside. Different names on them, of course."

Thalia picked up the envelope. It had been sealed with wax, but someone had already opened it. There was nothing inside but a single sheet of newspaper. She spread the page flat. The *San Francisco Pantograph,* April 14, 1896. The society page, filled with breathless accounts of debutante balls, news of forthcoming engagements, and half a dozen wedding announcements. On the other side of the page Thalia found only a jumble of advertisements. Nine years old, and the newsprint was already starting to yellow. "What is this supposed to be?"

Mrs. Von Faber helped herself to another cookie. "Use your eyes." She held out her empty cup for a refill.

Thalia turned back to the society news. There, among the portrait photogravures of brides stiff as waxworks, was a picture of her mother. Beneath it, the caption read, *Heir to Paxton Fortune Weds Widow.* In the text of the announcement, it said that Margarete Gruenewald, Trader, had married Lyman Paxton, also a Trader. In addition, Lyman Paxton's father was the Paxton, he was heir to the Paxton Trust, and he was working for the family firm, a real estate empire. The happy couple were already on their wedding journey and would not be receiving well-wishers at their palatial home on Nob Hill for another month.

Thalia closed her eyes to try to subdue her emotions so that her thoughts could come to order, but after only a moment she had to open them again to take another look at the image.

The likeness was unmistakable. The woman in the picture was older than she had looked in the wedding portrait Thalia had found among her father's personal effects. But it was the same person, no question. Margarete Gruenewald. Her mother. Her dead mother.

Thalia checked the date of the newspaper again. "This is from 1896."

"Yes, I read it." Mrs. Von Faber gave up waiting for Thalia and poured herself more coffee.

"My mother died in 1888."

"She doesn't look dead to me."

The Margarete Gruenewald in the picture had been alive in 1896. Thalia reminded herself it didn't mean her mother was still alive in 1905. But hope had other ideas. She could not help hoping.

If her mother was still in San Francisco, still alive, Thalia could find her. She could talk to her, she could ask questions, and she could find out why she'd been lied to for so long. Why had her father done it? Her mother would know his story. How many more lies of omission were there for Thalia to discover?

Thalia looked at the name on the envelope. CUTLER. "My father was still alive when this was printed. What was your husband going to do with this?"

Mrs. Von Faber shrugged. "I don't know. I have no idea what Johan's intentions were. But he did like to have influence. He liked to know secrets."

Thalia's father might not have known about her mother's re-marriage, but his story of her death was false. What about her baby brother? What had become of the infant?

So many lies. Had Nutall known any of this? Thalia considered the possibility but made herself dismiss it.

Mrs. Von Faber went on reminiscing. "I don't think Johan ever asked for money outright. He asked for favors instead. When he needed something from someone, he would let them know what he knew. He made it clear what would happen if they didn't do as he wished. Always, when he asked someone for a favor, they granted it."

In other words, blackmail. Thalia thought hard. Perhaps Von Faber had kept this image of her mother to use against her father? Or against her mother? Her mother had committed bigamy. She had married a Trader in San Francisco years after she'd married Jack Cutler. Could that knowledge possibly have been used to extract anything from her father?

Favors. Belatedly, Thalia remembered the Cadwallader Syndicate. "The noncompete clause."

"Such a fuss over that." Mrs. Von Faber stirred more cream and sugar into her coffee. "I don't understand contract law."

"Cornelius Cadwallader," said Thalia. "Was that name on one of the envelopes?"

"I called on him at his home first thing this morning. The look on his face." When she smiled, Mrs. Von Faber looked like a big Dresden doll. "He thought I was like Johan until I explained things to him."

"You mean he thought you were going to go on blackmailing him."

Mrs. Von Faber's soft chuckle had a faint undertone of scorn.

"As if I needed anything from him. Johan left me and the children well provided for. No, Mr. Cadwallader didn't understand me properly until I moved to put his envelope on the fire. Then he stopped me. Never saw a man jump so fast."

"Do you know what was in his envelope?"

"Yes." Mrs. Von Faber gave Thalia a sharp look. "Of course I know. I opened it. I also know that it is no one's business but his. But I'll tell you this. He was glad to get it back."

With a contented sigh, Mrs. Von Faber put her empty cup down on its saucer and brushed crumbs away. "Do as you please with that. I must be on my way. Four envelopes to go. People may not be glad to see me come, but I so enjoy how happy I make them when I go."

Thalia put the sheet of newspaper aside to escort Mrs. Von Faber out. She too was happy to see the woman go. Her thoughts were racing, repeating the same points again and again.

Her mother might truly be dead now, but in 1896, she had been alive and living in San Francisco. Her mother's maiden name meant there was no possibility of a mix-up in images at the newspaper. Nor could it be some chance resemblance between her mother and another woman.

In 1896, Thalia's mother had been alive. The announcement had said nothing about children. If her father had lied about her mother's death, had he lied about her baby brother too? Was her mother still alive? Was she living in a big house on Nob Hill with her husband and her son?

Anger began to tinge the shock Thalia felt, but it was a good kind of anger. It spurred her on.

Thalia's stunned wonder began to give way to determination. She had telegrams to send. She had letters to write. She would go to California herself. She would go to San Francisco. If she had to, she would walk to Nob Hill.

But she wouldn't have to walk, Thalia reminded herself. She would have Mrs. Von Faber's reward money to pay her expenses. Her first letter would be to the Dakota to apply for letters of transit on the cross-continental train.

She had lost her father. She had lost her mother, yet there was a chance she could find her again. She might even find she had a younger brother. Someone out there in San Francisco knew more than she did, and Thalia vowed she would find the truth.

Somehow, Thalia was going to get her questions answered. All her questions.

When Thalia returned to the parlor, she found Nell there, examining the sheet of newsprint with interest. "This woman is a relation of yours, isn't she? She has your nose and chin exactly." Nell folded the paper.

With a silent nod for his sister and a smile for Thalia, Nathaniel Ryker joined them and sat across from Nell. Even though she had to take long pauses to get through it without giving in to her various emotions, Thalia explained the whole thing to both of them.

"What a weasel Von Faber was." Nell passed the page of newspaper to her brother. "I don't see how he could blackmail you with it though."

Thalia folded her hands and waited as patiently as she could until he handed the newspaper page back to her. "I know the envelope says Cutler, but I think that must refer to my father, not to me."

"Von Faber might have planned to blackmail your mother. The day we met, he spoke of her with most unbecoming familiarity. He hadn't seen you since you were a child." Ryker dropped his voice to a mutter. "Which only makes his subsequent behavior worse."

"It must have been ghastly. I am so sorry I missed it." Struck by a new thought, Nell added, "Nat, I'm going to Sylvie's for the afternoon. She's planning a party. The entertainment will be staging a reading of *Twelfth Night* with Reggie and Bill and some of the others. She wants me to help her plan it."

"Indeed." Ryker's eyebrows climbed. "What's happened to your lessons in stage magic?"

Nell gave them both an apologetic smile and a little shrug. "I'm free now. I want to enjoy it for a bit." To Thalia, she added, "Since I've canceled it at such short notice, I'll pay you for today's lesson, of course."

"Certainly not." Despite everything, Thalia couldn't help smiling back at Nell. "I owe you my life, both of you. I can't possibly accept payment for anything."

"It was lovely, being your assistant," Nell said. "Now I can truly say I've appeared on the stage."

"Oh, yes. We still need to discuss that, you and I," Nat said to his sister. "I know it is too much to expect that you should ask me before endangering yourself that way, but do you think you might ever consider telling me your plans first?"

"You wound me." Nell's pose was indeed that of the injured innocent, graceful hand on heart, reproachful eyes turned heavenward. "I've just finished telling you my plans for the rest of the day. You never listen."

Ryker uttered a martyred sigh. Before he could reply, Nell sprang up and headed for the door. "I might not be home in time for dinner. I'll make Sylvie feed me there. Don't worry."

"On the contrary," Ryker began, "you *will* be home in time—" He broke off. Nell had already left them alone in the parlor.

Thalia said, "*I'll* be home for dinner."

Ryker's expression cleared. "I'm going to let Nell do as she pleases. Shakespeare plays, stage magic, whatever she wants. As usual. But there's no reason to wait dinner for her. Let's go somewhere. Let's do something. You need a distraction. Let's go out to a restaurant. Miss Cutler, will you do me the honor of being my guest for dinner?"

Thalia welcomed the thought. Her first impulse was to accept, but she checked herself. How could she consider going out to enjoy herself with Ryker? She had letters to write. She had things she must do. The thought of how much she had to do caught up with her, followed by a burning wish to put it all aside for now. Fatigue swept over her. The desire for distraction won out. It was all too much for her to deal with now. She would lay her plans later. "I would be pleased to accept that invitation, Mr. Ryker."

"Where shall we go? Oh, wait. I know." Ryker's smile flickered back in its brightest form.

They spoke in delighted unison. "Delmonico's."

"It's ages until dinnertime," Ryker continued. "What would you like to do with the rest of this afternoon?"

Thalia yielded completely to her wish to be distracted. "Now that I can do it safely, I would like to go outdoors. I would like to Trade and go for a flight—and a swim—in the Hudson."

"What a good idea. When we're not under siege by a manticore, I try to spend some time in the river every day." Ryker offered her his arm. "Please permit me to show you the way."

When Ryker led Thalia through the double doors into the Changing room, the place felt different to Thalia. The cold damp of the stone walls now comforted her. Thalia could tell the river was close. She might have Traded for the first time at Keith's Vaudeville Theater in Philadelphia, but this room was where Thalia truly had learned how to do it. She simply hadn't realized that the thread that bound the two sides of her nature wasn't fear, but anger.

Ryker skirted the pool as he crossed the chamber to the door to the nursery stairs. Thalia stood close and watched as he opened a second door, this one so well concealed that Thalia had never suspected its existence. This door revealed another flight of stone steps, steeper and narrower, that descended into darkness. "No lights here, sorry. We go down by touch."

Thalia drew in a deep breath. The air on the narrow staircase smelled of fresh water and living stone. "I can smell the river."

Ryker smiled at Thalia. "I can smell the tide."

They lost the light before they were four steps down the stairs. Thalia followed Ryker by touch and smell. Little by little, twenty steps farther down, daylight began. They kept descending.

At last, the steps came to an end at an arch blocked by a heavy wrought-iron grille. Set into the grille was a door like a bank vault's, complete with a combination lock. Ryker turned the knob back and forth in the correct combination. There was a serious-sounding click, and he opened it. "My dear Miss Cutler, won't you come out to play?"

Thalia followed him through the gate and waited, looking around, while he locked it and spun the exterior dial. Six feet on, the stone-lined tunnel ended. They were halfway down a grassy slope. Below them lay the Hudson River. Across the river were the wooded slopes of New Jersey, bright green with spring foliage. Behind them, the hidden steps climbed steeply up into the bedrock, back to the Ryker mansion on the hillside above, one mansion among many in Riverside. "How many years to make the tunnel, ten? Twenty? All so you could go for an afternoon swim?"

Ryker held out his hand to her. "My family built it long ago, but not just for swimming."

"Smuggling?" Thalia took his hand and they started down the slope, picking their way through the young trees.

Ryker chuckled. "I'd much rather call it free enterprise."

"Definitely smuggling, then." Thalia liked the feeling of Ryker's hand in hers. "So when you take your daily swim—?"

"Yes, this is how I come down to the river." Ryker scanned north to south and back. "Sometimes I don't want to come back."

Thalia frowned. "You want to stay in your other form?"

Ryker shook his head. "No, not yet. But at times it's a lot of responsibility, being the Ryker, running the Ryker Trust, managing the Ryker businesses, helping the extended Ryker family, and watching out for Nell's welfare."

"That last responsibility would be a lot all on its own."

They fell silent. Thalia let Ryker steady her when they reached the big rocks that made the breakwater at the river's edge. They balanced, still hand in hand, on the boulders as they watched the water passing. Somehow, it soothed Thalia's inner turmoil. "It has run like this forever," she murmured. "It will never stop."

"Not so." Ryker gazed out across the river to the New Jersey heights beyond. "The Hudson River is younger than it looks. The gorge was cut when the glaciers melted during the ice ages, most recently only a few tens of thousands of years ago. Think what it must have looked like when the ice was melting, full from edge to edge."

For a moment, in her mind's eye, Thalia could almost see the river as it had been at its height. The water had been far cleaner;

she knew that without knowing how. The air had been far purer. The world, even then, had been far from empty, but then there had been no taint of a city here. This part of the world had been wild, with only ancestors of the First Nations to watch over it. Thalia breathed, "Lovely."

"Lovely," Ryker echoed, but now he was gazing not at the river, but at Thalia.

Thalia gazed back. Her swan self recognized something in him, not identical, yet something akin all the same. "Is that you? Is that your seal half I see?" she whispered.

Ryker's smile had never been brighter. "I don't know what you see exactly. Let's find out." He Traded.

Thalia had a moment to admire Ryker as a seal, balanced beside her on the rocks. Then with a lithe twist he was in the water, and all that gleaming strength was on display as he dove and swam. She called, "Wait for me," and Ryker stayed near the rocks, but he moved effortlessly in and out of sight in the current.

In her eagerness, Thalia gathered all she had learned of Trading, yet she did not Trade. She stood alone on the rocks and let anger and fear run through her, but she felt none of the signs she'd learned to associate with her Trades, no chill, no tingling in her hands. If anything, anxiety ran cold down her spine, keeping her from Trading.

Wary of outside threats, Thalia turned in place, scanning the hillside behind her. There, at the brow of the hill, stood Tycho Aristides, the Skinner of New York. He was wearing his slouch hat and his big coat. At this distance, Thalia could not see what weapons he carried, but from his stance, she could tell he was well armed. As Thalia watched, Aristides sketched a wave to acknowledge her, then resumed his vigil.

The next breath Thalia took had a clear taste, but no scent she could perceive. Her hands were pins and needles, and a welcome chill slid through her. Eyes wide and arms open, Thalia Traded. She let herself move forward and down, sliding gracefully from the rocks to the river. The current bore her up. At first, Thalia swam in circles near Ryker, setting each feather in her wings to rights as he played in the current beside her. When she was finished, Thalia arched her neck. Ryker moved out to the center of the river, where the current was strongest. Thalia kept up with him. Together they let the river take them down to the harbor. Together, they ventured down to meet the sea.

Acknowledgments

Patricia C. Wrede and Susan Wolkerstorfer have made this book possible. I owe them more than I can say.

Stephani Booker, Charlotte Boynton, Fiona Clements, Kelly Jones, Jody Kaplan, Catherine Lundoff, Hal Peterson, and Catherine Schaff-Stump have contributed in countless ways. The mistakes are all mine.

Finally, credit where credit is due. Thank you, Penn and Teller, for the seven basic principles of magic tricks.